CW01666070

Flowers From

To Lee

An inspiring member of the Old Swinford writers!

Paul

13/11/24

By: Paul C Walsh

Contents

Dedications

This book is dedicated to all those in the future who embrace the struggles of human survival with courage, resilience and a sense of hope.

Acknowledgements

I would like to thank my fellow writers from the Old Swinford Group, in Stourbridge, West Midlands, for their helpful feedback and support in developing this novel.

Gratitude goes to Gillian Small from the writer's group, for her initial editing of the text, and to my partner Monica Ludwig, for her scrutiny of the story.

About The Author

Paul Walsh is a former secondary teacher and university-based teacher educator, now living in Halesowen, West Midlands. His first novel, 'A place between the Mountains,' was published in (2018) A second book, 'Hallowed Turf' followed in (2020), both through APS Books. www.andrewsparke.com. A third short novel, 'Rubber Soul,' will be available later this year.

Synopsis

The year 2227. There was a time when we believed that the earth would shield us from mankind's worst excesses. Humanity would cope with whatever challenges science, or the power of nature could create. Melting ice caps and rising sea levels had forced people to withdraw from coastal towns. We had survived limited nuclear conflicts, international food wars and extensive meteorite showers. But just when we hoped the future was secure, an unexpected phenomenon emerged. The sun began to burn more powerfully with each new dawn. Now, we were at the mercy of what came next.

In the UK, we called it… *The Change*

PART ONE

Unit 214. The Wastelands, England.

Sector Three. Formally Known As The Midlands.

May 4th, 2227

The others watched as John Byrne *** Hon. dragged his aching body over to the fireplace. He could hear his bones creaking, locked as they were, by the jaws of rheumatism. Severe pain was now a constant companion, with painkillers increasingly a thing of the past. His limbs jarred with every movement, competing with discomfort from old shrapnel wounds. None of this would change, and he knew it. A permanent legacy, a double-edged encumbrance, which tightened its grip on him and refused to yield like a vice of spiked nails. His debilitated frame was now waiting for the inevitable. Despite all this, he had not extinguished his thirst for hope. Not yet. But it was only a matter of time before nature took its course. A legacy of traumatic injuries sustained in the great wars that everybody had hoped would define the future of humanity. Experiences that he could no longer find the words to speak about.

Ignoring offers of help, he crouched down to light the kindling.

''No. Let me do it,'' he insisted.

Four figures stepped back into the shadows out of respect. John B, as he was known to them, had been their *Guardian of the Hearth* since the day they first arrived.

The embers sparked and crackled, then quickened into twisted flames like dancers across a lighted stage. John reached across for more timber. His 'new' arm effortlessly bore the weight of two measured cuts of discoloured, twisted silver birch. The old limbs would have struggled with their weight. He added these logs to the pyre. Not the sort of branches he would have ideally chosen. Old knowledge from his days as a carpenter. This wood burned and splintered too quickly, but it was all that was available in the rack. Satisfied, he recovered the diminished wood pile next to him and signed the inventory, like the meticulous protector of royal treasure. The watching eyes knew that the wood was more precious to them than any diamond or gold ornament. It would help to take the edge off the night chill. Help to keep them all alive.

"Jewels of carbon," he exclaimed, wryly. "A gift from the protected woods. We are grateful."

***

The existence of these resources was still considered by many as something of a miracle. Fashioned from the dust, saplings grown with a cocktail of chemicals, if the rumours were to be believed. Not that any of the faces in that room had met anyone from *Gnosis* and the *Green Zone,* where these marvels occurred.

These places were prohibited areas, beyond the reach of ordinary people who survived in the *Wastelands;* people like the extended family of John Byrne Hon.

The inhabitants of *Gnosis* and the *Green Zone* kept themselves apart. And why wouldn't they? The scientific challenges they faced consumed every waking hour of the day. Experts bravely battle new ground in the urgent quest to save our trees and edible plants. Wood that could protect everyone from the night cold, carved and cut to shape our needs. At least, that is what the news pods said.

He was in no position to challenge such proclamations. But John was troubled. Why was this information presented in such emotive, quasi-religious language? Were they casting themselves as survivalist prophets on a bio-chemical mission? Re-discovering how to grow plants and trees again without the nutrient-rich soil that had now been turned to dust. Was it right to revere them for keeping everyone alive, he pondered? That's what the news pods said. For on the outcome of their labours, and of those colleagues in other countries, would rest the precarious future of humanity. Who could disagree with such a prognosis? He did not. Whatever meagre benefits they enjoyed there were richly earned, he deduced, even if most other survivors across the country relied upon their wit and creative hands to survive, particularly out in the Wastelands, where people waited anxiously for each new breakthrough. And the initial signs were promising. So said the pods. No wonder these pioneers were now being revered like magicians of old, thought John.

But his face was lined with conflict. The felling of the trees, the burning of wood, the further release of more carbon, what an agonising conundrum of growth and death, he mused. Hadn't those carbon emissions contributed to the problem in the first place? And what of the future? If the domes that sheltered them failed. What would become of all of them? Speculations, unnecessary distractions. John knew there were more immediate things to worry about. Better not to ponder the implications of future calamity for too long.

***

His mind returned to the task at hand. It had to be done properly. Expediency demanded it. There was no room for indulgence.

''Only two logs. We know the law,'' he shouted, like a preacher reciting an ancient mantra. But this was no more than habit. John knew the words were unnecessary. Those gathered around understood the cost of exhausting their quota. They needed the fire to protect them from the plunging temperatures outside. When the sun went down. Respite for a few tenuous hours. Precious sleep.

***

Emerald, his youngest daughter, helped him to his feet. A young woman barely nineteen, with sallow, ashen features. A pallid face but not without beauty. And then, there were those piercing green eyes like jewels. It had been easy for her parents to name her. Like everybody else there, she was emaciated and gaunt, but her wiry frame carried strong muscular arms, the product of regular physical work. A woman used to responsibility beyond her years. Father and daughter's eyes are telepathically drawn to each other. A special bond born of mutual respect. Fused in recognition of what they knew lay ahead. More than just family. More than the blood ties she carried, as perhaps his last surviving child. When the time came, she would know what to do. He had taught her well. Her shoulders would carry unit 214's fragile hopes for survival.

***

Hawk pulled the heavy, tattered curtain across the window, pausing to savour the last moments of daylight. He stared at a glowing, mercurial sky. The scorching sun rapidly fading in streaks of fierce crimson. Flickers of black smoke rose from neighbouring homesteads, invading the skyline. Meandering smoulders a merging of lines, decorating nature's vast canvas. He ruminated that in different circumstances, it might have seemed beautiful. This was how he would describe such a spectacle to those who came after them. If anybody survived. Other people's children, but not his. At that moment, Hawk was reminded that he was alone. There was no one to pass on his name or story to.

He observed the firmament in its final moments. A patchwork of small homesteads, like his, waited for the impact. Were they just tokens of resistance, he rued, communities dangling on the edge of an abyss? Sending out a signal. Ordinary people clinging on to what was left of their dying world. And what of other places, other countries. Were they also living out this chilling reality?

***

Everyone knew that these signs were the lull before the storm. They knew what was coming. Helpless spectators in a vista, awaiting its nightly visitor. Nobody understood why it came. Not even the scientists. Some of them blamed the plethora of strategic nuclear explosions that ended the food wars. Had this devastation altered the weather? Or was it the mysterious shower of meteorites that had left their debris embedded in the earth? Whatever the cause, the survivors were left with blisteringly hot days and something more bizarre at night. Vast, marauding clouds, driven by nocturnal winds, crushed the colours below like the eruption of a terrifying pyroclastic blast. In Britain, they called it *The Change.* It blocked out the light and stole the lives of the foolish. Those unprepared or found outside without shelter.

The others in the room wrapped their coats around them and moved towards their night-time refuge.

"Come on, Hawk. We are waiting for you!'' Shouted Emerald.

The lightly bearded youth lifted his protruding chin, shrugged his shoulders, and walked across to join them. His narrow, bulbous eyes searched for a place to lie down. Emerald was sprawled next to her father's frame to share a little of her warmth with him. Hawk pulled the giant patchwork of misshaped covers and blankets across their prostate bodies and tried to find a space close to her. They spread out on makeshift mats, coiled in a collective foetal position, to combat the imminence of the cold. He stared at their frail outlines. To Hawk, they seemed like a line of vulnerable embryos. Peas in a protective pod.

Huddled together for warmth, unit 214 prepared for another night of survival.

***

John Byrne lay there listening to the stillness before the wind. He rarely slept well these days. Some people had adjusted by taking to their beds by 9.00 PM, prompted by fatigue or hunger. Not John. He was still a night owl. He tossed and turned to find a position for sleep. Lying on his side was not an easy option for a man with a hybrid arm. Grown in a bio-factory to replace the one shattered by an incendiary bomb in Morocco. An inner voice reminded him that he should be grateful. Not every amputee had received one. The benefits of being a war hero, he'd been told. But John knew he was no hero. Just a soldier who had been extraordinarily lucky. But he had learned that the army had an ulterior reason for this act of generosity. And it had given him a better chance to survive the aftermath. He rubbed his shoulder. Although the new limb sometimes felt real, there would always be that missing factor, that familiarity with the limb you were born with. The history. Memories. Those faded inoculation marks, scars from youthful sporting experiences, the discreet tattoo, faded and barely disguising the name of a young lover. He wished he could disconnect the arm for a few minutes. Feel the gap. Finger the tender tissue that cushioned his shoulder. There was the constant desire to scratch what he called his imaginary itch like an irritating spot. With a touch of dark humour, he envisaged being attached to an artificial arm. Maybe one made of metal, like in those dusty old sci-fi films he once watched from the ancient media archives. Robot John! He chuckled to himself at the thought of quickly assembling such a limb, especially in the case of a sudden evacuation.

John's insomnia was also fuelled by hauntings from the past. About his family. About what happened in Morocco, Turkey, and Spain. He tried to bury these nightmares deep within the recess of his mind, but the images always re-surfaced. At the heart of them all was Bethany, the woman he had loved for most of his adult life. The mother of his children. Torn from this world by a deadly virus. Tito, his son, a warrior moulded from the same clay, savagely cut down during the *Food Wars.* And what of his older daughter, Amber? Each day brought fresh doubts about her fate. Who knew whether she was still alive? Her last message had suggested that she was heading to the mines in the north. That was almost two years ago. The absence of news was another wound that continued to grow and fester within him. He tried to hold on to the unlikely belief that his older daughter had not perished. That she had somehow found her way to safety within those deep places. In the bowels of the earth where, even the great storms had failed to penetrate. Intoxicated by such anxieties, he finally gave way to exhaustion and the slumber his body craved.

A Regular Journey

Emerald opened her eyes. The others were still sleeping. Already, the oppressive heat of another day was forcing its stifling fingers into the room, seeking out gaps in the buildings. These were the diurnal moments she cherished. The shivers and numbness of night-time were slowly stripped away by a new warming sun before the temperatures became unbearable.

She disentangled herself from the knot of limbs around her and pulled away the blanket. How she hated that smell. The stale scent of bodies clinging to each other. She was not sure that most of them even noticed body odour anymore. Sitting up, her attention was drawn towards a small hole that had appeared in the roof above her. Through the fissure, Emerald thought she caught sight of something. The rare spectacle of a large bird flying high above. Was it a bird of prey in search of sustenance, she speculated, or was it escaping from incarceration at one of the new experimental centres she had heard about? Closing her eyes again, she imagined the creature swooping down and carrying her away from this nightmare world. There was her saviour, a mighty eagle, soaring through the skies, rising over defiant mountains and dusty plains, finally placing her body down upon a beautiful island far away. A place brimming with smiling faces somewhere imbued with human kindness. A place adorning the pages of one of those old cyber-holiday brochures, where people may have visited during the summer months before *the Change.*

If only… she fantasised.

But Emerald knew there was no flight from her predicament. Unless, by some strange wonder, she was welcomed through the gates of *Gnosis.* And that was not likely to happen. She looked at the branded symbol burnt into her arm.

'Not me', she muttered quietly to herself. 'Not for the *tainted.'*

Her destiny, like that of each member of Unit 214, was already mapped out. A bleak prognosis. It was accepting this fate that was so difficult. To remain trapped, incarcerated in the living hell they had correctly named the *Wastelands*. Ebbing out a meagre existence on the fringes of a volatile environment until they eventually succumbed. Given her prediction, it surprised her that more of them did not give up and take the logical outcome: suicide.

Before an emerging tear had fully formed, Emerald pulled herself up before discarding several layers of clothing. The young woman splashed her face and body with recycled water from the communal washing sink. Turning towards the drinking water filter, she consumed a small measure. It carried the usual distinctive odour of disinfectant. Still, it helped to clear her throat from the dust that had built up during the night. After dressing in double layers of light clothes, the young woman unlocked the door and entered the yard. She inspected the damage to the roof. Two heavy plastic tiles had been blown off by the night wind. Emerald opened her pocket and removed a small notebook.

She wrote the words: *Hawk. Replace the roof tiles* and placed the note in his mug before returning to the communal bedding area. She would be busy with other matters that day.

Her father was already up and had the morning pot boiling. The smell of nettles was overwhelming. He pushed the mug into her hand.

"Drink this, Emerald. We need to get going soon."

John and his daughter left the sanctuary of the house and slowly began to climb the ladder that clung, precariously, to the mound of rocks in front of the building. This embankment stretched across the perimeter of the compound, providing a sturdy shield from the elements. Three large numbers, '214,' had been etched onto a flat slab of sandstone that protruded beyond the wall.

It always took longer to ascend with her father. His pain was more tangible with each faltering day. But he was not prepared to let her make the journey alone.

Five minutes later, they reached the top of the wall, and Emerald passed the walking stick to him. Her green eyes lit up in the morning sunlight. Just like her mother's had once done, John observed. That is why they had bestowed the name upon her. A jewel to brighten their lives. A flower from the dust.

They stood there, motionless, gazing out on the landscape. Before them lay the empty remains of a once fertile terrain, which had flourished with fields of wheat, crops, and grass. Now, just dusty plains and folds of twisted rock as far as the human eye could see. The once-rich plant life charred to powder by the relentless sun. To their left, flanking what was left of the fields, stood the only thing that had not changed. Not for John. The Marlow Hills. Immovable, defiant features of the landscape, a gift from antiquity. Ancient rocks that were increasingly threatened at night by powerful winds. The trees and plants had gone. Angry gusts lashed her pillars with terrible force. As the weather had worsened, these hills had stood firm. And so must they, pondered John. A powerful metaphor for their own survival. He would concede that in their more exposed sections, the wind had left its mark, carving strange alien sculptures into the rock. These stood like wardens, defending the high places behind them.

He once knew these hills like the back of his hand. That is one of the reasons why he had returned to the area when the wars ended, together with the need to find his family. As a teenager, he and his friends had built dens in the nooks and crannies that abounded there and dreamed of adventure.

Her father paused, transfixed for a few seconds, with his head bowed, looking lost. A moment of despair. She linked his good arm to hers. The crumbled remains of these childhood fantasies were long gone. And so were Jake and Carlow, his best friends. Both cut down in their prime. Victims of the conflicts that everybody saw coming, but no one seemed able to stop. Shutting his eyes fleetingly, he saw their images. They were standing together, grinning, alongside him. Smartly suited in their army uniforms. Three friends, oblivious to the dangers that lay ahead. John considered himself luckier than some. He had only lost an arm.

A hand gently stroked his shoulder, interrupting his train of thought.

''Come on, Dad, the temperature will be rising soon. We need to go.''

***

The journey would take more than half an hour. She could have made it on her own much quicker. Emerald had pleaded with him to let her go on her own. But he refused. 'Too soon,' he argued. There were dangers there, so close to the protected domes. And John suspected worse things at the citadel, the bastion of the *Gnostics.*

Father and daughter walked along in silence. There was nothing new to say. The couple had made this trip numerous times. They screened their faces from the red dust that covered the ground and hung ominously in the air. It moved, surreptitiously, around their heads like serpents seeking refuge in exposed cavities. A furtive danger to the eyes, ears, nostrils, and mouth. It was all that remained of the soil that once surrounded them. The empty shells of scorched trees lay lifeless, peppering the land, while the charred bones of animal carcasses reminded them that it had not always been like this.

Their path bore left, and soon, the gleaming tower of the citadel came into view. A construction of exquisite metallic beauty, reflecting the sun's rays with dazzling effect. Like the appearance of a desert mirage or an ancient cathedral basking in former glory, she ruminated. How it contrasted with the lifelessness beyond its gates. With its ten-metre barricade surrounding the city, it presented a formidable sight. Emerald tried to imagine how different life was within its walls. There were stories. But she had never been there and, almost certainly, never would.

Her father gave her a stern look. "Come on. Our business is over here."

They moved towards a much more modest building in front of them. Hewn from local rocks, it resembled a dilapidated fort, austere and uninviting. A queue had formed outside the entrance. The waiting zone was lined with large pieces of stone as the two representatives of unit 214 joined the procession of people in the corral. Others scuttled away, holding on tightly to packages, knowing their lives depended on it.

After several minutes, they arrived at the front. An imposing sign, written in large black painted letters across the doorway, identified the place as *the Food and Water Distribution Centre.* Two armed guards fastidiously scanned the visitors for infection. Satisfied it was safe for them to proceed, the older guard, lean and haggard, with silver strands of fading hair, spoke to John.

''Your identification and fuel log number," he demanded. His colleague was looking curiously at the symbol implanted into the right side of John's head. Three asterisks and the letters 'Hon.'

"An honorary *guardian of the hearth*, I see,'' he bellowed mockingly. ''So how did you acquire that privilege then. Steal it, did you?''

He laughed loudly, then spat on the ground in a gesture of contempt.

''A long story, officer. Something that happened during the refugee wars."

John Byrne raised his fragile body to its full height and stared defiantly at the man.

Scowling, he guided his laser gun in his direction, provocatively resting the target lock across John's heart.

"You don't look much like a war hero to me, Mr. Just another shabby face among hundreds of *tainted* parasites!"

He turned to John's daughter. "But you, young lady. You might have something to offer me."

The guard moved closer to Emerald, wiggling his tongue licentiously and placing his hand on his groin. A grotesque spectacle. 'A gargoyle with no shame,' she frowned. Taking a step back from this invasion of her space, she remained silent. Her tormentor would not succeed in goading or embarrassing her. A steely glance would have to suffice.

Emerald recognised the anger surfacing across her father's face and whispered in his ear.

"Stay calm, Dad. Do not provoke him."

She pulled the plastic cards from her father's hand and thrust them towards the guards.

"They're all in order. Look! Food rations for Five. We will just pay and get out of here."

She took out four pieces of the new metal coinage and presented them.

"Three for the wood and one for delivery of the water."

The guards scrutinised the log and ID again.

"I have heard rumours about you, fella. Three stars, eh. And the title of honour. Be sure that I have marked your card today in more ways than one."

He winked at Emerald. ''And I will see you again, lady. Be certain of that.''

He stamped the log and shouted across to the wood carriers next to him. ''One large crate of ash and mixed wood. One tank of water. To be delivered to unit 214.''

''Now piss off, you two!''

***

They didn't wait around. Mercifully, the transaction had been completed quickly, and their hearth would burn for another fortnight. John and Emerald sauntered across to the building opposite the food centre. Emerald unzipped her trouser pocket to pull out the requisite tokens. They were abruptly stopped in their tracts by what they saw. The body of a man left bound and seated on the ground. The heated air had already collapsed the fullness of his shape, shrivelling his corpse like a deflated doll. The emaciated skeleton reminded John of bodies his platoon had come across in the battlefields of Turkey and Morocco.

The victim had been tied to a large rock, and his hands were restrained behind his back. A single laser blast had been dispatched through his head. Emerald followed the caked flow of dried blood that had meandered down his right cheek and settled at the top of his tunic. Here, the final moments of his life force had shuddered to a halt. She imagined it was her father lying there. How would she react?

A sign hanging around his neck provided onlookers with a blunt explanation:

There is only one punishment for the theft of food: Death.

In that moment, the desire to ever eat again appeared completely repugnant.

A stocky man with potholed burn marks across his face and neck approached the couple. He turned to them, shaking his head.

''Poor bugger. They say he stole some rice from the store. Just trying to feed his children. Now look at him. This is the third execution we've had here this month.''

John and Emerald did not respond. The latter was alone with her thoughts, fixated on the declaration attached to the body.

There is only one punishment.

She repeated the words slowly to herself. It only seemed yesterday that there were lots of different ways to deal with stealing, especially when there were such mitigating circumstances like starvation. So why was there now 'only one?' Her shock was turning to anger. 'What sort of people have we become?' she muttered to herself.

Emerald looked at the faces of the other bystanders who had gathered. How quickly everyone had embraced these new sanctions, she thought. It reinforced her view that there was little room for compassion in this new savage existence, let alone the possibility of tolerance or forgiveness. Their leaders said that these were luxuries they could no longer afford. The lessons of brutality speak loudest, they now announced. And yet. If anything fired Emerald's sense of hope, it was the importance of empathy. A willingness to understand and support those around them in desperate need. Especially now when conditions are so harsh. The mad daily scramble for resources and the cynical indifference towards those who had been left destitute by the *Change* was what got us all into this situation in the first place, she reflected. 'All we have done is replace one obscene reality with another.'

Her father didn't want to linger and waved her forward. They climbed the steps and entered the store. An oval ledge, set upon stone columns, formed the centrepiece of the room. Coils of twisted barbed wire surrounded it in tall connecting rows on either side of the counter. Behind it, they could see the earnest figures of the *carriers,* beavering away as they fetched food packages from the storage area.

Three armed inspectors were busy stacking packets of rations as they approached the ledge. One of them lifted his gaze to face his new customers. The increasingly rare sight of hanging folds of bloated excess belly fat suggested he was a man who still managed to eat well. Emerald thought he resembled an old bulldog.

He reached to collect five coupons from John.

"What about number 6?'" he queried. "You still haven't claimed rations for the sixth person.''

"She hasn't joined us yet."

"It's more than two years since you registered her. She's dead, old fella! I don't think you can count!'' (Both broke into laughter)

"Are all the others still alive?'' the second official enquired. "We check, you know!"

John B lifted his chin and scowled in defiance. "Yes. Somehow, we all manage."

Another inspector grinned, revealing an odious cavity of misshaped yellow teeth.

"Maybe we should start to cut these rations. After all, we do not want you getting too fat now, do we?"

He mockingly rubbed his stomach in a gesture of obese pride. John was no longer looking at him. He had retreated inwardly behind a screen. A space that protected him from the temptation to punch this cantankerous moron to the floor. A reckless reaction, he knew, that must be kept in check. The anger must remain hidden. Those old army disciplines. He needed to keep focused.

''Are you listening, old man?'' the inspector prodded him with his weapon.

''Please. He is in pain.'' Emerald interjected.

Mindful of the growing queue behind them, the store inspectors measured out five portions in old, dirty plastic bags and pushed them across the counter. The choice was not extensive. Small bags of rice, dried lentils, ground wheat for bread and a tub of green paste they called *sellium.* No one was too sure what it contained, but the authorities described it as a blend of minerals and a few vitamins. They packed the provisions into the two rucksacks on their backs and departed for home.

***

The suffocating atmosphere of late morning was doing its best to steal the last drops of moisture from their throats when they finally reached the compound. John dropped to one knee with fatigue. Hawk and another member of the community, Raul, were busy repairing the plastic bricks in the roof.

''You two are cutting it fine today,'' Hawk shouted down from the ladder.

''Yeah. You got my message about the tiles, then?''

''Of course. We are just about finished.''

He smiled. His gesture carried more than just a polite response to praise. His affection for Emerald was obvious to everyone.

''Have you checked the solar panels today?'' John shouted. Raul gave him a thumbs up.

''The connection is a bit choked with the sand, but I've cleaned it up. Enough to power the news pod,'' he added.

John B thrust his rucksack onto the floor with satisfaction. "Everything is OK. We eat and burn wood for another month.''

***

They were woken early the following morning by the sound of a loud engine. A dilapidated lorry, attached to a trailer, pulled up outside the compound. A crate of wood was unceremoniously thrown to the floor. Hawk and Emerald quickly scaled the perimeter ladder to meet their visitors.

"Hurry up and sign this, you idle buggers! We have plenty of other deliveries to make, you know."

Hawk and Emerald had been joined by Raul and another of the inhabitants, the woman they knew by the name of Hope. She had teased them shortly after arrival by unexpectedly dangling a snippet of controversy. "John had once known me by another name,'' she exclaimed but didn't elaborate. ''That's our little secret, isn't it, John?''

He had nodded awkwardly.

***

The four of them had already formed a human chain to carry the logs over the barricade of rock and into the compound.

"And do not even think about burning that crate, or this will be your last ever delivery!'' The petulant driver yelled at them.

"Now, where is your water tank?"

Raul raised his middle finger in a gesture of defiance. The very idea of seizing the crate and destroying it for firewood was preposterous. He was about to expand on his frustration when a hand appeared from behind to clasp his.

"Not today, Raul. Choose carefully when to fight your battles. There will be other days.''

Hope loosened her grasp and waved towards the truck.

''Over here, on the left,'' she cried diplomatically.

***

Too Much Time

It would have been a lie for anyone to pretend that the evenings didn't drag at the compound of unit 214. The same was surely true for each of the other communities. There was common agreement among the groups that much of the initial procrastination about their predicament was now banal and quite meaningless. All those endless discussions, the arguments, the apportioning of blame. The wisdom of a technological age was brought to its knees by power, greed and global inequality. What more was there to say? Each minute trapped in the darkness seemed to pass more slowly than the last. Tortuous moments of monotony as they tried to busy themselves under candlelight. A little reading, some household chores, and the endless thirst for news from the outside world. Such stories were fed into the compound twice a day via the crude screens set up by *Gnosis*. Sombre-faced newsreaders relayed a conveyor belt of information about the food wars and the damage caused by the *Change*. But their mood shifted as they shared details about what they referred to as the *Innovation Programme.* A plan to rebuild the country included the maintenance of clean water and food provision. Creating opportunities for work and greater social interaction. However, few, including the members of unit 214, had seen much evidence of any of this happening yet. Instead, those who lived outside the protected areas took a more pessimistic view. These newscasts were perceived as no more than cynical tools to indoctrinate and suppress ordinary survivors like themselves. Establish law and order and raise spirits. But the water remained suspect, people were still becoming ill, and the food provisions were meagre. People continued to die from curable illnesses. As for community engagement, each unit remained in relative isolation, mostly driven by suspicion and fear of their neighbours. The *Innovation Programme* seemed to have barely started at all. Still, it created something to discuss and contemplate in the long evening hours.

***

Emerald and her father sat in the warm glow of the hearth. She stared at him with the eyes of a mechanic inspecting a vehicle in need of major repair. His lower limbs were swollen and bruised, his left shoulder twisted by the constant weight of his new arm. But most of all, that gaunt look of someone who was running out of time. A man resigned to the fact that he was trying to hold back the inevitable.

“I don’t know if I can carry on much longer,” he whispered to her. “They are going to be looking to you for support sooner than I realised.”

Emerald had feared this. Those fierce brown eyes that once protected her and her brother and sister from harm were now dimmed. She had watched her paternal warrior gradually shed his armour and yield to the wounds that distressed him. The time had come for her to step forward.

John clasped the badge on his shirt. “Do you know how I earned this, my girl?”

She nodded. “For military courage, Dad. But you’ve never really told me what happened.”

“That’s because I’ve been waiting for the right moment.”

He cradled her hands in his. “I understand it has been difficult for you. I haven’t been the easiest person to live with during these troubled days. But I had to mould you. Turn you into a hardened survivor. It’s the only way.”

He opened the small brown box that he kept locked with a rusty lock. The key hung from a chain around his neck.

“These papers explain it all. Please, don’t be too critical of me. I did what I had to. To serve my country. To keep colleagues alive.”

He pulled out an old parchment. ‘’You don’t see too many of these anymore. Hand-written and sealed with a bond of authenticity. From the *House of National Defence.* A guarantee of safe passage for me and five others. The legal right to set up an independent community, a unit with full food rations and fuel allowance.''

Emerald was already reading the second page, entitled 'Acts of Heroism against Enemies of the State.' He guessed what she was thinking. John shook his head in self-deprecating fashion:

"I was no hero. Just a soldier doing his job. But it was what happened while I was at the front that will live with me forever. However, it's not that I want to discuss with you. It's about your mother.''

Emerald's heartbeat quickened. Her father had rarely spoken about Bethany before, despite her numerous attempts to engage him on the subject. All she knew was that Mum had been taken by a virus when she was a child.

"Before I speak to you about this, there are other things I need to go through with you. Be patient with me."

She wasn't really listening as her father ploughed through piles of information about the preparation and storage of wood and how the quotas could be accessed. The reasons underpinning the choice of trees chosen to grow under the dome. Types that would burn hot and slowly, like ash, or burn longest during the cold nights, like oak and poplar. Trees that grew rapidly, like silver birch, but also burned quickly. With temperatures plummeting to around minus twenty each night, every piece of information was vital, he said. She would need to know how to dry and season the wood, although that was becoming easier with the daytime temperatures. Where once it would take six months to remove the dampness entrapped within, it now only took a couple of weeks. He explained how to find and make kindling, what time to begin the process at night and how the ledger should be kept. This had to be accurate. If there was any suspicion that their firewood was being over-used or sold, then that would be the end of their fires. As his next of kin, she would inherit his position as a *Guardian of the Hearth,* nominated by him, for as long as the law was observed.

Emerald already knew much of this, like the back of her hand. She'd watched him studiously over the last two years as he had done his best to lead their small group.

"Tell me about what happened to Mum."

He rested the thumb and forefinger of his good hand on the greying beard that bounded his jaw and paused, searching for the words.

"How much do you remember about the final months of the *food wars,* Emerald?"

"As you know, Dad, I was young."

"Eight, I seem to recall."

"I remember you coming home on leave. We were all so excited. It seemed that you had been away for years."

Images of these episodes cascaded before his eyes. The unexpected opportunity to return home. To receive medical treatment for the missing arm. The delight of seeing his children again. The shock of seeing Bethany emaciated and weak. Her life, ebbing away. Her dark, sullen eyes were heavy with pain as the virus slowly ate away at her body.

"It was the last time we were all together," he reflected. "Mum, me, you, Amber, and Tito."

"I miss them terribly," she exclaimed. "If it hadn't been for Hope…."

"I know the debt we owe her. And I should have been here to help you all when Mum was fading away. Instead of being at the front. I will never forgive myself."

He hesitated. Tears began to form in the corner of his eyes. "I never saw Mum or Tito again."

Anger & Dreams

Hawk sat alone, temporarily shielded from the oppressive reach of the sun. Shaded by old protruding roof tiles, he stared out from the remoteness of the dilapidated annexe. A building that the other inhabitants of unit 214 shunned. Most of the day, these remains were exposed to the blinding heat. Apart from this one spot. The remnants of some old animal shed. Sometimes, he closed his eyes, twitched his nostrils and imagined that the elements had concocted a pungent odour from the past. Something to bewitch his curiosity. Crusted excrement in the corners, maybe, or the ghost of some domestic creature that once ate and slept there. He shuffled his body to accommodate the changing angles of the sun's penetration. Avoiding them had become a child-like game. Strange, he thought, how somewhere as prosaic as this helped to sharpen his concentration. Was it the stillness that drew him there? The elusive opportunity for privacy? Hawk wasn't sure. But it allowed the words he searched for to crystallise in his head. Words he needed to write down.

He wasn't like John, who wanted to take his memories to the grave. Hawk was desperate to expel the demons that the conflict had inflicted upon him. More importantly, those who came after would want to know about the insanity that unfolded. He was convinced that the television coverage had avoided showing the whole truth. The unstoppable madness of what people are prepared to do in war. The brutality, the humiliation, the starvation. Add the serious fuel shortages and large numbers of displaced people, and it was a recipe for disaster.

Politicians would talk about duty and heroism, but as always, they did what they had to do to ensure their own survival. After all, important figures had to be protected, they would say. To reveal the enormity of the crisis would surely have destabilised the country. If the nation were to prepare effectively for the aftermath, leaders would need to be economical with the truth.

But soldiers like him knew the truth. They were there at the front line. They could authenticate what took place amidst the anarchy and chaos. They knew what they saw with their own eyes. No one should have had to deal with what they encountered. A catastrophe that would scar all who bore witness to the events. Some, like John, maintained their silence. But Hawk needed another way to banish his nightmares. He longed to find some sort of therapeutic release. And, by articulating his own testimony, he would honour his fallen comrades. Men and women who paid for their courage with their lives. He would write an account of what really happened. John had counselled him against it. There were powerful voices who would not welcome such a manuscript. It might even cost him his life, he said. Still, if his writing made even a tiny contribution to the extensive debate about what went wrong, historians and writers would look favourably at his modest testimony. It would be worth the risk.

***

Hawk had found the bulky notebook in the bombed-out ruin of a bookshop in a village near the Greek-Turkish border days before the fighting stopped. What was left of his platoon was searching for something to eat. The shop was next door to what they used to call a supermarket. He'd wandered off and found himself inside the bookshop. Buried by rubble, under a broken cupboard, was the ornate outline of a writing pad. It was in pristine condition. Waiting for somebody to fill the pages with their angry words, he joked at the time. A thing of beauty, he thought, untouched by the contamination of war. It was the colour of the cover that first caught his eye: garish blue, with yellow petals protruding from the debris like an emerging Spring flower. The germ of an idea immediately emerged. "One day," he said, "I will recount what happened to an ordinary soldier like me so others will never forget."

***

Hawk shook the red dust from the cover and opened the notepad. He had already filled several pages with comments, notes, sketches, testimonies, and opinions he remembered from people he had encountered during the conflict. International journalists, local Turkish and Greek civilians, shopkeepers, and musicians. Russian troops, British soldiers, and refugees. It had been a melting pot of drama, human anxiety and tension. Here was his opportunity to stir the ingredients and clarify what emerged.

He browsed through what he had collected and began to re-read an article he had cut out from an American newspaper:

'Some would say that it started with angry groups of refugees on some well-known Greek islands. Places more accustomed to European tourists and untroubled days of holiday relaxation. Back then, there were oracular signs of what was to come…'

***

His regiment had been told that significant groups of people had started arriving from the north coast of Africa by sea, precariously packed into fragile boats and ships. Many were fleeing the rages of war and famine, traumatised by the increasing social chaos they left behind. Others, economic migrants, chasing the security of paid work. None of this was new. They had been arriving for two hundred years. But not in these numbers. His regiment's task was to re-establish order, working closely with Greek and other European military units.

***

He hadn't originally intended to join the army. Hawk was more interested in conservation. A man at his happiest crawling around wild, green places in his old rubber boots, protecting animals, especially the birds, and identifying flora. That's how he acquired the name. Like a bird of prey, swooping down on those who sought to damage the habitat of his feathered companions. Unfortunately, employment at conservation charities proved difficult to secure. After fruitless attempts to secure work with any of the Landscapes Trusts, Woodland Forrest Centres, or the Canal and River monitoring groups, he drifted into various kinds of casual work. There were bills to pay. He had a young child to support.

Saul had arrived unexpectedly, the product of a short liaison with a fellow conservation worker. Both, however, perished through disease and malnutrition within twelve months of the youngster's birth. The loss of his son and girlfriend left him bereft and devastated. For his own sanity, he needed to divert himself from this tragedy. He plunged his energies in campaigns against the establishment. Hawk spent much of his spare time online, challenging local landowners, businessmen, and politicians to protect the environment. It brought him into regular conflict with what he believed to be the enemies of nature. This included building companies and, occasionally, the police. He left the council house he had shared with his girlfriend, Lilly, and baby son; the reminders were just too painful. Hawk joined a group of eco-warriors and lived illegally in a small commune within a local private wood. He found work in garden centres and large farms in the area. Slowly, he built up some of the skills he would later rely on. The nurturing of edible plants, the value of woodcraft. His companions were an eclectic mix. One of the men he befriended had been discharged recently from the army. Trevor shared Hawk's interest in ornithology. An altercation with a local farmer one evening, in which Hawk sustained a black eye and bruising to his face, led Trevor to teach him some self-defence techniques. Exasperated by his vulnerability, he also learned about the operation of firearms. 'Learn to disarm an aggressor, and you'll stay alive longer,' his new friend explained. Hawk had laughed at the time, but when local thugs attacked the camp one evening, he was grateful for the skills Trevor had taught him. There was no need to discharge the shotgun he'd acquired. The fact that he had the confidence to carry it helped to prevent the situation from escalating. The local youths dispersed when challenged by Hawk and Trevor. Although he hadn't realised at the time, such confidence would serve him well when he was later conscripted to the ambitiously named 'Army Peace Corps'.

However, his true love remained the mysteries of the forest; the dexterity in moving silently through woodland terrain and observing his feathered companions from the trees. There were times when he wished he had been born one of them. Never enthralled with his birth name, Matthew, Hawk increasingly discarded it in favour of the name of a bird of prey that fascinated him. A creature whose grace and speed reflected its place in the ornithological hierarchy, a prince of the skies. After he was conscripted, where few were called by their first names, he threw the name 'Hawk' at his new comrades, and it stuck.

***

Hawk's mind returned to the refugees and migrants. What he was reading resonated with his experience there. Instead of finding a brighter future in a land of 'milk and honey,' the hopes of these newcomers had been left shattered on the beaches. For years, the welcome promised by the traffickers and insurgents had never materialised. Instead, they were greeted by angry residents, fearful that their own dwindling food supplies and jobs would soon evaporate with each new wave of arrivals. Centuries before, the first arrivals had been treated with limited compassion and sympathy. But attitudes changed as the numbers grew. Now, the authorities herded them into vast, gated enclosures at gunpoint that looked like concentration camps. This ramped up the tensions, denied the essential resources they needed and, unwilling to be corralled, violence erupted. Desperate men and women rebelled. Both refugees and locals suffered casualties. Rumours spread that certain foreign powers were assisting the newcomers with weapons delivered across the sea in an attempt to deliberately destabilise the region. Other European countries were shocked at the inability of the Greek military or the European Community to suppress the violence. They promised to send EU federal soldiers to assist. But even this proved problematic.

He put the article down and started writing.

''And I found myself part of that response,'' he wrote. 'Except we were not members of the European Federal Army. The United Kingdom had left the European Union more than two hundred years before. We were part of a newly formed peacekeeping corps. Comprised of non-EU soldiers from other parts of Europe, together with significant numbers of military support from the United States. Entrusted to help hold the line between Africa and Europe.'

Given the acrimonious circumstances that prevailed in that part of the world, Hawk was surprised when he received news of his destination. He'd expected more training before entering the war zone. Why had he joined? One arrest too many had forced him to recognise that he needed to develop something his parents had failed to instil. Self-discipline. The army recruitment day he'd attended sold a lifestyle where he felt that this could toughen him up. Hawk managed to convince his interviewers that he wanted to change. In truth, his skirmishes with the law were not deemed relevant. They were accepting almost anybody willing to sign up.

The British government had only agreed to send soldiers out of self-interest, some had said. A Europe in turmoil would not continue to provide the food trade Britain so desperately relied upon. And anyway, when they heard in their barracks that the Americans were also supporting the war, it was just like history repeating itself. And there could only be one outcome. As in 1945. That's what the lads in barracks had said.'

He put his pen down and continued reading the article.

'The boats grew larger and started to land on mainland Greece. Those who came were increasingly well-armed. Turkey initially agreed to support their neighbours with troops, but traditional tensions and prejudices prevented effective action. Some said that Turkey's recent admission into the *Federation of European States* had caused friction in parts of Western Europe. It was not what influential Northern European countries like Germany, The Netherlands and France wanted. But the old dream of an enlarged European Community was fading fast. Hungary and Poland had long since left, while Germany was considering its position. There was growing unrest there about the levels of finance needed to sustain the new EU infrastructure. And they had their own challenges to address. The continuous unrest about cries to restore fossil fuels and diminish food crops also kept non-aligned nations, such as Britain and some of the Scandinavian countries, fearful of closer commitment. Instead, they turned their allegiances towards an increasingly isolated America.

By the time Russian tanks had steamrolled into Ankara, the die was cast. Their battle was not with the Turks but with what they saw as the threat of a new caliphate of Muslim warriors from North Africa and the Middle East. Men driven by extremist ideologies and self-interest seizing the opportunity to fill the political vacuum. Many Turkish people were uneasy about military action against fellow Muslims. They felt bound together by poverty and faith. Some endured a standard of living that was barely much better than their new Muslim neighbours.

With much of Africa torn apart by war and political chaos, some could even empathise with their need to establish a new home in the southern European mainland. It hardly needed to be said that the Greeks saw this differently. And as events escalated, other powerful voices were drawn in. Iran declared support for the refugees, leaving the south of Europe wobbling on the edge of social disintegration.

'And that was when we arrived,' he added to his book with an almost nonchalant note. He started to sketch ghostly figures descending from a shadowy aircraft.

Hawk picked up his pen again and took several deep breaths. He was clear about what he wanted to add next.

***

'I remember arriving near the Turkish border, close to the Euros River like it was yesterday. The colours, the excitement, the smells of a mysterious new land. The banter and bravado of young recruits like me, keen to prove themselves. Most of them were naïve, bursting with adrenalin, fresh out of training, and on foreign shores for the first time. There was a macho atmosphere, an eruption of testosterone. But my own mood had been more sombre. I was more nervous about what we might face.'

He paused. 'Then we were parachuted into Greek airspace,' he scribbled. 'And everything changed.'

It all came flooding back. 'Warm rain is softly falling. We're about to clip onto the release bar above us, about to drop into uncertainty. I could still see the look on my comrades' faces. The bravado had evaporated. You could smell the fear. One of the guys opposite me had soiled himself. Another, Geoff Hutton, had wet his pants. All that bluster trickled away like the urine now staining his trousers. Frozen in silence, unspoken trepidation. Who would survive the onslaught? Who would even survive that first day? Not Hutton. He didn't survive the landing. Impaled through his torso by a tree branch.

"Our parachutes cascaded into the breaking dawn like kites on a summer breeze. My companions and I drifted down towards an uncertain fate.'

PART TWO

Sector I: Formerly Known As The Northwest Of England

The Black Meteorite Mines

April 25th, 2227

Amber threw her pick onto the floor and sank back, exhausted. Her right hand throbbed with the endeavours of several hours of digging. Extracting the mineral rock was not an easy task. The large plastic box beside her was barely half full, and the reality of what lay ahead filled her with foreboding.

From behind, a man's voice summoned her attention.

"Come on, girl, no slacking!"

She recognised the voice only too well. Cooper, the tunnel leader. He moved closer and began to run his rough, stumpy fingers through her hair. She flinched and pushed her locks back under the protection of her hat. Amber's repulsion for this man was hard to disguise. A nauseous feeling overcame her whenever he moved close. She could almost taste him salivating over her. "Wanker," she mumbled under her breath. Amber felt suffocated by the smell of his rancid sweat. It choked the personal space that she held so precious, down among the narrow passageways of the mine. She loathed him more with each new shift. Her supervisor, not for the first time, had paraded his sexual intentions. Two months earlier, he had forced himself upon her in an isolated part of the compound. Defiled and in despair, she had concluded at the time that death would have been a preferable option. Now, she imagined plunging her pickaxe into his groin and watching him bleed out. But it would not happen today. There were always two guards watching his every move.

Cooper's only salient feature was his experience of the mine. It certainly wasn't the brutal way he managed the female workers. But he did know his way around the underground passages and understood exactly the challenges they faced each day. That made it worse. He had worked alongside them as a digger for more than a year before he gained his promotion. Rewarded for reporting the theft of small quantities of the black meteorite by a couple of desperate workers. Individuals without the physical strength to make their quotas anymore. Two women were made examples of by the mine owners in front of the others. Without a recognisable police force or government protection, these people could do as they wished. Under the ground, their word was now law. Amber shuddered at the memory. Vulnerable souls were beaten savagely by the guards with their rifle buts until their cries turned to whimpers, and the whimpers turned to silence. Only one of them had survived. The other was the mother of two young boys. The assembled miners watched in silence. Amber could still recall her incredulity, her shame: the lack of protest, the pervading atmosphere of fear among them. None of the workers said a word. For some, warnings are designed not to be forgotten.

***

Cooper moved away, and Amber breathed more easily. She massaged her tired muscles in both arms. Then, she permitted herself a smile. A picture of her father's face had come into her head. He would have sent the little runt crashing to the ground with a single blow. Her protector, her guardian, her dad.

But it was not her lack of physical power that counselled caution. John Byrne would hardly recognise the transformation in his daughter. Two years spent digging out meteorologic rock had strengthened her body and, more importantly, her resolve to survive. She was a different creature now. Once, Amber had a head bursting with ideas and a body that was fragile. But that was in another life. This headstrong young woman in the second year of her philosophy degree at university was going to change the world, she recalled. A future in politics, academia, or journalism would consume her energy. Back then, she did not know one end of a hammer from the other. Artisans and craftsmen used tools. Not someone like her. But the world suddenly changed in a way no one could have imagined. The rigours and ambitions of academic thinking gave way to expediency, except in those early risings of post-apocalyptic optimism when the survivors talked of working in collaboration. Before desperation took root, and people did what they needed to do just to stay alive. Down below the surface of the earth, there was little work for philosophers. What was required were diggers, not procrastinators. People who could extract something that still had value or could be sold. That was if you wanted to eat.

"Amber"

She twisted her neck to see the more reassuring figure of Joel crouching behind her. The dust was still settling from the protective jacket, and he was shaking.

"I am done for the day. How about you?"

She frowned.

"I think I'm still a couple of hours away from finishing. Unlike you, I see."

She stared at the bulging yellow box he had dragged along. Overflowing with black ore. A second bucket, attached and quarter-filled, ensured his remuneration that day would be more than satisfactory.

"Don't fret. I'll share some of this with you."

He pointed to the box.

"I've got more than I need to make the weighing. Go on, take some of this."

She forced a gentile smile in his direction. Joel was one of the few people she knew who never demanded a price for his generosity.

Joel was also one of only two people in the mine she trusted. He had emerged as her confidant and protector in a place of constant danger. Although he never asked for anything in return, when he looked at her, she felt his eyes were filled with yearning.

Nothing further had been said in the six months they had known each other. But she knew how he felt. And the risks that such a declaration could bring. Immediate expulsion for him and a life of humiliation for her. Amber smiled and thanked him for his kindness. In truth, she was not sure how she would have survived down there without him.

With redistributed buckets, they strolled towards the lift shaft. It would take exactly three and a half minutes for the wooden elevator to release them from the caldron below. As the safety bar locked into place, Amber closed her eyes and used the time as a meditative 'bay', permitting herself a few much-needed private moments. She waited for the creaking noise of the pullies. These lifting ropes provided a background rhythm to shut out the helplessness. They blocked out everything around her that might eat away at her confidence. Weary voices, the constant coughing, the air of despondency that surreptitiously sucked the courage from their veins. But now, every lift journey was a metaphor of expectation. New stones, in a wall of resistance. And resist she must, to build resilience for what lay in the days ahead.

The small light above them gradually expanded until it exploded into brilliant sunlight as they reached the top of the mine. Amber blinked and opened her eyes. Shielding the intense heat with their caps as best they could, Amber and Joel retreated to the weighing centre with the other members of the shift.

Over a hundred miners emptied the contents of their buckets onto a large, multi-sectioned conveyor belt. Each piece of rock was separated, weighed, and scanned for its mysterious black composition before a value was given. Like an old cash till from the past, the machine at the end of the belt added each value and converted the final figure into a food coupon and, hopefully, some money. These would be distributed to them by one of the security guards. That was if their labours below had reached, or surpassed, the daily quota. This varied according to the identification label that followed their initial assessment. Just a crude analysis of physical capability. Put simply, everyone permitted to mine was classified as strong, reasonably able or baseline. Reduced to an A, B, or C. Badges were sewn to the overalls that miners paid for at the start of their employment. Joel's imposing physique and strength had earned him an 'A' status. Amber, like her friend Yolina, was in the category 'C' or borderline employees, which was reflected in the slightly smaller bucket to fill. If you failed to fill your bucket, you didn't get a coupon and you didn't eat. Three failures, and you would be dismissed. Cast out into a dangerous and unknown world. There were few ways a young woman or man could obtain food coupons outside the mine. Unless you possess a rare skill for which there is a huge demand. If not, it was contracted slavery to a rich family or prostitution. Better, then, to carry on mining ore into the early evening to make your quota.

And for some, there was another trial to contend with. Once the worthless rock shavings and debris had been discarded, each worker was required to stand in a triangular stance to be searched. This was always an indignant experience, especially if the searching guard was Ivan. He made it clear that he saw his job as carrying certain privileges. Chief among these was the excuse to molest the workers he lusted over during their search. Amber had quickly learned to disguise her attractive face with short, scraggy hair and enduring layers of dust. Her oversized tunic hung limply across her body, hiding the curvaceous outline of her breasts. The baggy grey trousers completed a dour image. It was designed to make her look older, less attractive, and blend in with the grime. And it did.

She crept tentatively towards the security line, relieved that her efforts had secured a token that day. Fortunately for her, Ivan was already indulging himself with another helpless victim. The anguished face of her friend, Yolina, stared hopelessly back. Her futile efforts to repel his invading hands, a humiliating experience. Amber knew only too well what she was going through.

Joel pushed her forward over the security line. This was not a time to loiter.

***

There was little time left to shower or brush the dust and sweat away. Hot food would be served to those with coupons, and it would only be served at 5.30 PM. It would be foolish to miss the opportunity for sustenance. Joel and Amber sat together in the canteen, trying to revive their energies. The thick porridge on offer hardly excited their taste buds. It might have contained vegetables, but neither of them was sure. The two friends indulged in one of their favourite meal games: exchanging fantasies about which gastronomic delicacies they most missed from the past. Whether it was chocolate, meat, or succulent fruit, it helped to kill time, not to mention distract them from the appalling monotony of what they were forced to endure daily.

Together with Yolina, the three of them had talked about leaving the deep mines and trying to make their way across the desert towards the Western sector, the *Gnosis* peninsula. There were stories that life was more bearable there. That people were supported by those in authority. Wood and food were more available. Some groups lived in supported units. Amber had her own personal reasons for choosing the area. It was where she had grown up. She dreamed about seeing her family again, assuming they were still alive. Amber's mother had perished in the pandemic, but she hoped her father and younger sister, Emerald, were still alive.

***

Joel's roots were much further away in Central Africa. His father had brought him to England from Nigeria during the fuel wars. To stay at home would have been suicide, he'd told his son. Fortunately, his father's business affairs had introduced him to important contacts. People with money could arrange to get them out of their increasingly dangerous home city, Lagos. The seventeen-year-old lad and his father, already grieving for his mother and two sisters, killed by occupying troops, had secured passage in a ship to Europe. It had cost his father everything he had. He yearned for the new life that awaited them in Europe. But salvation was about to be snatched away from the teenage boy and his father. An unprovoked fight on board the ship had deprived

Joel of his only protector in this world. Possibly a racist attack or maybe an opportunist mugging gone wrong. The captain's investigation had failed to establish the truth. The shock of his dad's murder understandably paralysed the youth. Luckily for Joel, Dan, one of the crew members who had seen the incident, took pity on the boy.

He secured extra food and water for the teenager and kept an eye out for his welfare during the last week of the voyage. By the time they had arrived in Greece, Joel had realised that he needed to become a man, and quickly. Be prepared to do what is necessary to survive. His physical strength and quick-wittedness would be put to the test to ensure that the family name was kept alive. Survival. One challenging day at a time. After working his way across Europe, he arrived in the UK. In the South of England, Joel came across someone who told him about the mines. About the black mineral that could be dug out of the earth and exchanged for food and lodging. In a fortunate twist of fate, he had arrived in the vicinity of the deep mines looking for work just as the *Change* unfolded. Like many others, he initially sheltered from the fierce weather below the ground. But once the storms had subsided and the new weather pattern became established, the rumours suggested that there was one place to head to. Where employment and food could be found. The place where the black meteorite was mined. He was sure there would be opportunities for anybody who could work hard to thrive.

***

Yolina was a petite, laconic woman who had also found her way to the mines through desperation. She, too, was a long way from home. The strain of recent events had left an enduring imprint on her features. The disappointments and humiliations of recent events in her life had torn away the pleasant smile that once lit up her face. Traumatised by what had happened, her deep blue eyes, once vibrant, were now dimmed, framed by dark troughs and creases. But with a crown of lush, blond hair tied back in a ponytail, she was still noticeably attractive. Originally from Lublin, in the north of Poland, Yolina had come to the West to find work as a teacher. Cataclysmic events had contrived to dismantle what confidence she once had, leaving her distraught and vulnerable. Nobody wanted a 'modern foreign languages' teacher anymore. Not in this new world. What masqueraded as the new government in Britain had more immediate priorities. An innovative new model for education would have to wait. It didn't require people like her. Having initially been employed privately as a French, German, and English tutor within an affluent family from Saudi Arabia, the increasing financial collapse resulted in her losing this job. The family returned to the Middle East, and Yolina was trapped in what was left of the UK. Any attempt to travel home to Poland would have been ill-judged and dangerous.

Yolina had been reduced to offering favours to influential men. That was how she ended up at the mine. Abandoned by a local official who had grown tired of her. Barely managing, as a 'C' worker, and already with two quota warnings. She was running out of options. She had come across Amber by chance shortly after Cooper's assault. Amber was traumatised by the violation in a bad way. Yolina knew more than most what to do to help this woman. She took her back to the accommodation block to clean her up and held her hands for some time. Both women knew that it was pointless to report him. Yolina drew upon her own experience of sexual assault to assist the victim in restoring some semblance of self-esteem. They became good friends afterwards.

All three of them had decided that they couldn't stay there much longer. They would break their contracts and head west, towards the *Wastelands*.

"Utter madness," Yolina had initially concluded upon hearing about the plan. But arrangements were already in place. There was no turning back, the other two declared. "We are leaving tomorrow," declared Amber. "Are you coming?" A nod of the head confirmed that there would be three of them leaving. Each of them knew there would be real dangers. They would need resilience. Keep their nerve. And, they hoped, enjoy a fair degree of luck.

***

Amber watched the other inhabitants of block C as they lay deep in slumber. It was 5.00 AM, and there was a quiet calmness in the room. This was interrupted, sporadically, by the usual nasal sounds of arcane sleep. Daybreak was already beginning to dissolve the darkness from the skies to herald a new day. She waited another five minutes to be certain they were all still asleep before rising from her bed and throwing on three levels of outside clothing, including her hooded coat. Her rucksack was already packed with food for five days, together with as much water as she could squeeze in. Alongside these supplies were added a few personal mementoes. An ornate mirror that she'd been told had once belonged to her mother, a faded picture of her family, a silver necklace, and a bar of fragrant soap. There was also a sum of two hundred and fifty-one money units, all she had scraped and saved together for such a moment. Nobody was too sure what such a sum was worth anymore. There was just about room for a spare pair of boots that she'd bought from a woman at the mine. All squeezed into a black backpack, ready for the journey she'd been planning for months. It may have been a step into the unknown, but now her heart quickened with the excitement of the moment.

Yolina was busy in Block B, making similar travel arrangements. Joel was housed further down the block and had been awake for nearly an hour. He was rehearsing the plan in minute detail and knew exactly what he was required to do. The accommodation building was not a prison, but the entrance was guarded at night. Private security ensured the safety of all the working inhabitants within the compound and prevented any outsiders from taking refuge there. The thought of somebody wanting to leave this protected haven would have perplexed the owners. After all, the outside world offered only freezing temperatures, violent winds at night, and searing heat during the daytime.

The three miners met at exactly 5.30 AM. They stood like shadows at the end of the accommodation area, peering out at the security fence. The plan was neither sophisticated nor subtle. Yolina would distract the first guard with suggestive gestures about how he might solve her insomnia, while Joel would creep up behind the second sentry and dispatch him to the ground with as minimal force as possible. Satisfied he had rendered him unconscious; Joel would join Amber in 'taking out' the second guard before he had the chance to either harm Yolina or raise the alarm.

They had studied the early morning movements of the guards carefully and knew they would not be expecting a threat to come from inside the compound. The plan started well, as the security guard known as Rico naively responded to the alluring charms of the young Polish teacher. His friend rubbed his eyes and laughed as Rico wandered over to the sleepless miner, who was engaging him in conversation. A single blow by Joel to the head of the second guard, Martes, sent him sprawling into the dust, where he lay motionless.

Unfortunately, Joel's attempts to incapacitate the lusting Rico didn't go quite so well. The security guard heard his footsteps, then turned to grapple with the Nigerian. But the absconding miner succeeded in snatching Rico's rifle from the ground. In the melee, a shot was fired before Amber picked up her friend's wooded pole and crashed it across the guard's head. He stumbled back and fell to the floor.

All three escapees ran for the exit as security lights lit up the yard. The trample of feet and angry cries rose behind them as the three friends burst through the gate into the half-light and disappeared into the early morning mist. They kept on running until their hearts felt like exploding. The icy crispness of the early hour froze their faces but pushed their legs to give even more. The outline of a ridge of rocks rose to meet them in the distance, and they headed towards them with urgency. Finally, the rocks enveloped their outlines as they collapsed, exhausted, behind dark boulders. The angry voices behind them began to subside. Then, there was only silence. It was clear they were no longer being pursued. Yolina could hardly breathe but tried to laugh as she hugged her fellow escapees.

"This journey is only just beginning," Amber reminded her sombrely.

"Ten minutes rest, guys," she gasped.

Joel blew his cheeks out in defiance. "There is no going back now."

***

With the sun's shimmering rays unfurling across the terrain, the fugitives frantically scoured the rocks for sanctuary. They needed to lay low, out of the wind, and rest to gather their strength for the next stage.

It was now 7.00 AM. They had until around midday before it would be too hot to continue. Five hours to negotiate that part of the exposed plains that used to be known as Derbyshire. The priority then was to find shelter, or they were in danger of becoming just another set of dusty bones in the ground. Amber reached into her jacket and pulled out a crumpled map.

"Where on earth did you get that?"

Amber permitted herself a satisfied grin. "I found it on the floor a few days ago, in the woman's toilet area. It's not complete, but it shows a good section of the route we might take. Guess we weren't the only ones thinking of leaving the mines."

Joel was busy scrutinising the map. "This section here, (he said, pointing) Between the hills and the Wastelands." There was a large piece missing. "Do we know what's there?"

Yolina said she'd heard rumours about a group who had cut themselves off from everybody else. Surviving by scavenging and other things. Amber shuffled nervously.

"What other things?"

"I don't know. Nobody goes down there to trade anymore. Guess we will need to be careful."

Joel kept his own counsel. He, too, had heard about the ones who called themselves the *Separated,* and much of what he had heard alarmed the Nigerian.

Their spirits fortified by cold tea and dried bread, they set out again, keeping close to the foothills of the moors. The walking was hard, and layers of clothing disappeared from their bodies as the heat became stronger. Their throats ached for fluid, but frugal provisions demanded discipline. "Only drink when you absolutely must," said Joel, "And then only a few sips," he added. It was vital that the water they carried be preserved until they found a spring or subterranean stream to replenish it.

Joel glanced at his old, battered watch. The one thing he had salvaged from his father's body. It read 11.45 AM. He took a dusty pair of antiquated binoculars from his bag and examined the contours of land to his left. Eventually, he spotted a break in the rockface.

"Looks like an overhang of rock, protected from the sun. Let's check it out."

Moving closer, they realised the feature was much bigger than they thought. A vast dome of rock had folded across the base columns like a potter had moulded clay into a giant lip. A distinctive ledge of flat stone lay underneath, giving it the impression of an open tomb. Outside, on the edge, the sun's rays shot down like laser beams. There was plenty of room for the three of them to lie down in the apertures and stay protected.

"Nice spot, Joel," Amber shouted.

"Can you two see if there is any old firewood lying around while I do some reconnaissance for water? We'll need to be ready for later."

Joel knew better than most where to look for water in such a landscape. As a boy, back in Africa, he and his friends would look for water beneath the dried river basins in the parched summer months. They had learned to identify the clues contained within the arid ground.

Behind the overhanging pillars were several small crevasses which criss-crossed the base of the rocks. He scanned the bottom of these ravines, looking for signs. He knew that sometimes it was possible for small plants to survive if an underground channel had sprinkled the area and any growth had remained shaded from the glaring heat. He climbed down into the first fissure, but there were only dust and stones there. However, his second investigation was more productive. There, shaded by a chunk of brown limestone, were three young plants, somehow thriving in the conditions. Joel gently caressed one of the stems, filling his nostrils with its rich green scent. It smelt moist and supple. He imagined being enveloped by thousands of such plants, stretching out as far as the eye could see. He scratched below the surface of the stems and, with meticulous concentration, traced the flow of damp, red dust. It seemed to be coming from underneath a large boulder behind them. With the help of a piece of razor-sharp rock, he began digging. The sweat poured down his cheeks as he hacked away. The debris darkened in colour as it became moist. Then, like the standing pools from the sudden storms he once recalled back home, water gently bubbled up and congealed in the dust. He pulled a piece of plastic from his bag and trapped the fresh water. Only a trickle, but enough to slowly fill his two containers. It looked cloudy but clean enough to drink, so he scooped some into his mouth. A little sour, but it could be swallowed. When he had finished, Joel scampered back up the crevasse. Placing four small rocks on top of each other to identify the spot, he walked back to the camp, humming an old Nigerian chant.

His friends heard him coming. They also looked pleased with their own efforts. Three small pieces of withered tree trunk were being hacked apart in readiness for a fire later.

"We should rest up here for the rest of the day," said a smiling Joel. "Gather our strength for crossing those plains." He pointed to the vast expanse of land before them. " Give me your water bottles so I can fill them."

Amber looked concerned. "Be careful, won't you."

He pulled his hood up and shuttled his way down the slope. "I won't be long." Joel was true to his word. He returned in less than twenty minutes with a tangle of old dried plants and four full water bottles.

“This will help get the fire going.’ He added.” Within an hour, the two logs were blowing some much-needed warmth in their direction.

After consuming some of the water, they lay down on their coats and tried to sleep. Yolina tossed and turned on the sandy floor, struggling to find a comfortable position, while Joel lay on his back, thinking of the challenges that lay ahead, before sinking into deep sleep. He turned to speak to Amber, but her eyes were already closed.

***

Yolina was the first to wake. It still felt stiflingly hot, but the blistering heat was starting to fade. Her footsteps woke the other two.

All three felt the energy returning to their bodies. “I don’t know about you two, but I’m hungry,” moaned Joel. They ate the last of the sellium with stale bread.

As the darkness started to descend, cloaked with its cold chill, they put on every piece of clothing they had and snuggled together tightly behind the glow of a modest fire.

Encounter

The night passed slowly, in irregular pockets of further sleep. Despite wrapping themselves tightly with the blankets they had brought, they couldn't avoid the frenzied bouts of shivering, especially when the fire fizzled out. Just after dawn, they crawled out to bathe in the early morning heat. They could hardly move their fingers or toes. It wasn't long before their metal mugs were boiling on the rocky ledge of nature's kettle, and the hot herbal tea raised both their circulation and their spirits.

The next couple of days continued to test their resolve in more ways than they could imagine. A pattern of long walks and weather-enforced rests made all three of them dig deep into their levels of stamina. Yolina was struggling with her left leg and started to limp. Joel had found an old tubular piece of plastic pole and fashioned it into an emergency walking stick. Amber was fatigued, beginning to suffer the effects of too little food, while Joel's throat felt sore and parched. Sleep continued to prove difficult for all of them with the howling winds and low temperatures. All three had forgotten what it was like to sleep outside at night without the insulation of a building. They had, at least, managed to find secure places to bed down. Abandoned houses and old caves provided some shelter from the elements. Evidence pointed to the fact that they had not been the first people to stay in these rocky hollows. Broken cooking utensils and crockery lay strewn across the floor. The bones of a human arm provided uncomfortable speculation.

On the second night, a four-legged visitor appeared at the entrance of their makeshift shelter. It was their heightened sense of cold-numbing restlessness that alerted them to the sound of growling. It lifted them from their mats just in time. A sinister, muffled sound filled the air as the wild dog salivated over the possibility of fresh meat. The hound jumped across the embers of the fire and clawed at Yolina's arm. Joel reached for the rifle he had stolen from the guard at the mine and cocked the trigger. A single shot reverberated around the cave, clipping the animal's ear, sufficient to provoke a release from his clasp of Yolina while it whimpered in pain. As if now enlightened by the language of danger, the beast slowly backed away, eyes glazed in frustration. Amber felt relieved, then scuttled across to comfort the visually distressed Yolina. Multiple layers of clothing had saved her arm from any serious injury. She could only guess what might have happened if the animal had not been alone or gone for her face. Another shot rang out. The women turned to discover that Joel was no longer with them. There was a disturbance in the bushes outside and the shadowy figure of their friend dragging his prey back to the cave. He broke into one of his infectious smiles.

"Guess not being able to sleep well out here has its bonuses," he quipped. "Meat is back on the menu!"

Amber nodded. "Thank God for the rifle."

"Don't thank God. Thank me! It would be silly to miss out on fresh meat."

Joel pulled out a large knife and began slicing the creature open. He used some of the spare wood and stones to make a primitive stove and laid strips of flesh above the fire.

"Eat as much as you can," he demanded. "We can't take much of this flesh with us."

***

They had calculated that it would take several days to cross the hill country before descending into the outskirts of the *Wastelands*. A journey of some 140 miles was spent dodging the worst excesses of night cold and midday heat, and that was assuming everything went according to plan. Amber opened the map, and the band of friends scrutinised the route ahead. All three still avoided the most urgent conversation that would not wait much longer. Crossing into the unknown land of the *Separated*. The escapees would have to rely on finding more drinking water once they hit the river delta. Beyond the waterbed, there was less certainty about where it would be found.

As they walked, there was no ignoring the growing despondency. It was only now, exposed to the stark emptiness around them, that they could truly comprehend their plight. A mission of madness devised in desperation. The occasional ruins that rose, like faded sandcastles on the seashore, brought reminders that humanity had once honed its creative forces to building communities before such insanity pointed science towards new monsters, the bombs.

***

The topography had started to flatten as they headed south towards what they hoped would be the remains of the River Severn. It was difficult to know exactly where they were, but the evidence suggested they were travelling roughly in the right direction. Some of the natural features of old Bridgnorth, with its mixture of dilapidated lower and elevated streets, had survived, while the dust-bowled basin that was once home to the river lay dry and parched. From the north, it presented a strange picture, like some great snake sliding across the foreground.

Back at the mine, some had said that all the rivers had quickly dried up after the *Change*. The only drinking water was now hidden deep beneath the ground, where moving water still carved new channels. But of course, this was what they had heard, not seen.

The three travellers walked towards the ruins in silence. Their waterbags were still a quarter full, so it wasn't vital that they found something to drink that day. By the end of tomorrow, though, it would be a different story. It was clear to Joel that Yolina was really struggling. They stopped to rest for a few moments.

"I'm feeling a little dizzy", she confessed. Yolina wiped the sweat from her brow and reached frantically for her dwindling water supply.

"Take it easy," Joel implored her.

Amber unzipped her rucksack and removed her old thermometer. She gently placed it in her friend's left ear for a reading. Thirty - eight point five degrees.

Slightly higher than the normal core temperature. She guessed that their bodies were all working overtime to cope with such conditions. Amber looked across at Yolina.

Their crumpled friend was close to a meltdown. Muscle cramps, exhaustion, disorientation. Eventually, a heart attack, Amber pondered. She needed fluid and rest.

"Five more minutes, Yolina."

They set off again. Each time they came across an old house or farm, they rummaged through the buildings that still stood, looking for anything they could eat.

As expected, anything edible, including food protected in tins, had long vanished. There was no time to waste salivating over empty tins.

Joel walked over to the edge of the latest house and stopped suddenly to gaze at the view beyond the garden. "Look," he pointed. The riverbed"

They gingerly climbed down into the empty basin which once resonated with the plunging waters of the Severn River. With each step, they also foraged for signs of damp ground, but no semblance or trickle could be found. Amber peered into the distance and identified a feature further downstream.

"That's our route. And here is where the map ends," she exclaimed.

"Yes," said a cautious Joel. "Where the *Separated* dwell."

A Hand Of Fate

That night was the coldest the travellers had faced so far. Crouched under an overhang of petrified river mud, they clung to each other for sheer life. The single piece of wood Joel found, partially buried in the sand, provided little warmth. They sat behind the flame, eating the last of the stale bread and dog. None of them slept properly. They all had indigestion. Amber couldn't stop shivering as the wind drove into their craggy nook, freezing any exposed flesh. Joel whispered to her that he couldn't feel his feet while Yolina was slowly turning a shade of marble blue.

Morning brought the release they craved, although when they tried to stand up, each of them wobbled like zombies.

They decided to follow the riverbed in the hope of locating an exposed water source. Each of them knew that the Severn had once been a mighty river, gushing forth thousands of tons of water and regularly breaking its banks to flood the land on either side. Now, it had been reduced to a dry canyon, more akin to a gorge within a desert. The occasional weed feasted on what moisture the night winds had left as a residue. But there was nothing to scoop into their containers. Yolina pulled the plant stem and tried to suck what fluid she could find in it. The taste was sour and stringy, offering little relief to her thirst. It made her stomach wrench, but there was nothing to expel.

" Don't despair," Amber whispered gently to her. "We'll find some water."

Joel suddenly stopped and stared at the large boulder to his left.

"What is it?" Amber queried.

"Look at the rock."

Yolina and Amber moved closer.

"There's some sort of image carved into it," she shouted.

Joel traced his finger around the outline of an old man sitting on a chair, possibly some sort of throne. Underneath was moulded the number '1.'

Within seconds, another stone. Another inscription. A question mark glowed from its surface, its yellow paint shimmering in the sun. Two more rocks appeared in quick succession, one bearing the rays of the sun.

"Any ideas, Joel?" Amber probed.

"Some sort of message, I think. But Lord knows what it means."

He had barely finished speaking when the ground collapsed beneath them. All three fell into a deep pit, landing painfully in a heap.

Before Joel had the time to utter the words 'What the…', three hoary ropes tumbled down the walls of the ditch.

A gruff voice rang out from above them. "Take the ropes!"

They looked at each other with trepidation. Staying down there was not an option.

Amber brushed herself down and stared at her companions. "Come on. We'll be ok."

She grabbed the rope and found herself being hauled back up to the top. The others followed suit. Just as she reached the rim, Amber caught sight of several shadowy figures hooded like monks. As they pulled her to her feet, a sharp blow to the back of her head sent Amber spinning to the floor. Joel and Yolina endured similar fates when they emerged at the top. All three of them lay on the surface of the smooth riverbed like fish waiting to be gutted.

Joel was the first to gain consciousness, brought around by a sharp pain in his face. He screamed in agony. One of his rescuers was plunging the point of his knife into his left cheek and working the blade around towards his nose. The cries of his companions soon pierced the morning silence as the cloaked strangers carved similar scars into their faces. All three of them lay bleeding on the ground.

One of the hooded men stepped forward.

"Now you are ready to enter our territory," he bellowed.

The visitors were hastily pulled to their feet, and the ropes secured around their hands.

"Come", the stranger instructed.

Yolina was still screaming, clutching at her face, while Amber struggled to hold back the tears. Meanwhile, Joel's eyes bulged with indignation as he screeched at his captors.

"What do you want with us?"

***

The procession moved quickly along the riverbed for several minutes. Amber counted about fifteen figures in hoods, each clothed in long dusty robes. She stretched her neck to try and catch sight of their faces but was prodded in the back to keep facing forward. Each captor seemed to be carrying a wooded pole and a stone-carved knife. None of them spoke except to poke them if they tried to turn around. Eventually, they stopped next to a larger rock on the left. Amber finally caught sight of her companions. Both carried evidence of bloodied scars on their left cheeks, shaped like question marks. She gingerly felt her own face. It throbbed with the mark of similar disfigurement. She watched as six of their captures started to push against the rock until it began to move. When the obstacle had been shifted, it became clear that it had been guarding an entrance to a tunnel. In front of them lay a twisting passage that descended under the course of the river. Once inside, the boulder was rolled back with an echoing thud as the prisoners were led down towards the darkness. Amber caught sight of Joel. Defiance shone in his eyes. They both tried to conceal the terror they felt about what might happen to them next.

***

Slowly, the light began to return in the passageway as it opened into a huge, gothic-like chamber. It was lit naturally by a hole through the roof. Robust blocks of sandstone seemed to hold the ceiling in place, like the pillars of some ancient cathedral. Maybe a hundred or so people were busy transporting various items across the cavern. Each clothed like their assailants. They fixed their eyes on the unknown visitors being led down towards the centre. As the procession moved closer to them, Amber realised there was something else they all shared: a scar on their left cheek, cut in the shape of a question mark.

Swollen-faced and bruised, the captives came to a halt below a raised ledge bearing an elaborate chair. The inhabitants of the cave stopped what they were doing and stood like statues, facing the ledge. They began to chant something slow and incomprehensible. A figure in a black robe appeared and sat on the seat.

"Bring them to me," he boomed authoritatively.

Still bound, Amber, Joel and Yolina were escorted up the steps that led to the rocky shelf. They stared at the man in black. Tall, emaciated, with piercing eyes and protruding dark, tattooed skin, he cut a menacing figure. His eyes examined each of them from head to foot. Eventually, he raised his arm and spoke.

"Why did you step into the land of the *Separated*?"

Amber cleared her throat and tried to explain the purpose of their journey. The man interrupted abruptly.

"Have you come to trade with us? If so, what have you brought?"

The visitors made no reply.

"What signs did you identify to give you the confidence to peruse such a foolish venture?"

"Which oracle did you consult?"

Amber gave Joel a bewildered look before hesitantly responding.

"We are just travelling through. We are heading across to the *Wastelands*. I have family there."

The mysterious figure in front of them stared blankly, with nonchalant indifference. He was clearly unimpressed.

"Only a fool would make such a reckless journey without something to trade. Without recourse to wisdom to empower you. Are you a band of fools, or maybe thieves come to rob us?"

"What are you going to do with us?" Yolina yelled in panic.

Their interrogator turned to glare at her.

"I might eat you, woman!" He laughed.

Yolina started to cry.

Joel had questions of his own. He tried to control his fear and pointed to his injured face.

"Why have your men marked us like branded animals?"

The man in the black gown shook his head.

"You have not been branded, dark-skinned one. Just prepared. We all need to experience pain to clarify our thinking. Your fate lies in the wisdom of the cards. Everyone here knows this and has gone through the process."

"What cards?" He shouted.

“Let me ask you a question. Before the *Change*, were you a religious man? Did you follow the morality of our corrupt and ossified world?”

Joel was taken aback.

“Like others, I did my best,” he retorted.

“Well, your best was not enough because you were enslaved by greed and power! This is what destroyed our world and reduced us to live like this. The evil that rests inside each of us must be controlled. But there is good news. We now have another pathway to follow. An intuitive choice which can empower you and unlock your inner mind.”

From beneath his garments, he pulled out a black card and held it up.

The people around them touched the scars on their faces and cried out in unison: ‘The wisdom of the cards. Show us the cards!’

Their leader replaced the item back in his tunic and stood up with both arms fully raised.

With a deafening authority, he bellowed, “The cards will have their say in the morning!”

The prisoners were frogmarched away to a row of small caves on the opposite side of the cavern. Their hands were finally untied as they were bundled into the hollow of the rock. A makeshift gate was placed across the entrance to prevent escape. Four dour-looking sentries stood behind the barrier, armed with spears, clearly resolved to ensure they stayed there.

Later, water was brought together with small bowls of brown paste. It was not dissimilar to the food they had lived on at the mine, but at least it quelled their hunger a little.

Ordeals

None of the prisoners slept well. Even when they were alone, and the cavern fell quiet, their minds were full of fearful imaginings. And they were not alone. Two figures on the other side of the gate were staring at them curiously.

Fatigue took its inevitable course, and their eyes finally closed. They finally awoke as the morning light started to penetrate the cavern. It wasn't long before six figures appeared at the gate.

"Come with us. It is time." They were bundled out of the cave and marched back to the central cavern. It was a mercy to have their binds removed.

The same dark-clothed figure was seated in front of them while the other hooded inhabitants formed rows of semi-circles around them. Another man moved forward carrying a box. The bounded captives stared inquisitively at him as he removed a set of cards and shuffled them vigorously.

A cry of 'Urgon! Urgon!' broke out as their leader rose from his seat. He turned towards the three outsiders.

"I am the interpreter of the cards. Your fate is bound up within the messages they convey. The decisions we all make have consequences. Choose wisely, and you might live. If not, the cooking pot may marinate your bones before this day is over."

The acolyte in front of him stepped forward.

"Choose your first card," he instructed.

The man moved towards Amber and held out the square box.

She reluctantly put her hand into the container and pulled out a card.

Turning it over, she saw a picture of a naked woman, surrounded by stars, pouring water into a pond. The man seized the card and held it up. "The Star," he announced.

Urgon stepped forward and drew Amber's gaze towards him.

"Your first card is encouraging. It represents a turning point. Some individuals can change their behaviour if they stop pretending. But not everyone is up to the challenge. We shall see."

Next, the man approached Joel. He was also encouraged to thrust his hand in and remove another card from the pack. Joel's image was of a carefree man standing on the edge of a precipice.

As it is held up, everybody around them shouts out, 'The fool!'

Urgon looks at Joel. "So, the card reveals that you are a breaker of rules. A taker of chances. We will test how far this will take you."

Joel's heart was pounding as he desperately tried to work out what test lay in store for him.

Finally, a shaking Yolina took a card. 'The Hermit!' they cried as it was lifted high.

"An interesting card to pull, young woman," boomed Urgon.

"The card is challenging you to dig deep, to discover who you really are. In the picture, the hermit holds a lamp. You must use your intuition to respond to your instincts. We shall see."

The hostages exchanged puzzled looks with each other. What did all this mean?

***

The captives were led back to their enclosure, but this time, each was placed in a separate cave. Amber did not have to wait long before visitors arrived.

Urgon stood in front of her.

"I have a question for you. If only two of you were permitted to live, which one of you should die?"

Amber's mind raced with possibilities. Was this a trick question? What criteria was he using to differentiate between them? She thought about Joel and his physical strength and integrity. The way in which he protected and cared for her. But what about Yolina? Such a reliable friend, her confidante. Veracious and always appreciative. In her hour of greatest need, how could she abandon her? Finally, there was the person she knew best of all. Herself. How could Amber measure her value against that of her companions? The answer she both dreaded and knew had to be given, now visualised in her head. She could not choose either of her friends. "The one to die must be me," she lamented.

Would not Joel and Yolina surely do the same if they were challenged to answer the question?

Her interrogator was waiting for an answer.

"I should be the one to die." She exclaimed.

Urgon's face betrayed not a flicker of reaction. Flanked by his four guards, he turned and left the cave.

Amber could hear her heart beating frantically. Had she just signed her own death warrant?

***

Joel was trying hard not to touch the scar on his cheek. The guards had brought a grey paste to his cell and urged him to rub a little of it into his facial wound. It would prevent infection, he said. Now, the challenge was to avoid scratching the still tender and itchy gash. He was distracted by the sound of Urgon's entourage arriving at the gate.

"Tell me, breaker of rules," the cloaked leader demanded. "To what extent would you go to save your colleagues from death?"

Joel's heart quickened. What did he have in mind to test his resolve? And, more importantly, would he be up to the task?

***

Urgon's assistant stepped forward and held out the box of cards. "Choose another card." Joel looked around at his adversaries. It was pointless to resist the request.

He pulled out an image of a woman holding a sceptre in both hands.

"These are symbols of the world's power. It speaks to you of life-changing choices and difficult challenges. How close to the precipice will a fool stand? We shall see," said Urgon.

They bound him and led Joel to the edge of a sharp rock edge. Below lay a thirty-metre fall onto perilous boulders. Traversing this precarious chasm was a sliver of rock bending out beyond the cavern wall.

"Choose your path carefully',' uttered the leader. "Halfway along the central bridge, it branches out in three different directions. Urgon looked at Joel.

"One of these narrow paths twist across the abyss to the safety of a cave. The other two lead into a bottomless cave system that nobody has ever returned from. There is a clue at the intersection to help you make a wise choice. Retracing your steps will not be an option. You will be met by the point of a spear."

His guards thrust out their poles in a vivid reinforcement of his meaning.

Joel stared at the bridge. He realised he was being asked to step into the unknown and might not survive the ordeal. Gathering his courage, he tentatively placed one foot on the bridge and started to walk.

The rocky overpass was barely navigable. He tried to keep his balance by avoiding looking down into the chasm. The only sound to distract his concentration was the faint trickle of moving water somewhere below.

***

Amber stretched her legs, trying to loosen the cramp that had set in. All she could think of was her friends. She'd heard the rustle of voices earlier and guessed from snippets of their conversation that Joel was being taken somewhere else. The sound of footsteps echoed around the outside of her cell. She, too, was summoned and frogmarched back into the main cave, where several of the congregation had gathered to witness her fate.

Urgon appeared with his assistant, carrying his box of cards.

"So, woman, choose your second card."

Amber nervously placed her hand inside the box and removed one.

"Just as I suspected," Urgon exclaimed. "The lovers!"

Those gathered bowed their heads and remained silent.

The prisoner gazed at her card. A naked couple peering up at a heavenly angel with his arms outstretched. The two words uttered by her kidnapper were blazed across the base of the picture.

"This is a card that points to love and lust," he continued. "Behaviour that belongs to the old world. It is only the new life created that is pure. We must tear ourselves away from such bonds between couples. Parents in the new world will be chosen by the community. Only those who are worthy will have this honour bestowed upon them. There is no room for casual sexual encounters now, with their diseases and unhappiness. They are dangerous and reckless. They cloud your thinking and must be eradicated in the ancient way. By pain."

Amber was terrified. What could he mean?

***

Two hooded females seized her by the arm while a third started to unbutton her tunic. They pulled her top off and removed her leggings and undergarments. Amber stood there naked, shivering, contemplating her fate. Urgon approached her, carrying a frayed branch of twigs in his hand. The wood gleamed in the morning light, reflecting slivers of sharpened bone. She was stretched across a bolder and fettered by both wrists.

An unknown male member of *the Separated* stepped forward. He disrobed and stood close to her.

Without warning, Urgon brought his makeshift whip down heavily across Ambers' buttocks. She winced in pain.

"Absorb the pain or give in to carnal lust." He commanded her. Amber could smell the breath of a would-be assailant standing behind her.

"No. No. Please. I don't want this."

Her sexual nemesis moved closer. She could smell his odour. Rancid and foul, like the whiff of rotting meat. His penis hung firmly, expectantly, ready to complete her humiliation.

"Your only hope for salvation is to bear the pain," Urgon screeched at his hostage.

Amber knew there was no choice. To be raped by a stranger and then, who knows what?

Or to endure Urgon's lash? Her choice was traumatic but not in doubt.

"She screamed as the whip cut into her flesh again and again. His aim moved towards her back. Amber closed her eyes and bit into her lip until it bled. Eventually, after several further strokes, she lost consciousness. A merciful silence to camouflage the suffering.

Urgon stood back, exhausted by his efforts. Unspoken murmurs of shock reverberated around the cavern. Some wanted to complain about the stranger's treatment but considered it unwise.

As Amber's beaten body was helped back to her cell, Joel and Yolina remained unaware of what had taken place.

The Polish teacher was pacing her area of confinement, desperately trying to make sense of what had happened to her friends. She heard screaming coming from the main hall but couldn't identify the victim.

Yolina and the other miners had heard stories about this strange group of people living under the ground in this area but hadn't anticipated such a hostile reception. Now imprisoned by them and awaiting an unknown future, she scolded herself for her naivety.

The lack of feedback from other travellers should have made them realise this section of the trip was far more dangerous than they'd thought. And it may cost them their lives, she pondered. Weighed down with her frustrations, she hardly noticed the guards approaching.

"Come with us," one of them demanded.

She was brought back into the main cavern. A hooded figure crouched, kneeling next to a boulder, scrubbing away red marks from the floor.

Urgon emerged from the back and stepped out onto the plinth. The guard released her binds and pushed Yolina forward. The hooded figures around her recognised the signal. They stopped what they were doing and gathered around for what their leader referred to as *illumination* time.

"Bow your head, woman, in the presence of the emperor."

The enigmatic leader handed the box to his assistant.

"Choose your last card," he shouted to her.

Yolina ran her fingers across the cards and picked one from the middle. She immediately handed it to her jailer.

The acolyte looked startled as he nervously held up the image.

"The Empress!" he exclaimed.

There were gasps from the audience. This was no ordinary card. It had never been chosen in the years they had lived beneath the river. Since their last empress, Samina perished. Urgon descended the steps and stood close to Yolina.

"Do you know what you have done, woman?" he enquired rhetorically. "No one has ever picked this card. Fate has visited us today. It belonged to my wife, Samina. But she was taken from us, from me, by the virus. So, what do you think this means? "

Yolina shrugged her shoulders in a gesture of confusion.

"I will tell you, visitor from the far shores of Europe. This is a call to keep boundaries. Understand where your true destiny lies. In this community, you are called to share the responsibility she relinquished in death. Your destiny is to sit alongside me as my confidante." Opening his face into a broad smile, he embraced her, whispering, "Say yes to destiny."

Ashen-faced, Yolina recoiled.

"I don't even know you!" she shouted. "This cannot be."

There were murmurings from the audience.

Urgon's expression darkened. His mood changed as he screeched angrily at her.

"The cards have decreed it, young woman. You have no choice!"

"Take her to my private cave."

A dazed Yolina was led away, tears welling up in her eyes.

Stumbling In the Dark

Joel arrived at the intersection where the stone bridge split into different directions. He stopped to reflect on Urgon's words. Where was the clue? The absence of any inscriptions or cryptic signs increased his angst. All three routes looked so similar. He was tempted to test one of the paths, but how far could he go before there was no way back?

'Don't be so stupid, man. Think!' he demanded of his rational self. Still fettered, Joel struggled to lie down on the ground. Slowly, he crumpled his body to the floor, closed his eyes and listened. Only those faint sounds of trickling water could be heard. Could the clue be linked to this? Joel turned his head in the direction of the right-hand path. The seeping of water could still be heard below him. He rolled over to the left and concentrated. What he could hear was moving water, but was this the same? Surely, it was louder, faster flowing, and more like a waterfall than a subterranean trickle. He climbed to his feet and listened again. He placed his ear to the middle ground and identified the previous clamour. It was the same as the one below on the right. So, could that be it? He retraced his actions. It had to be the left path, he thought.

Generating what bravery he could muster, the Nigerian delicately headed out along the left ledge. It became even narrower as it bent away behind a huge pillar of rock. A gentle trickle of water became louder as he moved further along. He approached the far side of the wall. Suddenly, there it was. Something from the past he had almost forgotten. Strangely beautiful and life-giving. A flow of fresh cascading water descends over the rocks. Joel started to weep.

Composing himself, he observed that the shelf he had traversed led into a cave at the rockface. With a look towards the heavens, he strode, nervously, towards the aperture. His heart was pounding as he arrived at the cave. Once inside, he squinted as the light forced its way into the far side. He could see a straightforward path from the far end of the cave, winding up to the main hall. A trickle of cold sweat oozed down his back while he fell to his knees. He had survived the ordeal.

In his relief, Joel hardly noticed the figure sitting in the corner of the cave. Perched upon a protruding stone, the shadowy image watched him carefully. It was a task he'd been entrusted with. Dressed like all the others, his brown tunic seemed to fuse into the surrounding rock like a camouflaged lizard.

Joel stepped back, startled.

"Congratulations, stranger. You have chosen wisely. I am here to welcome you back to us."

His guest gave him a cautious glance. Joel was not convinced by his words.

"Do not be afraid. Urgon will not harm you now. The cards have spoken."

He moved closer to Joel and whispered in his ear. "But I doubt you want to stay here." Walking back to his seat, the stranger suddenly turned back to him. Pulling back his hood, he revealed a sad face, strained, somewhat older than his frame. He beckoned Joel to him.

"I can help you escape from this place," he whispered.

Joel looked surprised. "Just me? What about my friends?"

"That will be difficult. The woman with the red hair has been beaten and shamed. Her body is weak. The other woman has been chosen by our leader as his new empress."

Joel was incensed. He grabbed the man by the throat.

"Do not harm me, or you will never get away. My name is Jonathan. I repeat. I can help you."

"Tell me! What has happened to my friends?"

Jonathan outlined the treatment meted out to Amber and Yolina. Joel puffed his cheeks in outrage as the details of Amber's humiliation were described.

"Those bloody cards", Joel exclaimed, kicking a rock on the floor. "I'll kill that bastard Urgon, if he's seriously harmed Amber."

"Be careful, friend. Urgon is not a man to provoke. His guards have strict instructions to deal severely with any threat to their leader. I knew two people here who have tried and failed. Your friend bore her suffering with dignity and will recover in a few days. I think Urgon thought you were in love with her and decided to test his hunch. The alternative outcome would have been worse, I think. It's possible that both of you may be allowed to leave, but I doubt it. The bigger problem will be securing the release of the blonde woman."

Joel bit his lip in frustration. "She's called Yolina, by the way. Listen. I'm sorry about grabbing you like that. It's been a harrowing twenty- four hours. I must ask you. Why are you helping us?"

Jonathan checked that they were not being watched and moved closer again. His eyes carried the look of someone who had shouldered many burdens.

"I've got to get out of here before this madness consumes me. If I help you to escape, you must take me too."

The rustle of chatter along the stairway prompted urgency.

"I will think about what you've said," Joel retorted. "But first, I need to check on Amber and Yolina."

Whispers

Joel's appearance back at the central cavern was greeted by some with surprise. Intermittent applause broke out to greet his survival.

Urgon and his guards approached his prisoner. "So, stranger. You have added wisdom to your courage. You will be allowed to live."

Joel was hardly listening. He only had one thing on his mind. Amber.

He scowled at the leader of the *Separated.*

"What have you done to Amber?"

Urgon looked agitated.

"Take him back to the cell. He needs to remember his manners."

Jonathan grabbed his arm and poked him roughly with his stave. He gave him a furtive look before escorting the Nigerian back to his holding place.

Later, as the *Separated* began to take to their beds, Jonathan appeared at the gate again with water and flatbread. The guards outside were dismissed by the visitor, and Jonathan walked into the cell.

"She is ok. They have given her something to treat her injuries. Amber was very brave and refused to submit to assault."

"Where is Yolina, our other companion, being held?" the prisoner enquired.

Jonathan looked perplexed. I think she is being held in Urgon's private cave at the back of the plinth. It appears that she has been earmarked for the role of our leader's spouse.

The Nigerian cast an incredulous look in his direction. "What?"

"I know it's hard for you to fathom, but it's in the cards. Whatever they suggest becomes law here."

Joel beckoned his visitor forward. "Tell me more about this Urgon. What sort of man is he?"

Jonathan sat down and thought about the question.

"He's a dangerous person. Increasingly volatile. Unpredictable. His behaviour has become more erratic over the last year. Some fear for his mental health. He's been increasingly delusional and harsh, especially with outsiders found around the riverbed. Many among the *Separated* fear him and are wary of his band of loyal guards. Others admire his ability to continually find food and water for the community. He was the first, almost three years, to stumble across these underground caves. His small group grew as newcomers chose to join him. Urgon was the one who brought the cards. One of Jonathan's' friends had told him that they looked like tarot cards. Urgon convinced them that there was ancient wisdom in following the messages that these individual cards portrayed.

He argued that following this creed would empower the fledgling community to make sense of their new lives and the barriers that lay ahead. One by one, the traditional values disappeared, whether they alluded to the old monotheistic or Eastern religions or to more secular beliefs. We think Urgon himself is from a Muslim background, but he never talks about his own family or faith. He's decried the old standards as tarnished by the world and forever linked to the destruction of the planet. Initial protestations, advocating 'self-help' and 'believe what you want' ideologies, were quickly quashed. About a year ago, some members left the group and took their chances elsewhere. The bodies of three of them were found two days' walk from here. Fatigue and thirst had destroyed them. They hadn't got much further than the far end of the river basin. He had their bodies brought back and roasted for their protein value. A warning to the rest of us. He forced us all to take part in eating their flesh. Some of us were physically sick."

He paused. "Other visitors have met a similar fate. You and your friends have been lucky. Regardless of what he says, I doubt if he intends to let you go. What I have told you should help us to concentrate our minds on the challenge of trying to leave this place."

Joel looked perplexed. "So, how did somebody like you end up here?"

Jonathan lowered his head. This would not be easy to share.

"We were refugees from the city. My wife, daughter, and I headed to the river basin in search of food and water. Like you, we were accosted and forced to accept trial by cards. Hannah, my daughter, chose a card with a symbol of death on it and was quarantined. They isolated her in fear of what misfortune she might have brought with us. Her mother insisted on staying with her, but I was not permitted to do so. They both grew weaker. Only later did I learn that their food and water rations had been drastically reduced. Hannah died in her mother's arms six months ago. My wife, Imra, couldn't cope with the pain and stopped eating properly. She blamed me for coming here. One day, she walked out along the rock ledges where you were and stepped off to her death. They said it was an accident. But I think a broken heart drove her to suicide."

Jonathan struggled to hold back a tear. "I think the only reason they didn't kill me was because of my medical background. I shared with Urgon that I had been an ambulance driver for ten years. Such medical skills are highly prized here."

Joel listened with empathy. "I'm sorry for your loss."

"They are both gone now. I just need a reason to keep alive."

He looked sternly at Joel. "Time is running out for the *Separated.* I go down to the underground river each day to monitor water levels and test its acidity. It is my job to report back any changes in the quality. But I can tell you that the supply is becoming sour. The underground stream is drying up. The food store is diminishing, too. Urgon has convinced the group that the old values, even ones he once subscribed to, are now obsolete. He's under pressure. He's done things that shocked all of us. Cannibalism is only one example. He has used torture to demoralise and alienate half the people down here. He wasn't joking when he threatened to eat some of you. Like I said, it's happened before. Look at me! Is it any surprise I feel disaffected or disillusioned? It sometimes feels like I've crawled into a grave, and I'm just waiting to die. Living underground like this is slowly destroying me. I need to get out."

"We must release Amber and Yolina," Joel insisted." Pack some things and try to locate our bags. He stretched out an arm and clasped Jonathan by the hand.

"We all go, or nobody does."

"OK. Leave it a couple of days for your friend Amber to recover. Then we will make our move.

Plans & Opportunities

Yolina woke up on a makeshift bed of old cloths and sand, feeling disoriented and in pain. As she struggled to sit up, she realized her head was pounding, and her body felt weak, as if she had been drugged. Next to her lay a mysterious cup; whatever it had, it certainly wasn't water. A scented candle filled the damp air with faded lavender, choking the atmosphere around her and making breathing difficult. Urgon was absorbed in a book in the corner of the cave, seemingly oblivious to Yolina's condition. She attempted to sit up in bed, but she lacked the energy to do so. It was evident that she had been drugged.

Urgon noticed her stirring, approached, and sat on the edge of the bed, gently placing his hand on her forehead. "Feeling refreshed?" he inquired.

Yolina flinched from his sticky palm. His hand moved down across her body and pushed against her breast. She wriggled away from his amorous advances, exclaiming that she was unwell. He looked at her, eyes burning with desire. With renewed fury, he clumsily pressed the full weight of his body over her and drew her close. Pulling at her clothes, he kissed Yolina with a lustful frenzy.

"Get off me," she cried. Urgon smiled and muttered.

"You will be mine soon enough. That is a promise."

With that, he rose from the bed and left the cave.

***

Amber cautiously reached up to feel the scar on her face, wincing as her fingertips brushed the still-tender skin. The cut was healing faster than the ones on her back and buttocks, a small comfort, amidst the dire situation. Her mind was a whirlwind of questions and uncertainties. Should they have set off from the mine with such blind hope? Why did they choose this risky path despite the ominous rumours? And most importantly, how could they possibly escape from Urgon and the Separated?

A sudden commotion at the gate broke the flow of her self-reflection. A tense, unfamiliar man approached her, his eyes filled with concern. With a sense of insistence, he took out a jar of brown paste from his bag and said, "This is for your back."

"You're not one of the usual guards who brings the food?" she asked.

"No, I'm not a guard. My name is Jonathan," he replied, furrowing his brow. After looking around carefully, he leaned in and quietly shared his purpose for visiting her. "I'm here to help you."

He could see the doubt in her eyes but was prepared for her hesitance.

"I have something else for you," he said, unveiling his cloak to reveal the rucksack she had brought with her. Despite being looted of dried food and cash, it was still relatively intact.

"I found it at the storage lock. Had your name tag on the outside. More importantly, I've also found your Nigerian friend.'' Amber's pulse quickened with this news.

"He is resting at the end of the tunnels. Like you, lady, he passed his ordeal. Joel is well and looking forward to seeing you.''

Lowering his voice, Jonathan added, "The two of us have been discussing our escape plan extensively." As he applied the paste to her wounds, she winced, to which he reassured her, "Don't worry. I used to be a paramedic in a different life." She flinched as his rough fingers worked the paste into her bloodied stripes. "They're healing nicely," he said, encouragingly.

Amber recoiled and asked him how much he knew about pain. "Quite a lot," he responded. "More than you might think. I used to treat people with far worse injuries than this.

And I'll leave the paste with you. I also understand about modesty'' (He slapped his bottom to indicate what he meant.)

She muttered an apology, barely audible, before pressing him for more answers.

"Yes. I, too, came here with people I cared about and loved. My daughter Isobel and my wife. Isobel was barely nine years old when she was taken ill. By the time we came across this community, she was really struggling. As always, Urgon insisted on consulting the cards. Poor Isobel picked one of the worst possible choices: an image of the devil. Despite our protests, he boldly proclaimed that her inner world was deteriorating beyond repair. Evil had grown roots in her body, and the girl had no choice but to accept it."

"Do not fear death," he pronounced to the assembly. "It is not something to dread. Accept the wisdom of the cards."

Jonathan began to weep. "They locked her away and effectively starved her to death."

He gathered himself again.

"And then, it got even worse. My spouse, Anna, was forced to choose a card too. The image of death, riding upon a white charger, was placed in her hand."

"Do not cling to old ways or situations that make us unhappy," Urgon said. "Embrace death as a friend."

Three weeks after Isobel perished and was overcome with grief, she killed herself. She threw her anguished body off the narrow ridges to the rocks and underground streams below.

"I was in turmoil. The two most important people in my life were dragged into a premature death. All I could think about was seeking vengeance against those who had torn my family apart. I tried, but my efforts were futile. Instead of killing me, Urgon recognised that I was of more use to him, alive. I've only survived down here by drawing upon my medical skills."

He took a moment to gather his thoughts. "All this time, I've been waiting for a chance to escape this place. You and your friends are that chance," he said.

He carefully draped Amber's tunic over her head. "Hopefully, the cream will start working its magic by tomorrow. I'll come back in the morning."

***

Joel's footsteps echoed through the main complex of caves as he wandered, lost in thought. A couple of the Separated greeted him cautiously, but most just looked away, shunning the Nigerian. The sadness in their eyes was palpable, and it weighed heavily on him. They seemed despondent, hopeless, and lost in Urgon's nightmare. Whatever madness lay under the river, it had not brought them contentment. Fear and weariness painted their faces, and Joel couldn't shake the feeling that there had to be another way, a better alternative to the life they were living below the caves.

Joel had been instructed not to contact his friends yet. There were too many guards in front of their holding caves, even for him to overpower. He'd been allocated a corner of one of the tunnels to lay his head that night. Best to investigate, listen, and learn more about these people and their bizarre existence under the River Seven. If Jonathan's words were true, Joel was determined to seek vengeance against Urgon at the right moment. For now, he needed to keep a level head, observe, and give Amber time to recover. Once she was ready, they would escape this wretched place.

An Unexpected Moment

Yolina jolted awake, her mind still reeling from the intense dreams she had just experienced. She found herself grappling with a jumble of memories from her childhood in Poland, including a surreal encounter with a Yolina from the past and a familiar landscape of trees and meadows. Amidst these recollections, thoughts of her infatuation with Tomas surfaced, as well as a fleeting desire to escape to her former peaceful haven. However, the harsh reality of her current surroundings couldn't be more different. Instead of the idyllic scenes she longed for, she was trapped in Urgon's cave, surrounded by a damp, musty atmosphere. As she realised her new partner had not returned, a mix of relief and anxiety washed over her, prompting her to hastily dress. And then, just as she began to gather herself, something unexpected occurred.

How are you today, Yolina? I trust that you are feeling better. We have some unfinished business to attend to.

He reached for the belt around his leggings and allowed them to drop to the floor. His penis emerged erect, with an eruption of blood vessels and desire.

Urgon threw off his tunic and moved towards her. Within seconds, he was pulling at her clothing. His hands were inside her top, caressing her breasts.

It was at that moment that she saw the knife. Ornate and gleaming in the half-light. It lay next to them on a makeshift table. Yolina relaxed and momentarily pretended to welcome his advances.

While he busied himself pulling at her undergarments, Yolina seized her moment. She reached across to the table and grabbed the weapon.

There are moments, she thought later, when you know what you are about to do, you will be judged as ill-advised. A rash decision in the quickening of time changes the course of the rest of your life. This was such a moment.

With what little strength she could muster, Yolina lifted the blade and plunged it into his torso. Urgon fell back, whining in pain. She pulled it out and stabbed him again, pushing him aside in panic. Wrapping the bedclothes around her victim, she turned him on his side to muffle the sounds. Yolina dressed again quickly. Her heartbeat throbbed in nervous confusion.

Urgon lay moaning on the bed, trussed up, she thought, like a giant insect larva. Yolina looked around. Had anybody else heard the cries? It remained quiet towards the entrance area. Surreptitiously, she crept towards her only exit route and paused to listen. The two guards at the end of the tunnel were engrossed in conversation, unaware of the drama that had unfolded. There was now an urgent need to find her friends, and quickly. But something caught her eye at the far side of the cave. Her rucksack. She felt an overwhelming urge to stop what she was doing and check that her personal mementoes were still there. Grabbing the bag, Yolina quickly pulled out the contents. What few souvenirs she cherished, the photo of her parents and a necklace given by the man she should have married, remained untouched. She often thought about Tomas, her only true love, and what might have been had he survived.

Yolina couldn't shake off the memory of rejecting him. She had convinced herself that she was too young to settle down and that their careers and unfulfilled travel plans were more important. But he insisted their love was unbreakable and vowed to wait for her return. Was it a compromise or just youthful foolishness? She never saw him again, and deep down, she felt certain of his death. It took six agonizing months before her worst suspicions were confirmed: he had been killed in the early days of the Polish-Russian conflict. As she refilled her rucksack, she knew there was no turning back now.

***

Urgon opened his eyes. There was blood on the sheets. He traced the crimson pattern with his finger back to his body. Oblique pictures flooded his head. They soon merged into one image: the face of Yolina. Screeching her name angrily and protecting his punctured rib cage, he sluggishly reached for the side of the bed. Once at the edge, with a painful lunge, he was sitting upright with his legs dangling. His new companion was nowhere to be seen.

"Imrie! Tony!" he shouted. "Get yourself in here. NOW." The two bodyguards sprang into the room. "Where is she?" The two men shrugged their shoulders and exclaimed that Yolina had told them that he was sleeping and not to disturb him. She had brushed past them with a comment about a message to deliver, and it was urgent business.

"You dozy idiots! Get the medic, Jonathan and find the girl. Look what she's done to me!"

***

Rising To the Surface

Yolina moved through the cave complex, head bowed, focused. The borrowed robe disguised her identification and veiled her like the *Separated* as she busied herself with bread baskets outside the caves where her friends were incarcerated. She eventually found Joel sitting alone at the side of one of the tunnels.

"What the..." Joel started to say, but Yolina quickly crouched and whispered to him.

"Quickly! We need to move. There's no time to explain."

Joel embraced the Polish teacher like she was family.

"Thank God you are ok."

"Maybe I am for a short while. But I've done something terrible. It endangers all of us," she continued.

"I Stabbed Urgon!"

Joel's face tensed with alarm.

"We need to act fast!"

***

Yolina and Joel stopped at the far end of the cavern and pulled back her hood. She tried to compose herself, but the top of her cloak kept falling back, irritatingly, in front of her eyes. The rim of the hood reeked with the memory of a former owner. Maybe another woman's anxieties, etched into the fabric and soaked with fear, she thought. Joel stood nervously beside her. She stared at the two guards who stood outside Amber's cell and braced herself. The thoughts she fumbled for finally materialised: confidence, self-assurance.

"Urgon wants me to talk to my friend," she spluttered unconvincingly. "Explain what he requires from us all now that I am to be his consort."

The two men shrugged their shoulders but let her pass. She remembered the small alcoves down the dimly lit passage. Opening the gate, she threw her arms around Amber's reclining figure. Joel was quick to join the emotional hug.

"I never thought I'd see you again," Yolina whimpered.

"Steady. My back is still sore from Urgon's whip."

She pulled herself up and grimaced.

"It's good to see you two."

Her Polish friend looked troubled. "We need to leave right away. Joel will explain."

***

Joel extended a helping hand to lift Amber to her feet, and the three of them cautiously made their way out of the cave.

"What about Jonathan?" Yolina asked.

"He'll have to fend for himself now," Joel replied.

As they entered the entrance tunnel, several cloaked figures emerged behind them, brandishing full-length spears aimed at them. Behind the guards, four others carried a stretcher. Urgon, with a furious expression, directed the group like a wounded animal. On a raised ledge, another figure cowered at the side, seemingly unnoticed by the group below. Joel recognised the person as Jonathan and gestured for silence by pressing a finger to his lips.

"Stay exactly where you are," a voice behind them demanded.

"You're going nowhere!"

With a sense of despondency, Joel gestured to his friends to halt.

"Urgon will demonstrate how he deals with such behaviour," the man bellowed.

Meanwhile, Jonathan had climbed the rocky steps at the side of the shelf and started to push against a cluster of loose stones piled above the wall. With a wave of his arm, he signalled to the escapees to step back before continuing his efforts to dislodge the rocks. Suddenly, amidst a flurry of dust and noise, several large rocks fell from the ledge and landed upon the guards. Broken limbs cracked in unison as the bodies tumbled in front of the escapees.

"Run!" Jonathan boomed as he clambered down to join them.

They scrambled away from the prostrate bodies of the injured. Joel picked up two spears and headed for the cave opening. It was still ajar. The blindness of forgotten sunlight overwhelmed him momentarily. "Quickly!" he shouted to his companions. "And try to shield your eyes."

The two men shepherded Amber and Yolina through the entrance and immediately rolled back the stone. Jonathan held his side and winced.

"You're injured," Joel exclaimed.

His helper pointed to the wound in his side. "One of them caught me as I picked my way through the injured," he explained.

They finally managed to close the stone aperture with one last hefty lunge. Joel pushed another boulder across the base of the entrance. "That should keep them at bay for a while."

Jonathan, exhausted by his exploits, collapsed to the ground. Joel lifted his companion's tunic to inspect his ribs. It looked serious.

"Go. I'm done for. Stay alive for me." He unbuckled his rucksack. "There's food and water in here for several days."

The former medic gave Joel a fatalistic glance.

"Come on, Jonathan. You can do this," Amber pleaded.

But his strength was diminishing. His life ebbing away in the dust. They realised he wasn't going anywhere.

"You must leave without me," Jonathan whispered.

"Head south. Keep away from the river basin. There are caves to the left of the riverbed. I'm

Ok. I guess I was never destined to leave this place. After all, Imra and Hannah are here. At least we will all be together again."

With that, he closed his eyes and joined those he loved.

***

The fugitives swiftly gathered their rucksacks and headed for the rugged terrain to the south. Amber struggled to keep pace with the others after their time underground. As they emerged into the sweltering afternoon, the harsh sunlight stung their eyes, and their parched tongues longed for moisture. In the oppressive stillness, they could hear voices growing louder behind them. Joel paused, pulling two spears from his backpack, and glanced resignedly at his female companions. "There's no way we can outrun them," he said with an urgency in his voice.

He quickly ushered the women behind him, seeking cover behind a towering sandstone pillar. Pressing a spear into Yolina's hand, he fixed her with a stern gaze."

"Do what you can."

In an instant, they were surrounded. Six shadowy, armed and dangerous figures closed in on the trio like predators encircling their prey. A menacing voice cut through the tension, "Come with us, or die here."

The absconders shared anxious glances and nodded their heads. If this was to be the end, then they had no choice. Joel gripped his spear and shouted at their attackers.

"For Jonathan!"

Two of the assailants launched towards him in a furious attack. As the Kenyan manhandled one to the ground, the other plunged his spear into Joel's left arm. He grimaced in pain and fell back. Two more of the *Separated* moved in and wrestled him to the ground, where he lay bleeding and helpless.

Another of the men wrenched the spear from Yolina's precarious hold and struck her across the face with its shaft. She, too, fell despairingly to the floor. All Amber could do was comprehend her imminent fate.

Suddenly, a swishing noise cut through the air like a startled bird's flight. It whistled through the clearing. One of the assailants fell to the ground, an arrow protruding from his chest. Then, another collapsed similarly. Amber looked around. Nothing. Another hail of arrows found their targets from unseen spaces behind the rocks. One of these penetrated an attacker's throat, and another plunged into the man's leg. As the dust settled, an eerie silence ensued.

Then, from the barren emptiness around them, a figure emerged. Cloaked like their attackers but carrying a longbow and spear. His eyes blazed as he cracked his spear shaft across the head of one of the men and down onto the kneecap of another. Only the two who were restraining Joel remained. They tried to grapple with the intruder. With frightening speed and the agility of a gymnast, he leapt across, plunging his lance into the man's stomach. The last of Urgon's men stood trembling.

"Tell your master that his days are numbered."

With that, he crashed the blunt end of his spear against the man's back and face in one swift motion.

"Run!"

The guard staggered away, grateful for his narrow escape. Joel reached out a hand to the mysterious savior.

"We owe you our lives, stranger."

"Indeed, you do." He looked around at his labours with satisfaction.

"Don't underestimate my loathing for what goes on under the river basin."

He walked around to inspect each of his victims. With a hefty jerk of his left hand, he carefully removed the deadly arrows from their bodies, wiping the arrowheads on their tunics.

"Normally, I'd bury them to prevent them being torn apart by wild animals, but in this case"

Amber turned to the man. "Why did you help us?"

He spoke quietly. "I am a *gatherer.*"

"But what are you doing out here on your own," Yolina quizzed.

"Oh, I'm not alone. There are others like me. We've been watching your movements since you first entered the area. Not many people have the guts to venture this far from the protected zones, so you aroused our curiosity. Most of us were surprised that you survived at the hands of that maggot, Urgon. We've seen how he destroys the lives of those who fall under his control. When I heard the ruckus at the boulder entrance, I had to act fast. You were lucky I was nearby. Some of your predecessors came before you and tried to escape him. Well, let's just say they didn't make it out alive. No one deserves that kind of fate. He made a solemn gesture, placing his right hand across his chest."

"My name is Marcos, by the way." He smiled.

Nervously, Amber and Yolina introduced themselves as they bandaged Joel's arm. Marcos crouched down beside them. "You can stay with us tonight, but we need to hurry. Urgon may send more assailants."

"And where is that?" Joel asked.

"Not far," Marcos replied.

As they made their way up and across the gentle outcrops, Marcos lent his shoulder to support Joel while Yolina did her best to help Amber. The river basin's twisted shape grew smaller and fell away, resembling the abandoned carcass of some giant, withered reptile. Disappearing down a maze of narrow canyons, they entered another concealed cave entrance. Descending further, they were greeted by tiny flickers of light that merged into an orange luminous glow. Marcos then discarded his outer robe and weapons, beckoning them to follow. Several people warmly welcomed the newcomers and offered them fresh water and a hearty stew.

"Eat and drink," they implored. "You are safe here."

The rescued trio were hungry but cautious. Amber looked around. This subterranean refuge looked a little like Urgon's underground base. Was this some sort of deception to ensnarl them again? Their eyes scanned the activity before them as they sat eagerly consuming the food. The contrast with this community was stark. They were smaller in number, about twenty people in all. Some went about their business with smiles on their faces, heads raised in confident posture. Amber and her friends had almost forgotten what the chatter of pleasant conversation sounded like. A sense of calm prevailed.

Marcos led the visitors into a side cave with misshapen pillars and clumsily hewed stone seats. Two older women arrived and gave them a warm welcome. "We are an independent community," one of them said. "We call ourselves *gatherers.*"

She carefully inspected the three outsiders.

“My son has not brought wanderers to our refuge for some time. Tell me, what you are doing here?”

Amber shared details of their quest to find her father and sister in the *Wastelands*. She described their time in the mines and what happened to them down in Urgon’s domain. The women listened attentively, studying the newcomers carefully.

Marcos’s mother closed her eyes, searching carefully for the right words.

“Do you remember how it was before all this? During those final days of the war, just before the *Change,* some of us started moving out of the cities. Many anticipated what was going to happen next. The signs were everywhere. The infrastructure had collapsed entirely. A lack of resources everywhere. Hunger, disease, hospital, and medical provision were all overwhelmed. People felt increasingly abandoned. Alongside all this, levels of State control mushroomed. Overnight, there were armed soldiers in the streets. But their presence didn’t reduce the violence and looting. It just exacerbated it. People were becoming desperate. Of course, the authorities had to try and restore some semblance of order amongst the chaos, but it just bred fear and dependency. An existence of desperate servitude snowballed. We wanted to live independently, but *Gnosis* didn’t like it. They wanted to control our lives. We made it to the river, but they sent soldiers to bring us back. Several of our kin died. They said it was dangerous to live out here.” The other lady, Jade, scratched a furrowed brow and interjected:

“Wasn’t it controlling attitudes like these that got us into this situation in the first place? Subjugation enslaves us to a culture of excess and wealth for the few and struggle for the many. My friends, we believe this mirrors the ongoing story of humankind, with all its empires and colonial powers. Like volatile tectonic plates pushing against each other, unsure of the deadly consequences. All it took was for man to develop the right weapons and the rise of global warming. The rest is now history. What did Oppenheim say about his monstrous invention, the atomic bomb, back in 1945:

When I saw its billowing cloud, I fell deaf and could hear nothing else.

We think it began a chain reaction in the development of nuclear weapons that eventually destroyed years of diplomacy and led to inevitable use. Aligned to atmospheric changes fuelled by global warming, we lost control of our weather systems, assuming we ever really had any."

She looked towards Jade for endorsement. Her friend added that a group of them had met with their facilitators, but it was clear they only wanted to coral them in homesteads, like the units established in the *Wastelands*.

Amber's attention had drifted. Her mind was elsewhere, towards her family in that same territory. It still seemed so far away. Her father had told her that he would return there if he survived the war and begged them to do likewise.

"So how have you managed here?" enquired Joel.

"Where do you get food and fresh water from?"

The two elderly women whispered to each other and beckoned them.

"You might like to see this."

They followed them down narrow steps to a chamber lit by a shaft of natural light. Yolina gasped. They gazed at row upon row of freshly grown stems supporting green flora. Some bore an unidentified fruit.

"The mines are not the only place that has the black meteorite. We've found it here, too," one of them proclaimed proudly.

"As for the water, many underground channels still exist. Look!"

They followed her glance towards the far side of the cave. A trickle of mineral water flowed through a smooth channel of rock.

"See. We don't have to eat people!" the woman laughed.

She continued.

"We have ventured further into the wilderness. There are some places that are not completely covered by dust. And something else. The black rock that fell from the skies has been found there, too. We have scientists among us who are studying the properties of the substance. We think it is meteoric in nature. During the meteorite storms five years ago, you might recall that the black rock appeared in the ground. Where you were living and working, in the black crystal mines, was the area that commanded the most attention because it seemed to have the largest deposit of the substance. However, we now know it is not the only place it fell."

She gestured towards four shelves filled with delicate glassware.

"Have you ever heard of chondrocytes?" she asked, but her question was met with puzzled expressions.

"They are some of thc oldest materials in the universe. Around four and a half billion years. Here is the fascinating thing. They contain organic matter and amino acids. These are carbon rich. And carbon-rich material contains the building blocks of DNA, like thymine and uracil. When ground and mixed with certain plant chemicals, it acts as a form of fertilizer. We are experimenting with bringing these plants out into the light for short periods to assess the process of photosynthesis. You have just seen the results."

She sat back, visually proud of her discoveries.

"These comets or asteroids rained down on us like a modern-day plague, but they have provided us with the tools to survive!"

"So," the older woman interrupted. "As I said, we don't need to acquire protein from human flesh. In our community, this issue is a fundamental marker, a symbol of being civilized. It tells us it is still possible to maintain some dignity, even in these traumatic times. It sets us apart from the beasts. We are not like the wolf. When he is hungry and unable to find food, he will turn upon his own, kill and eat the weakest, the most vulnerable. As you know, there are still lots of animals out there in the wilderness. Reluctantly, we continue to trap and eat them. This is only because we still need to supplement our diet. But our hope and expectations are that one day, we will be able to survive entirely on what we grow. Who knows? Any surviving creatures may eventually learn to trust us to leave them alone in the wild."

Amber still had some of the brown paste left that was used on her wounds. She started to rub a little into Joel's wound.

"Let me look at that," the woman asked. "You're going to need a few stitches. Come with me."

"I am told you fought bravely to protect your friends, stranger. Alas, such courage is not found everywhere these days. It will hold you in good stead for the challenges that lie ahead."

Joel felt awkward. He wasn't used to receiving compliments. He sensed a wisdom in this lined face before him, which both beguiled and strengthened his resolve.

***

Amber swiftly rolled up her left trouser leg and carefully retrieved a crumpled map from a hidden pocket sewn inside the garment. A sense of urgency washed over her as she studied the decipherable lines on the map. It was time to bid farewell to their gracious hosts and press on with their journey. The mysterious *Wastelands* were calling out to them, and they couldn't delay any longer.

Within Sight

Draped across a shallow, sandy floor, the visitors slept better that night than ever since leaving the mine. Amber woke early, distracted by Joel's snoring. Something sprang into her head. Words her father had once said to her many years before when they had been rescued by local people in a storm while out camping.

''Never forget, my girl. It's the kindness of strangers that keeps the pulse of humanity beating.''

''How true,'' she reflected as she mumbled the words again.

There was a covering of snow on the ground all those years ago. She closed her eyes and raised the picture from her memory. It sparkled and glistened in the cold air. How she wished to see snow once again.

Her thoughts were interrupted by a noticeably cheery Yolina.

''Hope you slept as well as I did. I could stay here forever!''

Amber raised an eyebrow.

''We both know that is not possible. Besides, we must be less than a week's walk away from *the Wastelands*.

Yolina hugged her friend. ''I know. It's just so good to be safe.''

Joel finally stirred and gingerly fingered his injured arm.

''How is it?'' Amber enquired.

''Sore, but whatever she rubbed into it has numbed the pain a little.''

Marcos appeared and beckoned them to follow him.

''I trust you slept well, my friends.''

They sat down, ate a greenish-brown stalked porridge and consumed fresh water from the stream below. Amber turned towards the elderly woman and Marcos.

"We will never forget what you have done for us."

"The best thing you can do for all of us is to stay alive out there. And to keep believing in the dream."

Amber looked puzzled.

"What dream?"

"We have spoken of little else," she replied with a gentle grin.

The trio waved their goodbyes and moved out in a westerly direction. Marcos accompanied them until they were completely clear of the river basin.

"Good luck, Amber. Stay safe. I hope you and your friends find your family."

With these heartfelt words, he bid them farewell and disappeared back into the morning haze, leaving a lingering sense of his presence.

***

They made good progress during the following days, continuing to sleep during the hottest hours of daylight and walking in the late afternoons or after dark. Vigilance ensured that they remained hidden mainly at night, moving silently and cautiously through the nocturnal winds. On the fourth night, the travellers took refuge in the remains of an isolated farmhouse. Joel was pensive.

"We must replenish these water bottles urgently," he reminded them.

Amber stretched out on the floor and yawned. Yolina suggested she join Joel in looking for water.

"There are the remains of an ancient well at the back of the yard. Let's investigate it," she proposed.

"If it's all the same with you, I'll stay here and try to get a fire going," her friend retorted.

The other two donned their outer coats and headed towards the yard. They quickly arrived at the well and stood, peering down into the darkness below. It dropped about ten metres to a dry basin. The metal bucket used to retrieve water was still attached to its chain. This hung from the remains of a hoist, balanced across the opening. It was supported by a double layer of bricks to strengthen the shaft and still looked secure. Joel thought it was just wide enough for a man to negotiate.

"It looks dry down there, but you never know," Joel exclaimed. "I'm going down."

He looked around for a rope. "Check in that collapsed shed, Yolina."

She emerged from the rubble with a big smile on her face. "Eureka!"

As Joel lifted his considerable frame over the lip of the well, it became apparent that the aperture wasn't as big as he first thought.

"You'll never squeeze through there. You big lump!" she teased. "I'll have to do it."

Joel was nervous about her descending into the well, but there was no other choice.

"OK but be careful."

Joel threw the rope over the overhanging beam and fastened one end to her waist.

"I'll lower you gently."

The faded brown rope creaked as it tautened with Yolina's delicate frame. She coiled and twirled her way to the bottom before arriving with a thud.

"I'm all right," she shouted up to him.

Yolina untied her protective harness and scraped a broken piece of rock into the well floor. Eventually, the earth became damp. Excited, she bellowed up to her companion.

"There's damp ground here. I'm going to check both side tunnels!"

Each of these openings had blackened with age and become strewn with debris. She stepped gingerly into the left tunnel. Two dusty branches and the remains of a dead rat were torn from the blockage. She carried on digging under the tunnel, and suddenly, the earth sank into a soup of brown water. Digging further, the pool widened and started to clear. Yolina summoned Joel.

"There's water, Joel! There's water down here. It's a bit cloudy, though."

"Keep digging! I'm sure it will start to clear."

With each plunge of the rock, the colour of the liquid lightened until it carried only the faintest hint of discolouring.

"It's running clear, now!" She shouted.

"I'll send the water bottles down," he yelled back.

Fastening their water bottles to the bucket, Joel carefully lowered them down to his friend. She took each bottle to the tunnel and filled it.

The replenished bottles were placed in the bucket and hoisted up to the top.

"You need to be careful getting back up here, Yolina."

The detached rope reappeared in the pit, and she carefully reassembled her winch.

Joel soon realised how much more difficult it was to pull someone up rather than lower them down. His wounded arm was still hurting, and he struggled to hold her weight. To add to his concern, the wind around him was rising. Pieces of broken rubble began to blow across the yard and bounce off the base of the opening. Meanwhile, Yolina was struggling to get a foothold on the inner lining of the wall. The pace of recovery slowed to almost a halt.

''I'm struggling to lift you out!'' he cried. His right arm was throbbing with pain. There was a crack before he could transfer the weight to his other arm. A piece of old plastic packaging shot across the yard and struck him on the head. He winced and slumped to the floor. The rope shot away from his fingers like an entangled fish escaping the fisherman's rod. Yolina screamed. Then, a thump and silence.

Joel pulled himself back up. ''Yolina! ''he cried. The Nigerian gazed into the hole. His face locked in paralysis.

''Oh my God! No.'' he blurted out. ''Yolina! Yolina!''

She lay motionless in the stillness of the well. He pulled on the rope and tried to animate her, but without success. In a panic, Joel ran back to the ruined house.

Amber had succeeded in building a small fire and was humming quietly to herself. The look on Joel's face panicked her.

He brushed the trickle of blood away from his left eye. ''Come quickly!'' he yelled breathlessly.

Within the well, Yolina lay motionless. Her head slumped at right angles to her shoulders. Even at that elevated distance, it was apparent that her neck was broken. Amber started to weep uncontrollably. ''My Yolina. My delicate Polish flower.'' Joel just sat on the ground with his head in his hands.

“I was hit by a flying object”, he muttered. ‘‘Lost my grip of the rope. My damaged arm couldn’t take her weight. It’s all my fault.’’

Amber felt that sudden gasping: she struggled to breathe and stood, rooted to the spot, unable to move. Her chest burned with the pain of loss. She just stared at the body of her friend, transfixed by grief.

***

They struggled to bring her lifeless body back to the surface, but their efforts fell short. It was as if their dearly departed friend had turned to stone, and they were attempting to lift a statue from the depths. Working together, they realized they lacked the strength to hoist her up. With the storm intensifying, they reluctantly decided to leave her and regroup the next day. Amber tried to comfort Joel, but neither soothing words nor her embrace could ease his anguish.

‘‘Leave me alone,’’ he sobbed.

Amber, lost in her own grief, ponders the absurdities of fate.

***

The following morning, as dawn broke, both stood at the well to complete their wretched task. Joel summoned every ounce of strength to take the strain off their friend’s corpse while Amber clutched the end of the rope. He didn’t say anything to her but was watching the tension of the twine as it bit into the brick support. He could see some evidence of fraying and bit his lip as the line came apart.

‘‘No! No!’’ he screamed as the rope snapped and sent Yolina back to her resting place. The pair sank to their knees, distraught.

Frustrations were distracted by the encroaching glare of the sun. Shielding their eyes, the pair made their way back to the house, head bowed in acceptance of the inevitable.

They tried to sleep, but neither could. Amber searched her memory banks for all the stories that made Yolina so special to her: their early meetings at the mine, their common bond in surviving the dangers there, their escape and the trials of being incarcerated by the *Separated.* In the end, it was an innocent accident that brought about her demise. Meanwhile, Joel has other pictures in his head. Why did he let her go into the well? He should have known the risks. But most of all, why couldn't he hold on to the rope? He was strong. Yes, his arm was still sore, and debris was blowing around, but why didn't he concentrate more?

With the late afternoon beckoning, they gathered their things and started to leave.

''Give me a moment, Joel.''

He waited at the door while Amber walked over to the well. She opened Yolina's bag and took out a silver cross she sometimes wore around her neck.

''I hope your god is listening, Yolina. You were a beautiful flower in this wilderness. Rest in peace, my friend.''

A single tear meandered down her cheek as she let go of the necklace, watching it disappear into the pit.

''Come,'' she gestured to Joel. ''We have a journey to complete.''

***

The landscape began to change as they moved further south. Sandstone hills gave way to expansive plains of dust where fields once thrived. The remains of human habitation grew more numerous. Villages, some with buildings still intact, lined their route. Individual houses peppered the horizon, like miniature blocks in a painting, and the remains of old vehicles lay abandoned along the roadsides. The morning light gave them an eerie ruddiness as if they had once formed part of some sinister gothic movie set.

They chose a remote cottage on the edge of one of the villages to rest in. It looked like it had grown directly out of the ground and was now a patchwork of the same bland terrain colours. Something once hung from the front of the building, twisted and parched in a patchwork above the front door. Maybe it had once screened the entrance with cascading wisteria or the reds and whites of roses, she pondered. Opening the door reminded her of stepping back into a children's storybook from her childhood. Incredibly, a few little pieces of wood were stacked next to the fireplace. Joel reached into his rucksack and removed his flint.

"I'll get a fire going if there is any wood around here."

Despite the extra bottles they had acquired from Yolina's bag, the water supplies ran low again.

"I'll look around later," Joel suggested. They ate their dried food in silence.

"I wanted to bury her, you know," Amber disclosed.

"I know. Me too." He reached across for her hand and kissed her fingers one by one.

She pulled herself closer and stroked his face.

"I love you, my big African!"

He embraced her with all the affection his heart could muster. They lay there playing with each other like awkward teenagers.

She gently reached for his tunic and began to unbutton it.

"Are you sure you want to do this?"

He moved his lips closer and kissed the woman he had loved at the mine for another three years before.

"I guess you've always known how I feel," she whispered.

Their union released a myriad of constrained tensions. Years of sexual frustration were cast aside as the energy exploded from their bodies, like the vigour of a startled flock of frenzied birds taking to the skies in migration. The couple clung to each other desperately as if to stop falling off the world's edge.

"All we have left is each other," she sighed.

"Unless we can find your father and sister," he added.

A New World

Amber first noticed the difference when she caught sight of the sign.

"Warning: Prohibited Zone Ahead: Do not Enter".

From their elevated position overlooking the plain below, the two travellers watched the skyline change from crimson red to olive and then to musty green. Below them, something was happening that was rather extraordinary. A partial view was possible. "If you creak your neck to gaze beyond the left side of the wall," she shouted across to Joel, "You will see it." Joel's gaze followed the direction she suggested. The view was, indeed, astonishing. Row upon row of young trees, baffling all the odds. Countless young saplings forcing their way from the dust into existence. All were hidden and protected from the outside world by what looked like miles of elevated support columns. These were reinforced by massive concrete metal bases. It looked as if they were designed like bridge supports to last hundreds of years. These connected to a ten-metre or so wall, which encircled the perimeter.

The whole area was sheltered from above by a giant, intricate dome. It glowed with the sun's rays in metallic colours unfamiliar to the couple. Like an enormous jungle canopy, the Towering above conveyed the look of some enormous fantasy cake. Its giant girders were bolted to the canopy above, while enormous rocks strengthened the blocks on the floor. Beneath this colossal umbrella grew various trees, each defying the barren reality they endured. They flourished with glorious green foliage. Although they were not as tall as the trees they remembered, there was no denying that they looked robust and healthy. Along the wall, a series of austere towers had been assembled at regular distances, manned by soldiers with automatic weapons.

The road twisted down to the edge of the *Green Zone* and ran parallel to the west wall. They passed three more warning signs to stay away, but it was the only road they could see.

“We’ll just have to risk it,” Joel grimaced.

But the appearance of the two strangers had not gone unnoticed. As they reached the wall, a booming loudspeaker message challenged them to stop and state their business.

“This is a protected tree area. Do not advance any further. Stop and wait for our guards.”

They became aware of the sound of accelerating engines in the distance. Then, within seconds, the screech of vehicle tyres filled the air. Two military vehicles stopped before the couple, and their back doors flew open. Several armed men jumped out and advanced towards Joel and Amber.

“Get down on your knees. Arms in the air!” their leader shouted.

The couple complied and sank to the ground.

Clearly agitated, a powerfully built man in full combat gear approached them.

“What are you doing here?”

Joel babbled an incoherent answer to the question and was met with a rifle butt across his face.

“Bring them.”

A dazed Joel was lifted into the second jeep while Amber was cuffed and frogmarched to the other vehicle.

Amber lowered her eyes and tried to control her sense of foreboding. She avoided staring at the three soldiers sitting opposite her. Everyone remained silent.

It must have been around fifteen minutes later that the small convoy arrived at their destination. She guessed they had put significant distance between themselves and the *Green Zone.* Amber tried to peer through the barred windows. All she could see was white stone walls and gleaming gates rising on both sides of the road.

This was not a preserved territory of protected trees. She had once seen a picture of these gates. Somewhere she had only dreamed about visiting: the white stone towers of Gnosis.

***

The vehicle's back door was flung open.

"Get out!" the soldier instructed.

With Joel reinstated at her side, they were marched along a series of dusty streets to a tall building on their right. The words *Security Centre* had been boldly carved into the lintel above their heads. They arrived at a large courtyard after advancing through several poorly lit tunnels.

''Choose your words carefully,'' one of the guards advised them.

Five uniformed men sat around a stone table, ruminating over a crumpled map. They eyed the two outsiders with suspicious glances. One of the men approached them and scanned the couple from head to toe.

''So, what have we got here, then? Saboteurs or simpletons?''

The others at the table laughed and gazed across at the unlikely visitors.

''We are travelling to the *Wastelands* to try to meet up with my family,'' Amber blurted out.

''And him?'' her inquisitor continued. ''Your bodyguard?''

Once again, the visitors were treated to a chorus of laughter.

His mood seemed to darken. ''So, where exactly have you travelled from?''

"The black crystal mines in the north."

"I find that hard to believe, young lady. Nobody in their right mind makes that sort of journey. Not these days. More likely, you two are among those crazies out there who are hellbent on destroying our work here and in the *Green Zone.*"

He frowned. "Either way, we will find out. Bring them to lab one."

The couple were bundled out of the room and taken to a side area with a row of metal bed frames.

"What are you going to do to us?" Joel shouted.

"Like I said, stranger, we will find out why you are here."

The captives were forced down onto the beds, and their hands and feet were bound with shackles. Amber winced as the iron rods bit into her scars.

A bespeckled man in a faded white coat nervously approached them. He was carrying a medical box.

"This will not take long," he blurted out, almost apologetically.

With fastidious precision, he removed two small syringes from the box and filled them with a light blue fluid. Meanwhile, the guards attached electrodes to the couple's foreheads and upper arms. Connecting wires protruded from a central device behind them and were fastened to the electrodes.

"Ready, doctor," one of the guards declared.

The medic leaned across Amber and gazed into her terrified eyes. It seemed to her that he displayed an element of hesitancy, even reluctance.

"Don't worry." This won't hurt. Just relax."

She felt compelled to follow the advice as the serum entered her vein. She struggled to keep her eyes open. Stretching her neck to the right, she caught sight of Joel. He was receiving the same treatment.

Amber became aware of a bleeping sound behind her: some sort of monitor. The rhythm of the sound merged with her heartbeat like some strange musical symmetry- a cacophony enhanced by the pulses she now felt in her head.

''We can begin,'' the doctor conveyed to the figure beside him. The familiar uniformed man stepped over to Amber.

''I'm going to ask you some more questions,'' he declared.

''Why were you outside the *Green Zone* earlier?''

Amber repeated her earlier reply to this question. Although she couldn't move her body, speaking was easy enough. The words rolled off her tongue without prompting. Her interrogator listened to the story of her escape from the mines and their encounter with both the *Separated and The Gatherers.* He raised an eyebrow at the mention of her father and their quest to find him. He looked at the monitoring machine, where the medic was studying the data displayed. The other man gesticulated with his thumb, nodding positively. The inquisitor moved towards Joel.

''Who are you, stranger, and why were you travelling so close to the protected trees today?''

Joel felt compelled to tell them everything he could remember. He couldn't have lied if he had tried. The doctor once again examined the responses for any inconsistencies.

Eventually, the guards unshackled the prisoners and allowed them to sit up. A small glass of water was brought for them.

''Drink this, then come with us.''

Joel and Amber were helped along the tunnel and back to the area where they were initially questioned. They stood in front of the same figures who spoke to them when they first arrived. The oldest of them left the table and stood in front of them.

''The solution we injected into your arm was something we have been perfecting here for some time. A truth serum: much more sophisticated than the brutal methods once used to extract information from those who might threaten our safety.''

Amber looked across to Joel.

''The good news for you two is that your accounts of why you were at the *Green Zone* earlier have registered a combined truth analysis of 98.8%, sufficient to allay our concerns. I must tell you that we are surprised, in fact astonished, that you've made it this far. Very few do. However, we are satisfied that you are not intent on sabotaging the work we have put in place. Therefore, you will be allowed to leave.

Amber blew a sigh of relief. ''Thank you,'' she mumbled.

''The effects of the serum will wear off quickly. We will give you some water and food for the rest of your journey but be advised: you need to be careful. Although the Wastelands are not far, there are still many dangers out there.

Amber embraced Joel in relief. Their rucksacks were brought in with the water and food promised. A short, balding man at the table came across to join them.

''Can I ask our visitors some questions, Sean?''

The soldier moved away with an officious salute and left them with the newcomer.

''My name is Richard Hartwood. I'm one of the leaders here at *Gnosis*. Tell me, what do you know about this place?

''Only what we have heard,'' replied Amber. ''Stories, rumours, you know. And, of course, the daily news podcasts. They have become our only connection to the outside world.''

She hesitated. ''Some question how accurate the reports are, especially the information about what is happening in other countries. We are convinced that *the Change* must have affected other nations too. Assuming most of the communication technology was wiped out there, it's still surprising that we don't hear more about what's happening beyond our borders.''

Richard interrupted her. ''You are perceptive and clearly intelligent, Amber. This is indeed a place that needs to lock in its secrets for several reasons that I cannot fully share. The truth is that we know more about what is happening nationally than anyone on the outside realises. As for the other nations, they have also been affected by the change, but in ways I cannot divulge. All I can tell you is that we have set up basic communication lines to share our predicament. Soon, there may be fewer natural borders between our neighbours and us. It's not just the rivers that have dried up. The seas are also evaporating at an alarming rate. Soon, we may be reattached to the continent, as we were many thousands of years ago. There may be new dangers ahead. The race is on to locate adequate amounts of underground water and grow food from chemicals. As you probably know, extracting drinking fluid from seawater has been possible for some years. It's all about storage facilities, given the difficult circumstances. The success in *The Green Zone* gives us great hope that this country, and other states, can overcome the immense barriers we face, like sustaining essential provision for the whole population until conditions are right to expand.'' He scratched his head while the tone of his voice deepened. ''Those we encounter at the perimeter of *Gnosis* tend to fall into one of two categories. They either want to damage our work or beg to join us. At present, neither of those options is possible. The city is not able to support all those on the outside yet. We are too small. Eventually, it may be possible. Only time will tell. As for the others, we will not tolerate those who feel the earth is doomed and are hellbent on destroying everything we are trying to construct. They are dealt with without mercy. For us, Armageddon is not an option.'' Joel spoke up. ''Most people I know seem to think this is a fairy-exclusive place. Only the most powerful and intelligent of survivors were allowed to come here. Is that true? For those of us on the outside, it feels like we are second-class citizens, desperately trying to stay alive.'' Richard's face darkened with the gravity of what he was about to say.

''We empathise with your plight, brother, but as I've just said, we cannot accommodate all the people out there: we would be overwhelmed. For that reason, we must deny entrance to Gnosis to all but the few who have the specific tools and abilities that we need.'' Hartwood signalled to one of the soldiers.

''It is time for you to go. It is clear to me that you have a great spirit and no lack of courage. It seems to have held you in good stead so far. Stay safe, keep alive. The country will need people like you. When the time is right, we may well try to contact you. Something tells me that your story is only just beginning.''

Amber and Joel exchanged curious glances. They picked up their rucksacks, noticeably heavier than they were before.

''We have added some supplies,'' explained Richard. ''You see, we are not monsters, despite what some outsiders think.'' He smiled and signalled to the guards to escort them back to the main entrance. Joel gazed at the landscape before them as the gates were shut behind them. He reached for Amber's hand.

''We're going to find them, you know. Your family. If they are still out there.''

PART THREE

Central Hospital, Military Wing

Athens, Greece.

14th October 2226

John Byrne*** Hon. lay motionless on the hospital bed. The ceiling fan above him revolved at speed with endless banality. He watched it whirling and buzzing like an aeroplane's propeller until his eyes fell away, dizzy, and blurred. It matched his mood perfectly. Trapped like a fly in a jar. Hospitals always had that effect on him. He tried to keep still. The doctors had told him it would be less painful if he limited his movements as much as possible. Easier said than done. An itching buttock, the cramp in his arm, the need to scratch his head, all immediately contrived to challenge such advice. It wasn't easy, and it wasn't the only reason he was vexed. Using a delicate adjustment of his neck muscles, he was able to turn his eyes to locate the other source of his irritation. Jorge, a French journalist. He was sitting on the chair opposite, pontificating about civilisation falling apart. This flamboyant orator, a correspondent from Paris, was recounting a story John had heard twice before that week. Jorge was bandaged across the crown of his head, the result of a small piece of flying debris that had swept him off his feet. From a distance, it gave him the appearance of a turbaned Sikh. Two young, wounded British soldiers were sitting up in their beds, listening to his rhetoric.

"You know what they are saying, don't you, Jean B?" he continued confidently.

"It's John, not Jean," he sniped. "You told me all this earlier, Monsieur. I suspect we might all need to get used to this extreme weather."

The journalist laughed and turned to the other men for support.

Raising an eyebrow, he continued his rant. "I hear that the tropical forests are struggling to produce fruit, and farm animals are dying in their thousands. I am telling you. This is not just a heat wave."

John B didn't need reminding about the situation. He had already seen first-hand the consequences of what happens when people can no longer grow food to feed themselves. They travelled to where others could. The look of desperation on so many faces at Ceuta, on the Moroccan coast, was etched into his memory. This once heavily fortified border separated Spain from her North African neighbour, who had been struggling to maintain order as thousands of men, women, and children arrived from the south. Their anguish was evident. Most of them were walking skeletons, clutching to whatever they held to be valuable. Each one of them was keen to proclaim about what they had left behind to anyone who would listen. He remembered the gaunt look in their eyes and the desperate words.

"The Sahara has grown wings, like a giant serpent, and devastated everything that grows." The words of an elderly farmer, petitioning him on one knee. What was he expected to do?

"We haven't eaten for days. Have mercy on us, we beg you," a ragged woman with three young children beseeched him.

Pulling his arm, another exclaimed, "Allah has abandoned us. You are our last hope."

John Byrne had felt uncomfortable as he fingered his automatic weapon. They'd been primed not to trust anybody. An old man, a destitute mother, A wide-eyed child. The enemy wore numerous disguises and came in many ages. And even where they were genuine evacuees, what could he do? He was there to keep order, not run emergency food kitchens. How was he expected to deal with so many desperate souls? It was certainly not his idea of soldiering.

***

Jorge continued his emotive diatribe.

"Anyway, I'm out of here tomorrow. Been recalled back to Paris."

His brow narrowed as his expression changed. "It's you guys that I feel sorry for. How do you say, 'Left in the shit?" The two young recruits laughed and glanced towards John, but he offered no gesture of reassurance. Just silent defiance.

"So, how long are we going to be stuck here, Sergeant?" One of them queried.

John lifted himself up against the pillow and looked at him sternly. For a fleeting moment, it felt like he was staring at his son, Tito. Same fresh-faced confidence, same disguised fear.

"Just as long as it takes to patch you up, son and send you back to the front line. As for me, they're sending this old warrior home for a new arm."

One of the young men looked at the shattered remains of John's shoulder. "I think we got away lightly, looking at what happened to you."

The other lad was staring at his jacket on the back of the chair. "See, you got a commendation then," he added. The three gleaming stars on his lapel had been caught by the sun's rays. From a distance, it looked like his uniform had been decorated with precious stones.

"I've heard they don't give those away lightly. Are you some sort of war hero?"

"No, son. Just did my job. Like you did."

Ceuta, Morocco

28th March 2225

"Heh, Sergeant, you didn't tell us we were going on holiday!"

Nervous laughter began to rise around their leader. Sg. John Byrne knew this was not a situation for juvenile humour. That's one of the reasons why he was still alive.

The cocky youth had already decompressed the temperature control in his suit and removed his helmet. He stood gawking at the sunbeds that framed the serpentine pool in front of them. The cool waters glistened invitingly. Before anyone else could speak, John thrust his rifle butt into the soldier's ribs.

"Ouch! What's that for?"

"Stupidity, son. Instead of switching off and indulging your feeble attempts to entertain us, you need to focus. Stay alert. Helmet back on, and that's an order!" He beckoned the men next to him. "You two join him in securing the perimeter. Use the drones to scan the area outside."

***

It seemed somewhat perverse, but John Byrne felt good to be back in Africa. He felt his destiny had drawn him back. Despite the possibility of death, the harrowing atrocities he had witnessed, and the injuries sustained when he was here the previous year, Morocco had become more than just a military base: it was more akin to a second home. The Midlander could have taken up an administration post or even an honourable discharge from the army. Byrne had certainly earned it. He was still getting used to the new arm. The connecting tissue pulled sharply against his shoulder while the grasping mechanism of his replacement fingers still felt clumsy and awkward. At least the trigger mechanism on his weapon could be depressed efficiently. Small mercies! What's more, six months of rest, nourishment and proper sleep had transformed his skeletal fame. He felt stronger, more refreshed, revitalised. But more than anything else, he had unfinished business here, at this gateway to Europe.

***

The other members of the platoon activated their laser guns and spread across the garden in cautious formation. They were flanked by two military AI robots. The only sound that could be heard within the complex was the chirping of a small flock of brightly coloured sparrows, seemingly agitated by the new arrivals. They perched on the cactus plants, stirring their feathers in a display of defiance.

John shouted over to the robot carriers to give him a toxicity reading.

"All substances negative, sergeant," the first soldier replied, verified by the second computer.

"No humanoid images evident," the second added.

Half the cohort moved into the building and advanced up the stairway to the bedrooms. There was little evidence that anyone had been there for several days. They opened the window shutters and shouted confirmations down to their commanding officer. Satisfied that the area was now secure and any immediate threat to them was nullified, Sg. Byrne raised his arm, then gesticulated to the men to lower their guns and fall out. The soldiers slumped in collective relief, unbuckled their pressure suits and sat down on the steps. Now, John could also relax. Removing his own helmet, He wiped the sweat from his brow. It rolled, irritatingly, into his eyes while he slowly breathed in the late afternoon air. For a few seconds, the fragrance of blossom overwhelmed him. It drifted across from a row of prickly pear trees nearby. Lifting the desiccated remains of an old piece of fruit, he pulled away the blackened skin and removed the pips. Without ceremony, these were dispatched to his trouser pocket. There was a place where he would attempt to germinate them. Symbols of the growth he wanted to bring about in this parched and war-torn land.

His thoughts returned to his men. A glance at his watch confirmed that they had been on the move for almost four hours. Gauging their mood, he knew they were tired and needed rest. This ostentatious mansion would provide sufficient protection for the night.

This was not the first palatial hotel they had come across that day. They were scattered across the outskirts of Ceuta, once forming a ring of opulence. A picture of the town that few would now remember. This building was set on an elevated outcrop of rock, shrouded by mature coconut trees and pines. There was little evidence that the place had been looted. John paced around the courtyard, absorbing the layout. The stonework was recent and modern in its design, embellished with vividly coloured artwork and effigies of North African wildlife. It was clearly built to accommodate wealthy clients. Behind its imposing metal gates and high, white-washed walls, it was clearly once private, a difficult place to penetrate. Somewhat overstated, he thought, with two mock watch towers mounted along the side ramparts. But it would make an excellent refuge for the night. Whatever the property owner did for a living, John suspected that he knew that the day would come when he would require such protection.

The men busied themselves up-packing their rations and restoring their energies.

"Drink your recycled fluid," John shouted. "Avoid the water here."

John Byrne climbed the towers and looked out on the desert. Already, the stars had emerged from the late afternoon sky to compete with their lunar companion.

"Stay alert," he bellowed to the guards on duty. "I want to know if there is any movement in those trees over there." He pointed towards the cluster of scrub land in the distance.

"Remember. There are people out there that will kill you for your rations."

He retreated down the steps and pulled out his own food. Turning to his lieutenant, John gave him instructions. "Change the guards in four hours, Blake. I need to get some rest."

John closed his eyes in anticipation of sleep, but all he could see was the terror of yesterday's conflict. A sequence of events prompted by the taking back of Ceuta's ancient line of fortresses. A rush of adrenalin, a momentary loss of concentration. The hidden sniper deadly for one minute before he could be eliminated. It was his own weapon that had lifted this enemy from his camouflaged trench, a sprawling coconut tree. Mission accomplished by the aggressor at the cost of his own life. Adorned in the distinct head covering of the *Polisario Front*, guerrilla fighters from the Western Sahara. Eliminating him was easy, but it was at the cost of two of his own men.

This was a new enemy. Not the throngs of migrant soldiers who sought passage to Europe. These men were hardened veterans of a long-running war for Western Saharan independence against the Moroccan State. A conflict that had spanned hundreds of years. Never had there been a better time to strike. Morocco was on its political knees, and a new enemy had seized the land. The soldier in John could understand their anger. However, the danger they presented was a major threat, as they were expert shots with a range of weapons. They knew there was a small connecting piece in the European suits that was vulnerable. Where the helmet joined the suit. With unnerving accuracy, their conventional bullets frequently found the Adam's apple.

Despite their superior weapons and protective suits, there was an unspoken fear about this shadowy, indigenous force and their ghost fighters. John was still reeling from the loss of his platoon captain, Ian Walker, who had been fatally injured by an incendiary bomb while securing the Tarajac Fort. They had got on well. It was a big loss, and he struggled to keep his feelings in check. He had lost too many people that he cared about in his life. Morale had also waned at the news coming from Punta Blanca, where thirty of their soldiers had perished. Stories about the treatment of several captured men had also emerged. Tortured and tied to posts as a warning to other invaders.

Byrne eventually drifted into sleep, muttering something about the need to secure the Melilla fence.

Marrakesh, Morocco

11th December 2522.

Before he left home that month, John Byrne had reassured his family that he would be back to celebrate the new year. His wife and daughters did their best to disguise their uncertainty about this. They knew when he was lying. The international situation was serious. TV footage of the early skirmishes at Melilla and the dock area at Ceuta provided little assurance to the families of soldiers heading out there. The need for significant reinforcements told its own story. Only his son Tito, who'd recently completed his own military training, sounded a note of caution.

"The officers at my base reckon we're going to be there sometime."

John maintained his pretence. "The forces we're sending are unstoppable, son. You'll see," but he disguised his gaze to avoid uncertainty about further scrutiny.

He embraced each of them in turn. "Be vigilant, girls, and look after your mother." He kissed Bethany with the affection built upon twenty-seven shared summers.

"I love you, big man. Make sure you come back to us, and soon," she pleaded.

He beckoned Tito over to him. "Promise me, son. No recklessness. Smell the danger. Remember those old camping trips we did. Keep your antenna on alert. Trust only the comrades you respect."

With that, he disappeared from their life. It was the last occasion they would all be together again.

***

The initial conflict in North Africa had failed to breach the European border. Spanish guards had manned the fence on African soil, as they had done for hundreds of years. But they had only narrowly avoided being overwhelmed by the sheer numbers of evacuees. Spain had been forced to employ the army to supplement this defence. Then, other European countries heeded the call to support them. But the situation was deteriorating. Despite the shared technology and weaponry of the EU and NATO, the number of armed refugees seeking entry to Europe continued to grow. Intelligence sources confirmed that people were leaving not just the Saharan states but also many countries beyond. Early reports had suggested it was virtually impossible to distinguish the paramilitaries from those on the move because of hunger. The armed insurgents belonged to several tribal groups. Allegiance was forged by a common desire to rid the continent of what they called the 'European cancer.' Despite their differences in history, culture and race, they had bonded together. The aim was not just to secure the northern coastline of Africa. That was only to be the first stage. The real objective was to launch a military offensive against Southern Spain. Quickly realising that other migrants camouflaged their presence, it allowed them to move furtively without recognition. What no one was prepared for was the level of brutality employed against their enemies and the unprovoked slaughter of civilians.

The headland towns had grown significantly over the centuries, and the inhabitants enjoyed prosperous lives. Commerce with Europe was buoyant, whether it involved the legal movement of fruit and precious commodities or the more surreptitious trade in illegal drugs.

NATO/ EU Military Base, Melilla (Morocco)

13th December 2224.

John sat on his bunk bed, inspecting the protective army suit. Seemingly paper thin, the alloy membrane was incredibly robust. 'Resistant to most things an adversary could contrive to use', stated the instruction panel on his right arm. Fingering the lock mechanism on his helmet, he traced the two points of connection. These were the weak points that they had been alerted to. Only there, could a laser gun, a bullet, or even an arrow, penetrate. He'd seen the injured soldiers on the news holding their throats. So many with the same type of wound, most of whom did not survive. Food for thought, he mused. John traced the narrow tubes which housed the water conversion unit and the excrement discharge container built into the lower side of the outfit. When engaging the enemy, there would be little reason to stop for bodily functions.

"If it wasn't for the need to eat and wash, you could live in these dam things, hey?" His bunk buddy interjected. Seamus's big smile broke the introspection perfectly. "These boots wouldn't look out of place in a Dublin nightclub!" He added.

John acknowledged the Irishman by playfully grabbing his lapel and pulling him off the top bunk. The full weight of his ninety kilograms landed on his friend's lap.

"Keep your hands off me, Jonny boy, or I'll have to bust that ugly fuckin nose of yours!"

The impromptu mock boxing match that ensued merely lasted a few seconds. Seamus smiled and headed off to make a drink. John had hit it off with the Dubliner immediately. Roughly the same age, in his early forties, the Irish volunteer had also left the building trade in Ireland. Unlike the many nervous faces around him, Sean lit up the room with his personality, humour, and positivity. He recognised in John a similar strength that belied his calm exterior. A reliable guy. The sort of character you would want alongside you when the shit started to fly.

John reached down for his boots and carefully eased his feet into them. They felt a little heavier than expected. Shiny, less comfortable than the ones he wore all those years before. John stood up to inspect his outfit.

'I look more like an astronaut than a soldier', he reflected. He looked at the faces around him. A moment of doubt surfaced.

"What the fuck are we all doing out here?"

But deep down, he knew the answer. His job had vanished virtually overnight when he'd been informed that the building company he worked for, would close by the end of the week, just like that. No reduced hour schedule, no call for volunteer redundancies, all due to issues linked to the global financial crash, the owners said. It seemed that nobody wanted a carpenter to help build those new shopping malls anymore. Unemployment support didn't even come close to paying the bills. And yes, he'd enjoyed his national service in the past. The temptation to join the military full-time was strong then, too, but staying with his wife and young family was more of a priority. Now, the children were old enough to fend for themselves. When the call for volunteers went out, he was strongly lured to respond. A peacekeeping force was what they called it. Drawn from a variety of European countries. And then there was the remuneration. A hundred level three digital purchasing units per week. Lowest tax code category. 20% bonus on completion of contract. They were told to ignore the media hysteria about local animosity and resistance. Most indigenous communities would welcome their intervention. Even at the two flashpoints on the edge of Europe: Southern Greece, where he knew that Tito had been sent, and the North African Spanish peninsula town where he was now based. Maybe they will understand our mission, John thought. But there had to be a reason why the package was so generous.

Three days later, he found out.

***

As they trundled along silently in their troop carriers, a blood-red skyline soaked the emerging dawn. An alert call with the familiar message came across their communication screen: *Engage suit locking sequence.*

"This is it then," Seamus, the youthful corporal sitting next to him, shouted.

John caught the tension in his voice. "We'll be ok, lad," the older man insisted. "If we keep our concentration levels up and our heads down!"

Seamus Morton checked the power reading in his laser again. "I'm ready for what may be out there, Byrne." But the man from the English Midlands remained tight-lipped.

***

It didn't take long to reach the fence. The first thing John glimpsed from the vehicle's barred window was the sheer height of the barrier that stretched away towards the sea. It looked more akin to some ancient castle wall than a fence. It sprawled across the peninsula like a great column, separating the desert beyond. Disembarking from the troop carrier, the platoon stood as a man, gawking at the spectacle. As they moved closer to the base of the construction, it became clearer what sort of obstacle it was. There were, in fact, three separate constructions built alongside each other. The outer level consisted of heavy pine wooden blocks fastened by large metallic straps. Directly behind was a wall of concrete and sandstone, which reinforced the outer layer. Finally, and closest to them, was the most recent addition. A metal framework of iron sheets housing a caged carriage transported people and equipment to the top. This must have reached nearly thirty metres to the summit. Here, a series of connecting platforms provided opportunities for surveillance across the several miles of scrubland and desert in front of them. About a hundred metres from the gate rose a sea of white tent tops, tailing back as far as the eye could see. Seemingly, thousands of desperate souls were hoping, waiting for their opportunity to leave the continent.

John's platoon walked past a section of the fence which seemed to have been clumsily rebuilt recently. The charred remains of its predecessor, like a black, skeletal vine, twisted out of shape and fractured, made further explanation unnecessary. Several dense layers of razor wire now crowned the metal ramparts around it, challenging only the most reckless to try to scale the barrier. But many still tried. John looked inquisitively toward Lieutenant Walker. "The aftermath of a firebomb, John. They almost got through this time", he added.

"What happened?"

"A group calling themselves *Brothers of Vengeance.* We're not sure how many of them there are. They are much more radical than the others who try to break through previously." He paused to light a cigarette. "It's not about the famine or the food wars for them. It's more about our presence here. They blame us for the food shortages in Africa. And they are well-armed. The barrier is seen as some sort of symbol of Western arrogance. Mark my words, they will try again."

John waited in line for the solar-powered lift. Twenty men crammed into a space more suitable for ten. Even in their temperature-regulated suits, the heat was stifling. It took seconds to reach the top. They fanned out across the top and took up their positions.

"Remember, stay vigilant," Walker communicated to them. No matter what happens, the fence must not fall."

The impact of these dramatic words eventually dissolved in the stillness of the night. The moon glowed gloriously as if to herald some new epiphany. Half a mile away, there were minor movements between the tents as people went about their ablutions or extinguished their fires. The only other sound to penetrate was the course shimmering of sand, driven across the ground by a gentle wind.

John and his comrades were relieved of surveillance duty at 3.00 AM and retreated to their new barracks. Most of the platoon were tired and hungry. He felt the same and joined those who slumped into their camp beds. They knew that tomorrow's patrol would place them on the other side of the fence for the first time, exposed to whatever dangers lay there. This was it, he reflected nervously. The training was well and truly over.

The Outcrop

Early next morning, the barracks were bustling with frantic preparations. Soldiers jostled for mirror space in the bathroom and did final equipment checks. Others did their best to line their stomach with a little breakfast. There was no knowing when the next proper meal would happen. At the briefing, they were told about their mission. Reports that several missing NATO soldiers had been spotted by satellite, camped in the ridge about four kilometres from the gate. Any missing combatants had been presumed dead, so this was something of a surprise. Satellite cameras had confirmed that there were uniformed figures moving about in the vicinity, and they were wearing distinctive NATO combat suits. Although there was no evidence of any transport nearby, there had been an attack on a platoon of soldiers the previous week. Walker refused to elaborate further on what had happened. Their job was to locate these men and bring them back to safety.

As they piled into the troop carriers, tensions were running high. What were the soldiers doing out there? Exposed, vulnerable. Walker remained tight-lipped. The journey was short. Little more than ten minutes, but long enough to play on their fears. As they pulled up opposite the main gate, a series of interlocking steel bars were released, and the gate opened. Immediately, there was movement and the flashing of mirrors from the tented area beyond.

“Quickly!” Walker shouted at the guards. With a tumultuous screech, the gate opened wide enough for the two vehicles to pass through. They closed them just as quickly as the troop carriers sped off in the direction of the tented community.

Engage suit locking sequence. Lasers on standby.

John clasped his weapon and tried to prepare himself for the unexpected. They sped through the refugee camp at speed and were soon past the tents, moving towards the elevated backdrop of rock and dried scrubland. The vehicles spiralled up the dusty pathway but were soon forced to stop by the terrain.

"You four stay with the transport," Walker instructed. "We go on by foot from here."

The platoon disembarked and headed towards the craggy outcrop.

AI support engaged and confirmed one of the robot handlers. The men moved cautiously in formation, behind the AI support, towards their hilltop destination. As they drew near to the summit, those at the front came to a sudden halt. Recoiled in shock, the communication came through: '*Soldiers down. I repeat, soldiers down.*'

Three pale, naked male bodies were bound and fettered to protruding rocks. Their skin emaciated as if all fluid had been sucked from their flesh. Each had been mutilated beyond recognition. But there was something else. One of the men had both an arm and a leg missing. Another had had a section of his back and buttocks removed. The ground around them was stained red with dried blood. The remains of various human body parts lay scattered next to an extinguished campfire.

John swallowed hard to avoid throwing up. "Nothing could prepare you for such savagery," he admitted later. Byrne didn't know, but other colleagues had found this unexpected confrontation with sadistic cannibalism too much to absorb. A sickening taste had risen in many of their throats, chastening the souls of soldiers who thought they had seen everything. Helmets were quickly abandoned with reckless candour. The need for fresh air was overwhelming. A cold, cosmetic message from AI hit their screens: It stated the obvious.

'Body status analysis complete: Combatant units no 6157, 61520, and 6240 expired. All operatives now on standby: Grade A alert; Do not remove helmets. I repeat. Do not remove helmets," the message continued.

Hastily, the troops regained their focus and obeyed the instruction. The men took up a circular formation and waited. But not a sound to lift the tension. There seemed little evidence that the perpetrators were still around.

The group moved tentatively along the narrow path that divided the imposing ridge. They came to a clearing and peered at the precipice beyond.

'No unidentified life forms confirmed within 200-metre range', the AI support announced.

John looked around. Although he couldn't put his finger on it, something was wrong. He approached Walker but was waved away.

'Not now, John". He turned to Corporal Morton. "Take six men and bury the remains of our comrades.'

The rest of the platoon stood there, scanning the rock formations for confirmation, even though there was little movement.

Lieutenant Walker gathered the soldiers together.

'It seems the comrades we are looking for have fled or have been murdered, like the three poor souls back there. We'll wait till they've been buried and then head back. You can stand down to alert level 'B' but keep your weapons close to you.'

"How could they do this, Lieutenant?" Werner, a tall Germanic soldier, verbalised his despair.

"Who knows. Hunger, revenge, the need for information. What matters now is that we apprehend and eliminate those responsible as soon as possible."

Twenty minutes later, the grave diggers reappeared, their task completed.

"All human tissue buried in marked graves, Lieutenant,' Corporal Morton reported. "Still no evidence of hostile forces."

Just as the rest of the platoon assembled to leave, the AI robots display a new message to the men:

'Unidentified life forms approaching the camp.'

***

A flash of silver caught the light. That familiar glow that radiated from the UN combat suits, even on the warmest of days. Eyes stretched, squinting to identify the newcomers. Were these the soldiers they'd been looking for?

Laser guns lowered. The men in front of them seemed unarmed. Affirmation. Shouts of welcome. A lowering of concentration, just for a few vital seconds. It was all that was needed for their 'lost comrades' to reach behind their backs. A well-rehearsed manoeuvre. Explosive devices were quickly seized from small army rucksacks. In an instant, the bombs were hurled at them like frenzied fast bowlers on a cricket green. The crack of laser strikes the assailants' necks, too late to prevent their deadly gift.

The last thing John remembered before passing out was the ringing in his ears and the anguished cries of his colleagues.

***

Burning flesh. The distinctive smell of human life incinerated in gruesome violence. John choked with the pungency of it all as he returned, coughing and spluttering, back to the conscious world. The pain was everything, and more, he had thought hell to be beyond the imagination of any depiction. He lay there, unable to move. The sounds of suffering overwhelmed him. Comrades crawled through the sand, screaming. Some on fire. Others, like him, lay motionless on the ground. An aching pain gathered momentum in his head, stabbing away and spreading to his shoulder. Then he saw it. Or rather, he did not. A gaping hole was all that remained of his upper arm. The rest of the limb lay hanging, limply, by his side. He forced himself to hold back the fear, the tears. Was this it? His final moments of life?

In his delirium, he barely noticed the figure approaching. A man crouched down and instantly clamped what remained of his arm with a medical support strap.

“That should secure it,” he whispered confidently.

“Ah,” John screamed.

“Shush now, Byrne. And this will suppress the pain for a while.” He took the morphine device from his pack. “Try to keep still. You’ve lost a lot of blood.”

Finally, a recognition of the facial features. It belonged to Morton.

‘Ever the pragmatist, the casualty asked about the numbers. How many lost, Seamus?” the wounded man croaked.

“Many. Maybe ten dead. Another fifteen or so injured. It’s bad.”

“Are you ok, Corporal?”

“Cuts and bruises. I was lucky. At the far side of the camp. Unlike Lt. Walker.”

John looked dejected.

“What’s left of him is over there.”

He pointed to the twisted, charred corpse to his left.

“And the attackers? “

“All three dead, but their plan clearly worked.”

He scrunched his face in bitter acknowledgement of the situation.

“We were too slow!” His raised voice hardly necessary. “Saw the suits and just assumed they were our guys. Feckin hell!”

He turned to John. “Anyway, old man. Don’t you think about dying on me. I need you alive.”

Byrne tried to raise a smile. "You must be desperate!"

"Maybe, but you have just been promoted to Corporal!"

***

Seamus Morton knew the drill. If your commanding officer was killed, the next in command stepped up. It was as simple as that. That's what the training manual said. No 'ifs or buts', emotional turmoil cast aside in favour of the bigger priority: the need for army discipline. Despite all this, Seamus almost pissed his pants in panic. He grabbed his communication pack urgently and sent the necessary message.

Rescue mission required. Ambushed by alien assailants. Several fatalities. More wounded. Lt. Walker is dead. In urgent need of support. Corp. Morton. Acting Officer in Command.

The response was ambivalent. "Understood, Morton. Hold your position and await further orders."

The night air descended like a shroud over the platoon. The stench of death was everywhere. Still no *further orders.*

All told, there were just twenty-three operatives still active. They formed a cordon around the injured and waited. Eventually, the response came from the other side of the fence:

Night rescue problematic. Hold position till morning. Rescue imminent.

Seamus Morton could feel the tension. Who else knew they were trapped on top of the outcrop? Some of the men tried to seize a couple of hours of sleep, but the wailing of the injured made it difficult. John Byrne was one of those. He'd experienced pain before, breaking his leg playing rugby and rupturing his Achilles heel in a climbing accident. Both were many years before. Now, away from those he loved, he felt vulnerable, defenceless, frail, but most of all, scared.

John slipped into sleep with the aid of another morphine shot. As the desert brushed itself down to welcome another day, John woke, startled by movement. Was it a bird or a mouse? The sentries had already engaged their weapons and trained them on the scrubland around them.

There was a rustling sound behind the rocks in front of them. But where were they? Enemy attackers eventually started to emerge from concealed holes on the hillside. Each carried a European laser shield, protecting them from the UN guns in front of them.

A voice boomed out in broken English. 'Hand over your rations, or you will suffer the fate of the three men you buried yesterday'.

Morton had to gamble. No sign of reinforcements yet. There looked to be around fifty aggressors. He signalled for his men to lower their weapons and throw their food packs across to them.

Three cloaked men put down their shields and walked across to collect the packaged supplies.

"Is this it?" The assailants mocked.

"Then you will need to hand over the bodies of the dead, too."

Morton had heard enough. He gave the order. Those who could, opened fire, aiming at any small gaps around the shields.

The battle was short but intense. Their attackers were well-armed. Although several of the assailants were killed, the platoon also sustained further losses. With only nine soldiers left to protect the injured, Morton made another difficult decision. To surrender. Maybe they would let the injured live. Maybe the rescue craft would arrive just in time.

He was now struggling to hold on to all he valued about common values. Surely, there would be some compassion for the injured.

The aggressors moved nearer. In an instant, the defenders had been seized and bound. A man emerged from their numbers. Lean and haggard, with a protruding broken nose and piercing brown eyes. His face bore the marks of several conflicts.

"I am Ahmed."

His eyes trained on the small number of UN men in front of them. He shouted something in Arabic to his colleagues. They seized the soldiers and removed their suits.

"Which of you is in charge?"

Seamus Morton spoke up. "I am the acting lieutenant for this platoon."

Ahmed laughed. "This is not a place for actors. What I want is information, foreigner. Tell me. How does the locking sequence work at the gate? The steel one, where the vehicles emerge from. Tell me this, and I will let you live."

Seamus knew in his heart that this was a lie. He was already a dead man. The acting lieutenant had little knowledge of the mechanism they spoke of and knew the wrong answer would be fatal.

"I think there are three levels, but not sure of the sequencing or opening codes."

Ahmad walked across to the other soldiers.

"Wrong answer." With a single blow from his sword, he decapitated one of the injured UN survivors.

"I will ask you again, Morton. Do not attempt to buy time. I know more soldiers are ready to leave the base."

Seamus Morton turned marble white with fear. Even if he knew the codes, he couldn't betray the platoon. He mustered as much courage as he could and shook his head.

"Ah!" Shouted the fuming Arab as he raised his sword arm again. The head of Seamus Morton hit the ground with one violent blow of the blade and rolled through the dust in front of John's unconscious body.

The assailants began to mumble between themselves. Something was up. A man appeared from the tunnel with a message. Two further military troop carriers had already left the base. Some of the assailants were already preparing to disappear back down the hidden rock opening. Gathering dust clouds signalled the imminent arrival of the UN rescue pods.

"Kill them all!" Ahmad shouted as he moved back towards the tunnels.

***

John had only heard part of this unfolding drama. He lay in the dust, for all external purposes, dead. He could hear the cries of members of his platoon as they perished, one by one. Murdered purely for what the uniform stood for. He waited and watched before pulling a body across his and hoped for a miracle. He closed his eyes and articulated his dying wishes. But no one came to finish him off. Instead, everything went quiet. With his good arm, he pushed the corpse that lay on top of him to the side, pulled himself up to a sitting position and looked around. The bodies of fellow soldiers lay scattered everywhere. Some mutilated. All dead. Even those he knew had only been injured. He inspected his damaged shoulder. The bleeding had now stopped, and the support strap appeared to be still in place. Somehow, he was still alive.

John became distracted by the whirling buzz of rotas as the sound gathered momentum. In clusters of rising sand, the vehicles landed. Behind the suits, it was impossible to gauge what expression these men carried as they conducted their grim task of checking the bodies. The AI robot gave a scientific inventory. *Thirty- nine dead. One survivor.*

Two medics noticed Byrne sitting motionless on the ground. They administered further pain relief to him and checked his shoulder support.

"Whoever put this on knew what they were doing," one of them voiced knowingly.

"He was my friend."

The other medic gazed curiously at the wounded man. "You're something of a hero, son. The only survivor here. You'll be getting a medal, I'd say!"

But John didn't want a medal. He wanted his friend, Seamus, back.

He wanted Lt. Walker back and all the poor souls lying on the ground around him.

***

"Hello, Corporal Byrne. According to a message sent back to base, you were acting corporal when Morton took Walker's place and, what's more, the last man standing. A true officer. Senior officers are going to want to talk to you when we get back to base."

John Byrne was hardly listening. But when he returned from the camp hospital, the subsequent de-brief would change his life in ways he could never have anticipated.

A Compromise

A week passed by, and John was learning to adapt to the loss of his right arm. ‘Thank God it was the right one’, he told the medics at the hospital base in Ceuta. “I’m so left-handed I could hardly butter bread with the other.”

They told him he’d been lucky. No gangrene, no infection, to complicate recovery. However, he’d sustained other injuries in the bomb blast. There was shrapnel lodged in his leg and above his left hip. Some pieces of metal had been removed, but others were lodged precariously close to vital organs. Best to leave them alone and monitor their impact. John didn’t need telling he’d been seriously injured. His body had already confirmed the damage. Time would tell what impact these injuries would have on his future.

***

The meeting with senior military staff would take place that afternoon. He was intrigued to know what else they required from him. They’d fitted him out with a new army jacket to wear. ‘The least they could do’, he thought, given that there wasn’t much of the old one left to accommodate his changing body shape. He’d already gone through the events of that day with senior staff. The half-eaten comrades, the trap involving camouflaged NATO colleagues in stolen suits, the initial casualties caused by the bombs and the massacre of survivors wishing to surrender.

Three high-ranking officers sat before him in the meeting room. Their ribbons and shoulder markings confirmed their status. He guessed at least one of them was a general. When they introduced themselves, his suspicions proved correct.

“Good afternoon, John,” said the rotund, avuncular man in the centre. “It’s been a few days now since the tragedy. I hope you’re bearing up despite the discomfort." He was fingering a small object that looked metallic on the table.

"In acknowledgement of your courage, we are going to award you this medal today." He held it up in the light for John to see. It glowed golden yellow, supported by an attached line of blue ribbons. "If you leave the army now, it might help you to secure work back home. But let me warn you. Things are increasingly difficult. The economy has almost collapsed."

He stared inquisitively at the injured soldier.

"But that is not the advice we want to give you. It will be no surprise to you to learn that both the immigration situation on the borders of Europe and the food wars are not going well. Our NATO forces have suffered significant losses. The *Polisario Front* has joined up with several other Saharan tribes to rid the continent of foreign troops. A campaign of murder, torture and even cannibalism has spread. Many local friendly tribes and city dwellers have been brainwashed into believing that the fence at Ceuta is about to fall. They see this as an excellent launching pad for a full invasion of Spain from the south."

An older-looking member of the panel leaned forward and interrupted. "The truth is, Byrne, we have a much bigger issue now looming. Russia has indicated that it is prepared to launch controlled nuclear missiles on any group that threatens its borders. America has said the same. China remains isolated from Europe's woes, watching and waiting. All this is worrying news, having a negative impact on persuading people to come forward to join up. At a time of such national security, we need to boost the image of the army. In short, we need heroes to inspire greater recruitment. A time is coming when a man's reputation may be all he has in this world. And we would like to enhance yours."

He continued. "We want to use your story and image to inspire others. In return, a second-class medal or even a third might be available. These awards would carry more pay and prestige. If you agree, we will send you to Europe to receive a new bionic arm, moulded from your own

DNA, according to the latest scientific breakthroughs. Just imagine it, Byrne – a new arm like the one blown away."

John was certainly interested in the last offer. He'd heard how effective the technology was. Some had said they couldn't feel the difference between the old limbs and the new.

John cleared his throat and spoke up. "I am flattered by the proposal. I'm guessing there is far more commitment to enhancing the image of soldiering here. I know the dangers of this work. In some ways, I feel honoured to receive such an offer. Permit me to speak bluntly, sir. I'm not a military expert, but as you will know, I have served in the forces for several years. There were things that happened out there, beyond the fence, that should and could have been avoided. Poor reconnaissance and intelligence, for starters. I'm not looking to blame anybody in person. They all fought proudly in difficult conditions." He paused for a few seconds of reflection. "I lost comrades I respected and loved. I also have a son who serves in the NATO force on the border between Greece and Turkey. No idea if he's still alive. Could you help me to find out? This would be another reason to do this for you and, of course, the support of my children back in the UK."

The uniformed heads around the table engaged in whispered conversation.

"So, it is settled, then," confirmed the general. "There is one stipulation, and it is huge. You must undertake to conceal all details of the events surrounding the deployment and activities of platoon 26 last week." He peered down his glasses at John Byrne. "The army will conduct its own enquiry into what went wrong. You will be called to speak confidentially at this hearing soon."

Byrne nodded.

"And when can I receive the new arm?" he inquired.

"All in time, lad. All in good time."

***

John Byrne received the letter by hand. They had promised to contact him on that Monday, and they had been true to their word. The soldier asked him to sign in acknowledgement of receipt. With a formal salute and the required signature, the messenger left John to open the correspondence on his own. He sat down at the table and stared at the printed name: *Lieutenant John Byrne ** Hon.* Was this an error? An elaborate military stamp on the cover encroached across several bold letters: *TO BE OPENED BY NAMED RECEIVER ONLY*

General Baker had promised him a promotion, but this was something else. Two grades. The rank of lieutenant! He used his finger to wrench it open and eagerly read the details. The promises made, together with what was required of him, were clearly laid out.

He would leave the following day to travel to a military base in Turkey, where the operation on his arm would take place. DNA samples had already been taken from him and were with the medical team. The regenerative process would take several days, but once complete, his new arm should function as well as the old one. He was less comfortable about the narrative he had bought into. Once he was able to manage stage two of the recovery, namely his physical rehabilitation exercises and medication, he would be sent back to the UK to help with recruitment events for the army. There was also mention of visiting front-line troops in the key conflict areas.

***

John knew he had been lucky. It could have been him left dead in the Moroccan desert, like Seamus Morton, Lt. Walker and the rest of the platoon. At the same time, he was proud of his newfound status. What would his son Tito have made of it? Or Bethany? Sweet Bethany. Lt. Byrne sat back and caressed his wounded shoulder, smiling as he basked in his good fortune.

Tito

Tito had been looking for a job for almost three months. Despite leaving senior school with good qualifications, options were limited.

"I don't want to go to university," he'd told his disappointed father. I want to see more of the world. I'm going to join the army. Just like you did when you were a bit older than me!"

John, momentarily speechless, was torn between his desire to dissuade Tito and his understanding of the allure of military life. He knew that this new conflict was not about politics but hunger, and Tito's enemies did not wear uniforms. His son, barely two years older than he was when he became a soldier, wanted to make the same mistake as his father.

"Don't you realise what's going on out there, son? This is not a normal peacekeeping mission. The European borders are under siege. These are desperate situations."

"So why are you signing up again, Dad?"

John gripped his teeth in annoyance. The boy wasn't supposed to know. Not yet. His wife turned to glare at her husband and interrupted.

"Well!" exclaimed Bethany, with more of a touch of sarcasm. "We'd all like to know the answer to that one. When were you going to tell the rest of us?"

She had done her best to deter John from joining up. The media couldn't disguise that military casualties were increasing by the week. Everybody was concerned. These were extraordinary times. But financial pressures were building for everyone back home and certainly for the Byrne family.

John realised that he had to bring more money home.

Bethany had not been well for several weeks. She felt fatigued, stripped of all energy. It was as if her heart was only operating at a limited capacity, permitting just enough blood to keep her vital organs functioning. The local doctor was unsure what was wrong with her. She had started to struggle with the demands of her IT job and had been forced to take temporary leave. Bethany knew several people were waiting in the wings to step in if she failed to return soon. Being unable to work was not a realistic option. Medicines were expensive. Food and energy bills had climbed alarmingly throughout the year and showed no signs of abating. John's carpentry wage only covered the essential bills. He'd presented her with a compelling case to earn more money for the family. That meant a return to the army.

***

Tito Byrne had looked at alternatives. Tested the water. Some interviewers told him he should attend university, but Tito's mind was made up. He was going to become a soldier. He hadn't told his parents how advanced the plans were. After all, a nineteen-year-old didn't require anybody's permission.

***

While John was playing his part in keeping the shores of Greece free from armed African insurgents, Tito and his regiment had arrived at the Turkish/ Greek border, unprepared for what they faced. Not even their military leaders had realised how quickly the situation was changing. Initially aligned with their European allies in defending the peninsula, the Turkish army had fragmented. Some units had challenged the moral legitimacy of attacking fellow Muslims, albeit invaders from another continent. The sight of these starving brothers and sisters of Allah aroused significant sympathy. With several of the tremendous authoritative centres of Islam around the world fuelling this compassion, some adherents saw the opportunity for a new caliphate to rise from the chaos.

Like his companions, Tito had walked into a storm. Men from different parts of the world carried out an ambush of tactical simplicity. There was no escape. Cornered on the edge of a small town, three kilometres from the shores of the Mediterranean, they faced an enemy, both in front, behind and to the sides of them. Private Tito Byrne and his colleagues fought bravely. If his father had known, he would have wept with pride. A targeted bomb dispersed the bodies of three of his colleagues from their protective trench. What was left of his friends lay scattered and broken in the dust. The rest held their position until their laser guns ran out of power. They died in a hail of bullets as enemies converged from all directions. The body of John Byrne's son lay motionless on the ground. The glory he sought was left strewn alongside his blood-splattered neck.

Hope

It took a sense of humour to live through such precarious times with a name like Hope. Barely a day went by without somebody reminding her of the irony. But the woman who had befriended her boss, Bethany, seemed comfortable with their teasing. Harmless banter, she mused. More importantly, it distracted them from probing too deeply into her background. There was a pot of dark secrets about her past that she would struggle to explain. It had taken several months to sum up the courage to share any of it. She knew it was the sort of story that would polarize opinion. Bethany's intuition had raised several questions about her new staff member.

The time had come to enlighten her. Hope had kept it to herself for too long. She confessed that she struggled to connect with her new colleagues when she arrived at the Technology Centre nine months ago.

"You were, like a wounded animal, luv! Your radar signals locked, your personal antennae in complete listening mode, as if you were trying to identify signs of danger," added Bethany.

"That's why I reached out to you. You were the only person I felt would understand me."

Bethany leaned forward; her eyes filled with understanding. "Everyone needs someone to talk to, Hope. I've seen your hard work, commitment, and attention to detail. But sometimes, when we need to work more collaboratively, it helps to share a little more of ourselves. You seem to be such a loner, and that's okay. But I'm here for you, ready to listen whenever you need to share."

The executive from 'Smiths Technology Support' was frustrated with her host.

"You're a strange one, Hope. Such sadness in that face of yours. Whatever giant hole you fell into in the past has scarred you. Whatever it is, such a burden should be shared."

That Tuesday evening, Hope took a step towards healing. She invited Bethany over for a meal, a gesture of trust and openness. Bethany, intrigued and sensing the significance of the invitation, agreed to join her the following evening.

***

After work that night, her new friend made a delicious pasta bake and opened a large bottle of red wine.

“Everything you think you know about me is a lie,” she confessed bluntly. “What I tell you now must go no further. Even if you sack me.’’ The fear was evident in her words. “My life depends upon it.”

‘’Where to begin,’’ she muttered. “My name isn’t even Hope.”

Bethany sat back, startled.

“You can trust me.” She reached out and gently placed her hand on top of Hope’s. A metaphorical gesture to reassure her pensive host.

“Go on.”

Hope grimaced. Her mind was elsewhere. “You remember my interview? It must have been more than a year ago. All that difficulty you had obtaining those references.” Her friend nodded.

“Yes. I thought we were going to lose you before you even got started.”

“You almost did.”

Hope narrowed her eyes. The weight of her imminent [7]announcement hung heavily on her shoulders.

“I lied to all of you. There were no references. Those stories about my previous company collapsing. A fire in the Human Resources suite destroying records. Staff moving abroad. A serious illness. Lies, all lies.

When the references finally arrived, they were no more than fabrications. I found someone to write them for me, or should I say, paid somebody."

Bethany was speechless. Eventually, she forced a question from her lips.

"Why? What on earth did you do that?

"Your skills seemed extensive. You had clearly worked at a high level of….

Hope interrupted her. "I know. But much of it was learned in prison. I had plenty of time."

Bethany reached for her wine glass."

"Prison. What on earth for?"

"Murder."

And my real name is Irma. Irma Eastford.

***

Bethany sat back in her chair, clasping raised hands behind her head in frustration and bewilderment.

"Give me one reason why I shouldn't sack you first thing in the morning. Go on! Tell me why I shouldn't. What on earth happened to you, Irma?"

Her colleague calmly began, with open candour, to explain.

A tale of appalling injustice unfolded during the next hour. The man Irma fell in love with worked in the 'Wellness Substances' industry, specializing in cosmetic mind-changing drugs. He travelled a great deal, but Irma was content with the limited time they shared together. It wasn't long before she accepted his invitation to move in with him.

They had talked about marriage and made initial plans. In retrospect, Irma admitted she should have seen the signs. It began with a supposed funding issue. A request to borrow money from her financial savings. He said it was only for a couple of weeks until overdue payments were made to his bank. He knew she had inherited a sizable fund from her mother, a renowned medical surgeon in London.

"I fell in love with a man who seemed to be everything I dreamed about," she said, "But all this time, he was just using me."

"When I started to refuse, he turned violent. I tried to share what was going on, but neither friends nor family members believed me. Jacob was just so plausible, so charming. They gave me quizzical looks and shook their heads. Even when I showed them the bruises on my wrists and face, they were not convinced. One night, the violence escalated. He returned home in an angry mood. Jacob wouldn't tell me what was wrong with him, but I knew something serious must have happened. ''I need this money now,'' he bellowed. "My life depends on it," I begged him to tell me, but he refused. "Better you don't know the full details," he exclaimed.

''Transfer the money now,'' he demanded. I stood my ground and demanded an explanation. His response was to punch me in the face and kick me while I lay collapsed on the floor. I managed to raise myself and ran into the kitchen, but he caught me by my hair, dragging me back to the ground. Once again, I struggled to my feet and reached across to the knife rack. When he attacked again, I lashed out in terror. The blade caught him across his neck, severing an artery. There was blood everywhere. I tried to stop the bleeding, but it was hopeless. I rang my medical mobile support unit, but by the time they arrived, he was dead. I sat there holding him in my arms till the medics took him away."

Irma paused as if frozen by the trauma of the account. She struggled to hold back the tears. Bethany could only throw her arms around her and try to comfort her friend.

Once composed, Irma shared the next bombshell. "The police brought me in for questioning. Initially, I wasn't aware of what was unfolding. I explained what was happening, but my interrogators seemed unconvinced by my version of events. Witnesses had seen us arguing in a restaurant the previous evening. Two of them claimed that I had threatened him. The level of anger picked up on the restaurant customer welfare analysis was high. Not surprisingly, Jacob was his usual calm persona. And before you ask, the reason for my fury was that he told me I would need to sell all my investments ASAP to pay his debts!

The police presented a different interpretation that shocked me. They had found no evidence for my story and kept referring to my anxiety levels. Readings from the CCTV camera drones outside our house showed unusually high levels of personal instability. No wonder I was nervous. I was about to tell him I'd had enough and was leaving him. They kept going on about my nervousness and angst. The arrest readings seemed to confirm this. But of course, my readings would be high. I'd just defended myself from a serious attack!

What I wasn't prepared for was the letters the police found from Jacob at the house. It claimed that it was I who was pestering him for money and that he was afraid for his life. I just couldn't see the point of laying out these lies on paper, but he was clearly covering himself if anything happened to him. The second document was a new will, leaving the house, which he owned, and his other assets solely to me if he should die.

My attempt to investigate his professional finances met with a wall of silence. All sorts of confidentiality issues and government barriers emerged. He was clearly well-connected. Finally, they charged me, not with culpable manslaughter but with murder. They said I had motive and opportunity and was in a heightened state of instability. Only the latter was true. I lived the last few months convinced that if I failed to sign away my inheritance, he would kill me.

Irma dropped her head into her hands.

"I was given nine years in a high security correction unit. Managed to get out in three, though," she whispered.

Bethany poured them both another glass of red wine. "Please continue."

"I would no doubt still be there but for a stroke of luck. A prisoner in another institution, keen to negotiate a deal with the authorities, confessed that he had worked with Jacob on a heist to steal thousands of financial units of *trepium.* This was a top-of-the-range hallucinogenic recreational drug that Jacob's company was marketing. When he realised the company were on to him, he decided to deflect attention away from himself by fabricating a story of an avaricious girlfriend determined to steal drugs from his company. Prisoner 35274, his partner, had led him in to crime."

Bethany interjected, "So, how did the courts view this development?"

"There was a lot of bluster, accusations by lawyers and further police scrutiny about the case. Eventually, the judge ruled that there was a strong likelihood that I had been the victim in this sorry saga and, given that I had already served three years, ordered my immediate release. However, finding an appropriate job with a prison record proved difficult. Employers were suspicious. Although they didn't say the words to me, you could see the doubts they harboured in their faces. 'No smoke without fire,' she mouthed while shaking her head. That's why I hit upon the idea of forged references. As you saw, my technology skills were sound, but I knew you wouldn't take me on with my background. So, there it is. The whole tangled tale of my downfall. I killed him by accident, but who knows what I might have done to him if I had known the full story."

From that day forward, the two women grew closer. Hope started to help her friend with child-minding. She was still her boss and even secured a modest promotion at the company. It was shortly after this that Bethany began to feel ill. At first, she dismissed it as just a touch of indigestion. But it developed into something more ominous. Bouts of regular pain and loss of weight. The body scan confirmed her private suspicions. Stomach cancer. Moreover, it had spread virulently.

During this period, John was away with the army and didn't realise how serious the situation was. Bethany put on a brave face: it was better that her husband didn't see her at her worst. She knew he would try to come home and nurse her. That wasn't his forte, and she doubted he would secure extensive leave of absence.

By the time she told him, Bethany was nearing the end. Hope stayed by her side throughout the final days, supporting the children. Barely in their early teens, it was a terrible shock.

When he received the news, John was inconsolable. He felt he had let his wife down. Strangely, it drew him closer to Emerald, Amber and Tito. And when he returned from the war for good, there was somebody he would secure a place for in unit 214. That person had done more than anyone to support the woman he had loved all his life. Hope.

Raul

The man from Malaga had always considered himself fortunate. He used to believe that people make their own luck in life, a byproduct of careful planning, mature choices and the avoidance of reckless lifestyles. His parents had driven this philosophy into him as a boy, and it had served him well. In moments of reflection, he knew their success had given him a significant springboard to mould his business ambitions. With a mother from England and a father from Spain, he and his brothers were no strangers to frequent trips across the channel. He recognised the potential for almost tropical growing conditions that the last century had brought to Britain and harboured an ambition to move there in the future. That was until the *Change*, or *El Cambia*, as they called it in Spain, brought all this to a traumatic halt.

Some of Raul's friends had nicknamed him *Suerte Uno,* the 'lucky one.' To an outside observer, his fruit-growing business had thrived with each passing year. Critical decisions about expansion, especially in the overseas UK market, had reaped rich dividends. Settling down to family life with the clever and engaging Lucia had provided him with a solid marriage and two delightful children. Even those who were sometimes hard to please, like her parents and some of her best friends, were won over by his charm and energy. His life was the envy of many until that fatal day when heavily armed foreign insurgents entered the city. They said it couldn't happen, not in Malaga. A prestigious port city and regional centre. Nobody realised how life, as they knew it, would simply crumble away. Just thinking about those events made him feel nauseous, sometimes physically sick.

Later, he told others that one of the best things he ever did was bump into John Byrne. John was a soldier at the time, posted to support their Andalucian allies after Spain signed a unique collaboration agreement, having recently left the European Union. A chance meeting with the Englishman outside a *Pharmacia* near the port probably saved both their lives. Foreign insurgents had attacked the platoon that John was working with, firing a laser rocket in their direction. It exploded near them, sweeping both men off their feet. Raul, a local civilian, was simply visiting the chemist to pick up a prescription. Although shaken, Raul appeared to be OK. He shook the dust from his clothes and saw the man in uniform crumpled on the floor. Byrne, however, was in the wrong place at the wrong time. As John hit the pavement, concussed and bleeding, this local stranger dragged him away from outside the pharmacy into a narrow alleyway. Despite the risk to his own life, Raul then crept back to the pharmacy for bandages to bind John's head. As the insurgents moved forward, he helped the English soldier into an army vehicle nearby for evacuation.

Before he left him, John asked the stranger his name. "Raul. Raul Lopez, senor."

"Thank you, Raul. I owe you a debt. I hope to pay it someday."

"*De Nada* (don't mention it!) And if you ever need some fruit" He broke into a wide grin. ''I'm your man!"

With that, he reached for a business card and placed it in the breast pocket of John's jacket.

Two days later, John Byrne called upon his good Samaritan to thank him properly. His forehead was still bandaged, and he was on the mend, apart from suffering from an almighty headache. When John learned that Raul's work necessitated occasional business visits to the English Midlands, he insisted that he visit him when he was on leave so he could show him around. Raul held him to his word. But two days into the Spaniard's trip that following year, and without warning, the skies darkened, and the meteorite showers began. The winds destroyed everything in their path.

The man from Malaga found himself unable to return home. The European borders closed. Martial law prevailed across every European state. He didn't know it then, but his country had experienced similar weather phenomena. All he could do was wait.

John returned to military duties. When he finally came home for good, he was surprised to hear that Raul was still in the UK. He tracked him down to the remains of a nearby village. There, he found a pale shadow of the man he remembered. Reduced to a combination of begging and casual hard labour, it was clear to Lt. Byrne that Raul urgently needed support.

"There is nothing for me back in Spain anymore," he lamented. Raul showed John the letter. His wife and children were dead, victims of the terrorist bombing campaign that had continued to plague the southern communities of his homeland.

He began to weep. "I can't even get permission to go back to Spain to bury them".

John addressed him stealthily. "My time with the military is coming to an end, Raul. You see this arm. That is the only reason I tour the broken armies of the federated UN, attempting to encourage recruitment. Why was I in Malaga that fateful morning? Fulfilling a contract. Two years, I promised them. 'Inspire them with tales of valour,' they said. 'Make them proud to serve the cause, so others will follow them.' But do you know what? I've changed nothing. Those young soldiers look at me and see themselves as younger, more confident, and more able than I. Pitched along a path to glory. The adrenalin of youth. Playing their part in baulking against the invasion from Africa. Destined to be heroes. I tell them I was fortunate, but they soak up the embellished story of my final days in Morocco. The last soldier standing. Survival despite the odds. Maybe they need to hear something like this to push away the doubts and fears that they hide. Especially when you stare into the eyes of the enemy."

John wiped the sweat from his brow and gazed at the sky. "The one thing we cannot change is their desire to survive. These people who have abandoned Africa are desperate. One day, we are going to have to compromise. Reach some agreement about sharing our resources in Europe, or the conflict will never end.

Raul nodded. "What will you do when you go home to the UK, John?" He turned to him. "I have papers here to set up a small community for six people. We will have fuel and food. I have already allocated five places. So, one vacancy remains, my friend." He paused. "It is yours if you want it."

Raul looked stunned. He'd heard about such communities in the *Wastelands*. It was certainly preferable to scratching around government buildings looking for paid work. The Spaniard lifted his head and embraced John. "Gracias, amigo. Muchos gracias. Maybe there is still a little luck left for me in this world".

***

When John returned, he found Emerald in the ruins of his old family home. A small cottage in the hamlet of Lurnham, a part of the country once known as Worcestershire. Although most of the rich vegetation that once filled the undulating fields that bordered his house had now disappeared, along with neighbouring woods and forests, there was no mistaking the distinctive position of his old house on the edge of this rustic, stone-clad village. The wisteria bush that had clung to the front of the building, adorning the entrance with fragrant blue flowers each year, was now no more than a shrivelled tangle of twigs. He stood in front of what was left of the building, memories tumbling uncontrollably from his head. Only the reassuring sight of the Marlow hills, nestling in the distant skyline, provided much reassurance.

Like a cascading picture book, the images of those he loved, fell into view. Bethany, Tito, Emerald, and Amber. Somehow, despite all the challenges of recent years, some of them had survived. Alas, not Bethany. Nor Tito. As for Amber, he could only hope, but that was rapidly fading.

He remembered buying the property all those years ago. "We can't afford it," fretted Bethany. "The payments are too high." He smiled as he remembered his words at the time.

"Don't worry, my love. We'll find a way."

***

John opened the rusted gate and knocked on the door. Emerald's gaunt figure emerged with a massive grin on her face. "Dad!" She hugged her uniformed visitor with every sinew she could muster.

"You've lost weight, Emerald".

"So have you!"

They laughed, and she led him by the arm into the living area. John's attention was drawn towards the east wall. "What happened here, Emily?

"Part of the structure took a tumble in the night winds. We've been fixing it with whatever materials we can find."

"We?" John repeated, somewhat confused. He had not even noticed the young man sitting in the shadows of one of the room's corners. He turned to his daughter. "Who's that?" giving the stranger a cautious glance.

"That's Hawk, Dad. He's been helping me with the wall".

John gave him a quizzical look and studied the robust repair job done to secure the perimeter.

"We used only rocks and cement, sir," Hawk explained.

"You've done a good job, lad. I'm not sure what would have become of the place. Thank you."

John observed the reinforced rock barrier. "Has it been tested against the worst of the night winds?"

"It wasn't too bad last night, Dad, but we had a couple of challenging nights earlier this week."

John's attention was now drawn towards a section of the rear roof.

"It will take a fortune to replace all those panels. And that's if they are available. The old place is really struggling with these new weather conditions."

While the evening drifted into nighttime, the two men learned a little more about each other.

“No, Dad. He’s just a friend,” Emerald responded to her father’s goading. “We met at work. He helps me with stuff.” John raised an eyebrow.

“Really?” He delivered with a wry smile. ” Does he live here?”

“No. Hawk lodges with a family at the far end of the village. We’re not in a relationship if that’s what you’re asking.” She paused as if to reflect on her words. “Not yet,” she added provocatively.

Hawk sat alone at the kitchen table, scribbling in a notebook.

“What are you writing?” enquired John.

“Oh, just some notes about the war. I’ve decided to write an account of what happened to my regiment.”

“So, you were with the army, then?”

“Yes.” He looked at Emerald’s father. “Emerald has told me about you. I’m sure you, too, have many stories about the war. “

“I do, but they stay right here. (He pointed to his head) Some tales are best left untold.”

The older man beckoned his young companion to join him outside.

“We’re just going to take a stroll outside, Emerald. Before the temperature drops.”

She cast an inquisitive glance towards her father.

“Don’t worry, Em.” he smiled. “The interrogation will be light!”

Emerald watched them enter the yard, engrossed in conversation. At that moment, she saw her younger brother Tito alongside her dad. Animated, eager, brimming with ideas. Was that why she felt drawn to Hawk?

The more John listened to Hawk, the more he warmed to him. Despite the difference in age and experiences, he'd found the lad's enthusiasm infectious. It stirred memories of his son. He turned to him and spoke bluntly.

"What do you think of Emerald then?"

Hawk fumbled for a response."

Sheepishly, he mumbled, "She's special. A very special friend."

"Mm." John could read his affection for her in his eyes.

"And does she feel the same about you?" he enquired.

"I think so. But it's sometimes hard to tell."

"Anyway, I'd best be returning to my lodgings before the night winds start," declared Hawk. John clasped his hand. "Maybe I'm wrong, but I think Emerald is quite taken with you, Hawk!" A flicker of embarrassment flushed across his face.

"Listen to me. This old place of mine is clearly falling apart. It won't survive for much longer. That's why I have accepted an offer from the military hierarchy. To form a small community in one of those vacant units, become what they call a *guardian of the hearth*. I'm going to visit one in the *Wasteland* tomorrow. What do you know about these places?"

Hawk's eyes narrowed as he fingered the identity micro-chip buried in his arm. "All I know is that they exist for the few. A couple of hundred small communities dotted across the *Wastelands*, mainly old, stone, isolated houses or former farm buildings. No more than five or six people in each. The authorities supply them with food, drinking water and wood to burn. They are very strict about the rules. The group must pack up and leave immediately if there are any transgressions. You can imagine what that means. I met someone who was ejected from a unit near here. Somebody died there, and they kept collecting her rations. Armed men came to evict them the morning after they found out.

Anybody trying to return is likely to be shot. Besides, they will have another group in there before the end of the week." Hawk sounded agitated.

"We may have fought their fucking wars for them, but most of us will never be invited to enjoy the relative security of such a place. Remember. Most of us are considered *tainted.* Forced to live on the outside, fend for ourselves, like modern-day lepers." There was bitterness in his voice. ' ' But you, Mr Byrne. You seem to have won their favour. Whatever happened in Morocco is clearly appreciated by the new powers. Some of us have heard rumours about you. The only one to survive some sort of massacre. Lauded by the military leaders. I've seen your face on the recruitment posters. You know, the ones encouraging us to sign up for the army."

John smiled and placed his hand on the lad's shoulder. "This new world still carries many traumas and injustices that the old one did. But there is a chance to build something better. In the meantime, what is most important is to survive. That's why I will take their offer. All being well, I can move there with Emerald before the end of the month."

As these words dropped from his mouth, he turned to look for a reaction. Hawk looked dejected by the news. "You seem to have shown great kindness to my daughter, Hawk. I appreciate that. There's a spare place in my unit. Would you like to join us?

Hawk found his composure. "Me?" He looked emotional. "It would be an honour, sir. An absolute honour."

A New Home

John had been surprised by the swiftness of the response. He'd expected to wait several weeks before a unit became available to move into. However, barely five days after completing the contract details, the official picked him up at 8.00am and headed out through the morning haze to look at Unit 214.

The man in the faded blue overalls thrust his right hand out in John's direction. "I'm Luke. Luke Peters. Heard about your exploits in Morocco. Respect, man." He winched as he straightened his twisted leg. "Did some service myself before I caught one in this leg."

John shook his hand and broke into a cautious smile. "Guess we are both lucky to still be here."

Their vehicle rattled across the uneven surface as it headed away from the village.

"214 is a slightly unusual site. A bit isolated but perfectly inhabitable," the driver exclaimed.

Despite the devastated landscape, Byrne recognised where they were going. It was about fifteen miles west of his village cottage, in sight of the Hills. He had grown up barely ten miles from there. The farm was hidden within a small crater, surrounded by sandstone walls, below a dusty, featureless plain. From a distance, it looked vulnerable to the elements, its rooftop barely peering above the level of the land.

"Don't be put off by the isolation," he continued. "The old farm building was built below the surface for a reason. Once you climb down into the crater, you are protected from the worst of the elements." As an afterthought, his companion threw out a reassuring caveat.

"You're lucky this unit has become available. The organisers recognise a man with your military record deserves special treatment." John followed his guide down the steps to an old farmyard house. As they entered the main building, he inhaled a familiar odour and recoiled. The fading stench of death.

"What happened here?"

His companion shook his head.

The story that emerged was worrying. "We think the four occupants perished quite suddenly. Poisoned by their lack of attention to detail," the accommodation officer shared nonchalantly. "These water pipes require regular maintenance, you know," he added," People need to follow the instructions."

John had a gift for knowing when he was being lied to.

"So, the pipes are contaminated?"

"No. Not if you keep them clean. Don't worry. We have rectified the problem. The bloke fancied himself as some sort of engineer. Set up a filtering pump. Thought he was being clever if you ask me."

"The smell will disappear soon. We didn't find them for several days."

"Them?"

"Yes. Four bodies."

The more he learned, the less convinced John was about the account.

"And you say there is room for six here?"

"With a squeeze!" Luke laughed.

As the two men, John and Luke, moved around the complex, John kept his thoughts to himself. The place was filled with antiquated furniture, each piece carrying its own story. The usual clutter of misshaped plastic tubes, wires, and bits of metal added to the mystery of the place. A collection of old rugs and blankets were piled up in the corner of the main room, close to the open fireplace. It didn't look like it had been lit for a while, adding to the eerie atmosphere.

"You'll not find one like this," Luke exclaimed, his voice filled with a mix of excitement and mystery. John already knew the choice would not be extensive. He'd asked several people in the area, but their responses only deepened the mystery.

"I'll take it. When can we move in?"

***

Before a week had elapsed, John Byrne had moved his modest possessions from the cottage in Lurnham, to unit 214. Three shaky bed frames, a faded settee and chairs, a set of wooden drawers and some basic cooking utensils. A modest and frugal testament to a lifestyle largely devoid of materialism or avarice. Army life had taught him that real needs were very few. Emerald had inherited her father's lack of covetousness. She packed an increasingly uncluttered set of clothes alongside a well-worn running kit, some drawing materials, a dusty violin, and her old laptop. The laptop barely worked, but at least it stored some important photographic images from the past. The violin lacked a string, and her artistic tools now facilitated using only three colours. None of this was unusual in this new minimalist existence. All this could be carried on the back of a truck when transporting their possessions.

John's most prized possession was removed from the front room wall and carefully wrapped in cloth. A family painting. Part-payment for carpentry work he had done for an artistic customer many years before. The colours had noticeably faded, but their features were still prominent. Bethany, as he remembered her. Stoic and beautiful. The girls, Amber and Emerald, are wide-eyed and bursting with energy, and Tito is mischievous and strong. An image of the life they once shared before the world fell apart.

There was little point in leaving anything. The scavengers would already be hovering in anticipation. There would be no going back. But there was something he needed to do before abandoning the family base. John had been thinking about this task for weeks. He realised it was unlikely, but a parent never gives up hope. What if Amber was to return? How would she find them? He had to leave a message that she would see. But how? He had stood staring at the naked wall from which the painting had hung. The space had been framed by the repeated build-up of dust and grime. A blank page. Framed by rock. It would be here that he would place his message in large, white paint.

Amber

Your sister and I are alive, holding on to a glimmer of hope at government unit 214. We live in the belief that you, too, are safe and hopefully well.

Dad

He finished by writing the date next to his name.

That night the night winds threatened to claim at least one of the supporting walls, making the old place a perilous shell. However, he clung to the hope that this, the sturdiest of the fortifications, would endure and, with it, the message. The ravages of war had turned human beings into vultures, devouring anything else that was left.

Emerald was quite upset about leaving the cottage. There were so many memories steeped in the fabric of the place. In the final weeks of her mother's life, her petulant younger brother, Tito, and an older sister she had looked up to and still missed. And her father, the one unfaltering pillar in her life until the army snatched him from her grasp. But he was now back for good, although the war had clearly taken its toll. They both knew that his body was broken and, eventually, she would lose him, too. As for Emerald, she was no longer the naive young girl her father left behind. The new world had toughened her up, as it had to. Life was now mainly about survival.

***

Emerald was secretly thrilled when Hawk shared her father's suggestion about him joining them at their new home. In recent months, John's daughter had grown closer to her affable companion from the end of the village. She initially wasn't sure what he and her dad would make of each other. Grizzly, battle-scarred, over-protective veteran father meets charismatic, opinionated young visionary: it could have been tense! John's youngest daughter recognised what her father was doing, which helped to facilitate the next chapter of her life. Britain was no longer a safe place for a young, vulnerable woman on her own. If the friendship between them grew into love, then so be it. John knew he could no longer protect her. His time was ending.

The Farm in the Crater

Emerald, Hawk and her father moved to unit 214 a week before Spring used to arrive. Now, each month was virtually the same. The *Change* had put an end to all seasons. A relentless package of bitter nocturnal winds and blistering hot days assaulted their senses with monotonous consistency. They busied themselves, reinforcing the doors and walls of the main building. There was no shortage of stone in the vicinity. They set about stacking heaps of sandstone slab across the corners of each room. The fireplace was cleaned out and ready for their first delivery of logs. Hawk had proved to be a source of surprises. Not only had he persuaded a friend to drive their belongings to the new home in his works truck, but he'd also managed to acquire some sizable chunks of elm wood to tie them over. He appeared one morning carrying a large axe in his hands. A weapon as sharp as his wit. 'Can't have us freezing to death before we've settled in,' he quipped.

Rooms were swept of dust, and heavy curtains were beaten mercilessly to release their choking dust. They'd been promised a delivery of wood in three days, coinciding with the arrival of the other members of the new community, Hope and Raul.

John paced outside the perimeter, looking like a man suffering from toothache.

"We need to secure the building from intruders," he shared with his two companions. "And I don't just mean with your impressive axe, Hawk." He smiled at the young man and slapped him, gregariously, on the back. "Come, we have work to do." Beyond the buildings lay a flat ledge of rock that circled the farm. John opened one of his large boxes and pulled out a coil of barbed wire. The two men fed the wire around the compound, attaching rusty old cans to the line, finally securing the barrier with larger rocks.

Three hours later, John looked satisfied with his work but was exhausted. "That should alert us to any unexpected guests," he bellowed.

“Who will be sniffing around out here? “Hawk probed.

“I don’t know, but it’s best we have some warning. Just in case.”

Emerald stood watching the two men she cared most about in the world. A sense of contentedness brushed through her head. ‘It’s going to be ok,’ she thought and permitted herself a smile.

When Hope and Raul appeared later in the week, unit 214 was almost fit for habitation. John and Hawk had repaired sections of the roof that had lost tiles or boarding and reinforced the outbuilding, including the remnants of an old barn. A vat of contaminated water had been mixed with a bit of concrete to form a functional binding paste. Added to lumps of pulverized rock, it produced a helpful barrier to keep the elements at bay. As promised, a consignment of mixed wood and drinking water and some bags of dried food had arrived. “Don’t waste it,” the heavily armed guard yelled at the residents.

“You’ll need to collect subsequent food parcels from the distribution centre. Every two weeks.’ Opening his bag, he measured out five sets of coupons. “Here.” He thrust them into John’s hand. “You will need these.”

He summoned his driver to help unload a large plastic fluid container. “Go easy with the water,” he continued. “Remember to add the purification tablets, or you will become ill.”

And with his final instruction given, he beckoned his partner back to the vehicle.

“Good luck, Unit 214. You’re going to need it, stuck out here.”

PART FOUR

Fire Ants

The main path before them circumnavigated the walls of the *Green Zone* and led them out in the direction of an emaciated basin that was once the River Severn. There was an eagerness in how they moved, in anticipation that their journey was coming to its end, even if there were no certainties about what they would find. Maybe another seven days, Amber thought, but it was only a guess. Joel had regained full mobility in his arm, courtesy of the healing powers of Marcos' mother. Amber, too, was feeling physically stronger. Her abuse at the hands of Urgon, a rescinding memory, with the scourge marks almost healed. She stopped abruptly in her tracks and realised that she had momentarily forgotten about her companion, Yolina. Barely an hour had passed over the previous two weeks without her thinking about her deceased friend. She closed her eyes and framed an image of the beautiful Polish woman she called her best friend. A tear meandered down her cheek before she gained composure. "I will never forget you," she whispered to herself. "Never."

Joel gave her a vexed look.

"I'm all right. I'm just having a moment.

With the sunlight pounding the surface of the land, they took shelter in an abandoned house and sat down to eat before trying to get some sleep for a couple of hours. They were surprised to discover that the donated rations were quite generous when they opened their rucksacks. There was a green paste mixed with something pepperish, which carried the scent of cabbage and five large flatbreads. At the bottom of her bag, they found something neither of them had seen for a very long time: apples. Although they were small and a little sour, the two pieces of fruit were beyond delicious.

They slept better than they had done for many weeks and woke to the late afternoon skyline turning maroon.

***

As the day broke, the two companions set off on the next stage of their journey. They followed the wide path heading south. Each of them walked in silence, keeping their own council. In truth, there was little new to say. Amber, alone in her thoughts and not for the first time, is rehearsing the possible situations they might find in the *Wastelands.* Would she meet her father, and if so, what state would he be in? What had become of her little sister, Emerald and had their family farmhouse survived the weather? If anybody could wear a survivor badge, it would be her father, she thought wryly. Despite hearing about the casualties in North Africa and the Greek islands, she had comforted herself with what she remembered about her dad. His cautious nature, meticulous planning and, most of all, his ability to smell danger. Had such traits and skills enabled him to survive? Countless other fathers were out there, equally well prepared, but they still returned in body bags. She needed to think about something else, and Joel provided the opportune distraction she needed.

"Look, Amber, over there. Down by the old river basin.' His attention was captivated by the structures that emerged from the morning mist, their forms gradually taking shape.

"That Joel is the remains of the city of Worcester.'

He shrugged his shoulders in a gesture of bewilderment. "Never heard of it."

***

Like all UK towns and cities, it bore the marks of destruction brought about by the *Change.* Some of the housing on the city's edge had been completely flattened, reminiscent of the impact of a tornado, sweeping through and lifting almost every brick from its place. Towards the centre, however, the more prominent structures had fared better, with a couple of familiar landmarks still standing. The dense walls of Worcester Cathedral still stood proud, although a section of the roof had fallen in. Likewise, the familiar feature of St. Andrew's Spire still rose into the sky, albeit it now looked like it had lost the top of its pinnacle.

"You know this place, then?" Amber's companion, Joel, quizzed.

"Oh yes. We came here on days out when I was a child. You might find it hard to believe now, but the river then was once wide and fast flowing. The books we saw in childhood had pictures of the water. It frequently flooded the surrounding fields and estates, isolating homes and leaving some stranded and cut off. But that was long before us. I can vaguely remember we hired boats once and canoed a small section that still had a little water on the outskirts. We could walk almost to the middle of the riverbed. They were happy times, Joel." Amber's voice was tinged with nostalgia.

He shielded his eyes from the menacing heat. "I, too, remember what it was like to be on the river. Back in Nigeria. Fishing with my father. "His face dropped. "We need to take cover for a few hours before we're burnt alive here," he snapped. "Come. Let's look for somewhere over there."

They moved surreptitiously through street debris, looking for a suitable building. Joel strengthened his grip on the staff he held in his right hand. "Keep your eyes peeled. We might not be the only ones here." Amber spotted a relatively intact shop on their left.

"Let's try this one," and beckoned him across. It looked like one of those old paper shops selling newspapers, tobacco, and confectionery. The contents of the building had been stripped to the bone like everywhere else. There was little chance of finding anything interesting to eat. They moved slowly through the shop and found a room at the back. There was a sofa and chair, a partly burned table and a fireplace. Amber read his fire-lighting intentions. "Better not, big man. We don't want to attract attention."

With a shrug, he embarked on the ascent. 'Let's uncover if there's a resting place up there.' The exuberant cheer from above needed no further clarification. He emerged, a wide grin adorning his face. 'I'm a mastermind,' he declared, his satisfaction palpable.

“In case you’ve forgotten, Mr. It was me who picked this place!”

Amber threw herself into the old sofa and watched the dust rise above her head like a halo. “I could fall asleep right here.”

Joel was busy reading a leaflet on the table. “What’s that you’re engrossed in?”

“Some sort of poster. These look like the giant ants we had in Africa.” He passed the sheet across to her. Alongside the image of the giant insect were two words: *Fire Ants.*

Josh looked more closely. “Don’t recognise this shape, though. Ours have red bodies and are much bigger. Looks more like it’s been drawn by a child.”

Amber was more intrigued by the reverse side of the paper. Three words and an exclamation mark.

We are ready!

“Don’t look so serious; we’re not about to be abducted by giant ants.” And with that, he laughed boisterously. “Come on. Let’s see if there is any drinking water around here.”

***

The visitors hid their bedding upstairs behind storage boxes, grabbed their rucksacks and moved back into the street. Weaving in and out of the buildings, they checked every cupboard and storage place in the vague hope of finding food or fluids. But like all the structures they’d come across before, every can, bottle and container of water had been lifted from the site long ago. In truth, the best they could hope for was maybe an old chocolate bar trapped behind a vending machine or cabinet, somehow missed by frenzied human hands when they stripped the place bare. They’d once found a can of unopened orange fizzy drink in the kitchen of an isolated cottage. It had fallen behind the fridge. Amber will never forget that first sip, an assault on her tastebuds that lingered and shook her body into bubbly spasms. Joel had burst into a bout of uncontrollable coughing with the tingle of the experience. Sweet luxury! It had been such a long time.

She smiled at the memory and was reminded why they still painstakingly searched each building with a flicker of hope.

Joel stood at the doorway, frowning.

"What is it?"

"Come here. We've got company."

Four figures stood at the entrance of the shop. Two of them were brandishing what looked like antique firing devices, while the others carried wooden poles improvised with metal points to create spears.

"Who are you?" cried one of them.

"We are just travelling through. On our way to the *Wastelands*."

"So why are you here?"

"Just hoping to find some water and food," added Amber.

One of the men thrust his spear aggressively towards Joel, while another grabbed his bag. He pulled out the contents and scattered them on the ground.

Amber turned to her companion with a look that demanded his composure. They had been here before.

"Just food and water," the man shouted across to the short, balding figure with the gun behind him.

"Bring me the girl's bag."

Amber unbuckled her rucksack and flung it to the floor. Each item was similarly unpacked and examined.

“We told you there is nothing of value in them.”

The scrawny youth in front of her looked disappointed. His emaciated frame bent down to re-pack the bags and threw them across his shoulders.

“Come with us,” the older man demanded.

Joel prepared once again to be bound.

The other man sensed his reaction.

“Don’t worry. You are not our prisoners. We just want to talk to you.”

***

The group walked into the city, eventually turning into a side road. They entered what looked like a large hotel building, immediately descending a set of stairs to eventually arrive in a cavernous room. Joel saw more images of the insect displayed on the poster. These images were pasted onto the walls and flew from improvised flags around the hall. Both Amber and Joel shuffled their feet in understandable nervousness.

“Please. Sit. Food and water are arriving. Apologies for the abrasive treatment by our guards. We cannot be too casual with security. *Gnosis* spies are everywhere.”

The visitors turned around to see a tall, statuesque man with a long, ash-grey beard. He watched their arrival with studious care before speaking to them.

I am known here as Quinton. One of the seniors.”

By now, others had gathered in the hall to look at their visitors.

The promised nourishment arrived on slate plates and drinking vessels. There was flatbread and a green vegetable that tasted like cabbage.

Joel relaxed. A question surfaced from his lips. "Why would Gnosis be spying on you?" he asked.

Quinton started to chuckle. "Where have you been, young friends, these last couple of years? Clearly not around here." The others in the hall joined in his laughter.

Amber interrupted her companion. "You are right. We have not been in this part of the country in recent times. We have travelled from the black crystal mines in the north. I am trying to find my dad."

"Well. You are an intriguing couple. This is an extraordinary journey you claim to have made. Some might say foolhardy, certainly dangerous."

Amber lifted her head proudly." I lived here before the change when I was young.

"And now you want to unite with your family?"

"Yes. My sister and father, if they are still alive."

Quinton gave them a pensive look. "We all have people to find,'' he reflected wryly." So, you don't know who we are?"

He seemed convinced by their blank expressions.

His eyes narrowed. "They call us the *Fire Ants"*.

He beckoned across one of his female colleagues. "Tell them, Sita, what this means."

She pointed to the images around the room. "These pictures remind us of how we should behave to survive. Humans emulate the patterns of nature. More specifically, imitating the organisational skills of our eusocial insect friends, the fire ants. Like them, we now live in the ground. We think we are slowly losing our sense of touch and communication with each other. Ants are particularly good at using pheromones, a secreted chemical that draws a social response from other ants. We copy their tactics when we forage for food. Marking storage points and unblocking obstacles.

The critical point is that sustenance is brought back and shared with the colony. There are not splinter groups feathering their own nests while others go hungry."

Quinton introjected, "Under this post-catalytic government, supported by *Gnosis,* the many go hungry and thirsty, while the few prosper. This is fundamentally wrong. It is a pathway into chaos and the ultimate destruction of all of us."

Joel was intrigued by the images. "Tell me. Why are your ants painted red?"

Quinton, his expression now marked with severity, spoke. "Because we are fire ants! In the wild, these creatures contain a stinging bite. They strike to defend their territory, and so do we. And like the fire ants this sometimes requires self-sacrifice. Did you know that if attacked, they sometimes perform an act of suicidal altruism? Poison sprays out from their heads. To stay strong, we, too, must be brave and sometimes heroic. The military arm of the government, with *Gnosis,* try to hunt us down because we won't conform to their elitist model of change."

Amber's attention was drawn to a dozen or so people, clad in unique attire, entering the room. They sat in rows, their eyes fixed on the two individuals in the centre who were engaged in a form of martial arts.

Sita watched her interest. "All our 'human ants' engage in unarmed combat training, just like their insect friends. An attacked worker ant can fling its body backwards to escape threat. We might have to do similar things at times.

One of them was staring inappropriately at Amber. She felt his eyes all over her body as his hands gestured suggestively.

“Ignore him. He is keen to mate. The time is right for him, but like many down here, he is without a woman.”

“Well. This one isn’t available,” announced Joel as he glared at the young man.

“Daniel. Enough!” the elder shouted, and the teenager shuffled away, mumbling.

***

As Joel and Amber finished their food, they noticed tensions between two of the group's older members seemed to be rising. Quinton suddenly turned towards his visitors. "So, what skills do you two have? Can you grow food? Can you fight?"

Joel rolled up his sleeve to reveal his fast-healing wound. "I bear the marks of combat. The fact that I am still here tells its own story."

Amber interrupted. "My back is lined with scourge marks from the river people further up the country." We have endured much suffering along the way. And we know how to strike back."

The older of the two men nodded his approval. "I'm sure you do."

‘’The thing is we need to recruit young people with the spirit to challenge the authorities. People who share our passion for re-grouping and establishing a more egalitarian existence. It is unacceptable that meagre resources are still shared disproportionally by the few.’’

The other man waved a hand to his companion and addressed them. "We have tried talking to the authorities and separately to *Gnosis,* without success. Instead, we are met with intransigence and the threat of violence. We now have little choice. We must take down these tyrants so that the poor have a voice. Many of our *fire ants* have already perished in the cause."

His companion raised his voice with an impassioned plea. "Join us. Abandon your old family ties. Unless we succeed now, there might never be another opportunity. Fight with us."

Amber and Joel sat in silence, afraid to answer. They had come too far to abandon their journey, so close to the finishing line. And yet they couldn't help but be impressed by the passion of these people. Some of what they said made sense, but was the talk of direct action really the way forward?

Sita moved more closely towards them and started to draw on the ground. "This is the SESF. Better known as the 'Swanston Electronic Storage Facility.' Do you know what type of place it is?

Amber recalled it was one of the largest storage centres in the country before the *Change.* "Didn't it hold most of what we used to call the 'cloud,' she added. "All those old pictures, messages, etc., we were supposed to keep forever."

Sita nodded. "It was the main storage plant for the Midlands. Built deep below the earth's surface, on several levels of an old, discarded mine. Hundreds of complex computers are custodians of every electronic communication we ever send. I ask you: what was the point of it all? Every tedious, boring email that left our laptops and smartphones saved forever so we could satisfy our lust for data." She turned to Joel.

"Tell me. How do you think they managed to save all this information?"

Joel shook his head. "I guess they did their calculations and designed the site to accommodate the ever-increasing need."

Sita drew a glance from Quinton. "Let him tell you." Quinton rubbed his salt and pepper whiskers and muttered two words. Then, he repeated them more loudly. "Water and electricity."

Amber looked confused, but Quinton continued. "Back in the 21st century, when we started to collect all this electronic information, the prototype storage centres were relatively small. Most people didn't think much about how they operated. Increasingly, fewer people were involved in maintenance and storage issues as AI robots started to manage them. Like many of these sites, Swanson was hidden away in an isolated area, away from public gaze. The key thing was that they required large amounts of accessible water to cool down their computers, together with enormous quantities of electricity. Given the importance of technological storage to the country, nobody questioned the cost of this on the environment. They grew bigger and bigger as the decades passed by. People eventually started to see how they were draining local rivers to keep the equipment at low temperatures. Moreover, the percentage of the national grid given aside to powering these sites kept rising. Eventually, it would become unsustainable."

Quinton paused to clarify his thoughts. "What they didn't share was exactly how much our power needs were draining the land of natural resources. Yes, *the Change* may have turned our rivers to dust, but digital technology gave it massive support in emptying the inland lakes and rivers and exhausting power supplies."

He looked at his two visitors. "This time, it will be different. We have no choice but to engage in direct action. Like I said, we need more people to make this happen."

Amber didn't need to consult with her companion. "We will give you our answer later," she said.

***

Both were surprised that they had been allowed to leave so quickly. The darkness was already starting to creep across the night sky, silhouetting the hills as they headed back along the street to the shop. Everything was as they left it. Their bedding remained hidden upstairs, and Amber busied herself to make up their makeshift bed. Joel couldn't help but notice the blankets had been placed together on the double frame. He knew when she felt insecure.

It wasn't until they started to talk about eating something that Joel panicked. He realised his rucksack was missing. "Oh shit! "He exclaimed in frustration. ''I must have been distracted. I've left it behind."

"I need to go back. It's got all my food and fluids."

Amber looked anxious. "Looking for your supplies? They will know we are not returning. It's too dangerous."

He broke into one of those big grins that she always found disarming.

'' Don't worry. I won't be long. I'll keep them guessing about our intentions. You start preparing some supper. Be back soon."

With that, he was gone in a flash, running out of the shop and back towards the large hotel complex. Amber watched him disappear down the street, running like someone late for their train. Trains. She hadn't thought about such things for years.

***

It didn't take Joel long to get to the hotel. He was increasingly quick on his feet despite a heavy muscular build. Weeks of constant walking, sustained by meagre rations, had returned his body weight to that of a teenager. Amber's companion stopped to wipe the sweat from his brow. Slowly, he descended the motionless elevator stairs with caution and heard voices below. A faint chant of 'fire ants. We will be heard,' now filled the chamber. As he entered the room, fifty or so pairs of eyes fixed their gaze upon him. Joel moved towards the side room, where they had been questioned by Quinton and Sita, to see if his bag was still there. He hardly recognised the heavily disguised pair as they walked past him. The chanting changed as some individuals formed different sounds, projecting them like distraught animals in danger. Joel had no idea what was happening. Quinton was now watching him and responded to his bewilderment.

‘We’re developing a new code of distress calls inspired by the ants,’ Quinton explained, a hint of a smile playing on his lips.

“Pheromones”

“What?”

“Like a secreted chemical. Brings a response from the others. We don’t leave our colleagues behind.”

‘Glad you’ve decided to join us,’ Sita’s voice cut through the tension. She stood before him, dressed in faded combat gear and holding an automatic rifle.

“And where is the woman?” Sita queried.

“I’m just collecting my bag so we can eat tonight,” he responded nervously. “We might join you tomorrow.”

The fire ant leaders exchanged telepathic glances.

“He’s seen too much!” cried the impetuous youth who had accosted them earlier.

“He’s right” added Quinton. “This one comes with us.”

Joel felt the hand on his shoulder. At that moment, he knew he should have listened to his travelling companion.

***

Amber stood outside the shop entrance for the third time in twenty minutes, gazing towards the city centre. She thought she’d caught sight of him at one point, but her eyes must have been playing tricks. It was no more than an emerging shadow from the fading light. Her head was now reverberating with possible scenarios. All of them were problematic. Why wasn’t he back? What had happened to her companion? She opened her mouth and placed a small piece of dry bread between her teeth, rolling it back across her molars to distract herself. It wasn't working. She considered her options. Stay and wait, or head out to find him. For the first time, Amber began to ponder the terrible implications of losing the man she had slowly learned to love. She couldn't stop the tears from starting to appear. With all they had endured, Amber wasn't sure she could carry such a burden.

***

Joel whispered to the tall man jogging alongside him. "Where are we going?" He turned his head sufficiently to grunt something about finding out when they arrived and turned away with a resolute look. After about fifteen minutes, the group of activists, numbered about twenty, left the vulnerability of the open land and took refuge in the remains of what had once been a coppice of elm and beech. All that remained now was the skeletal bark of fallen trees and the large holes that had housed their root base. The wood had long vanished to needy homes. The group split into groups of three and four and scampered into these craters. Joel found himself alongside two women of indeterminable age. They appeared like soldiers, partly disguised by sand-coloured outfits that looked like they had been clumsily stitched together. Their hair had been carefully pinned back inside camouflaged hats to help hide any obvious individual traits. To complete the outfits, each woman wore a beige mask across her face. The only obvious sign of identity was a red ant's logo sewn into their tunic's left sleeve. Joel sighed at the contrast such a bold statement made. Despite all the chanting and bravado back at the hotel, these two red ants looked tense and distinctively frightened, almost terrified. They looked across at Joel with disdain. He realised there was an understandable degree of suspicion about him.

Joel hadn't seen Sita or Quinton since they set off. He persevered with his questions. ''What has happened to your leaders?" he quipped.

The older, more rotund of the two women closest to him, placed her firearm on the floor and turned to shush him.

"There is more than one mission taking place tonight, stranger," she muttered.

Joel scratched his head. What exactly had he walked into that evening? He picked up the hand-made spear they had given him for *protection* and ran his thumb across the blade. He would keep his head down, just as they had demanded and try to escape as soon as an opportunity presented itself.

After a few minutes, a strange, bird-like sound filled the night. It was the signal to move on, and the fire ants scrambled from their holes. Another fifteen minutes of careful movement brought them to the edge of the Malvern ridge. The foreground ahead of them was lit with large standing lights, fully activated by any movement on the ground before them. One of their numbers rolled a small, cat-like robot into the illuminated space. It immediately elicited a full charge of light and the appearance of a pair of large, aggressive guard dogs. With barely a whimper, each animal collapsed to the ground, victims of the silent arrows discharged by two of the visitors. "Stay close,'' the younger woman shouted to Joel as they began to run towards the visible building in front of them. "There will be armed guards inside."

It wasn't until he was almost at the entrance that Joel could identify the bold lettering above the door:

Midland Area 2 Electronic Storage Facility: Authorised Personnel Only

He followed the others as they burst through the security door and, with the aid of stun weapons, took out the solar lights. The sudden sound of laser fire broke the silence in the passageway. "Those without guns, fall back," one of the men shouted, and Joel complied immediately. One of the women he had shared the bunker with fell to the floor, her torso seared by a defendant beam. The smell of burned flesh choked his nostrils, leaving him temporarily nauseous. As he turned to help her, an arm pulled him away.

"Don't be stupid, or you 'll be next," he yelled. The exchange of fire lasted several minutes until the area fell quiet.

"I think we are in," another man bawled as the surviving invaders stepped over the bodies of the fallen and stood before an imposing door. "Stand back!"

A homemade explosive device destroyed the lock instantly, and they walked into the main facility area. As far as the eye could see, there were endless rows of computer units. "What is this place," queried Joel. The red-haired man next to him offered a curt response.

"This is where every sad detail of our electronic life is stored, like some vast automated ocean of data. Give me a hand here, big fella," Joel helped him pull the heavy body of one of the guards out of the way and stared at the glazed expression on his face. "Yes, it's a robot. It isn't human. Don't stand there gawking at it. We have work to do. A maximum of three minutes is needed to smash the cable distribution boxes and do as much damage as you can to the cooling tanks. Go!"

The fire ants vented their fury on the machines in a blaze of gun blasts and laser-fuelled explosions. Joel used his spear to puncture some of the distribution cooling pipes, stamping on others and throwing a large container at the nearest computer panel.

Almost immediately, a cry was heard from the entrance. 'They are here! Time to get out.' The entrance passage was buzzing with new sounds. As he looked outside, Joel caught sight of a military *helizoom* descending from the sky. Several heavily armed soldiers were already starting to plunge down, powered by their individual booster packs.

"Run for your lives."

Joel began to head across the open land with Aura, the young woman he had shared the bunker with earlier. Suddenly, a suited figure crashed across his line of vision, and the now familiar smell of wounded flesh filled his nostrils. Aura let out a painful cry and tried to support her injured arm. As the soldier lunged towards Joel, he managed to turn sideways, thrusting his spear as hard as he could towards the assailant's throat. The man reeled away in pain, holding his jugular vein.

"Quickly!" the African gestured and led his wounded colleague away from the clearing. Despite her discomfort, they soon managed to distance themselves and their pursuers. The fugitives stopped for a moment's rest and looked back at the ongoing drama. Many of the others had been less fortunate. Aura's arm was bleeding openly. Her terrified expression conveyed a desperate need for reassurance.

"We can't return to the old hotel," she frowned. "They will be waiting for us."

"I know where we can go," he yelled.

Choices

In Joel's mind, there was only one destination to take. The sweet shop and the reassurance of Amber's welcome. Under cover of twilight, as the ruby sky sought out the gathering clouds of darkness, the fugitives aimed to weave in and out of the city buildings undetected. At least, that is how Joel saw it. As they approached the outskirts of Worcester, the night firmament was lit up with familiar shapes. Two *helizooms* were hovering above the temporary base of the *fire ants*. Powerful searchlights scoured the perimeter of the hotel.

"It's just off the main street. Five more minutes," Joel pleaded with his distraught companion. Despite supporting her un-injured side, the pace was slow. Just as he contemplated carrying Aura through the final section of the journey, the shop came into view.

"Wait here," he instructed her. "I'm going to check if it's safe." He gently disentangled himself from the woman, leading her to a raised outcrop of concrete. There she rested, hidden from prying eyes.

"Please. Don't leave me!"

She watched him dart around the neighbouring buildings like a predatory cat, searching for prey. At last, he shuffled through the front entrance and stepped into the dusky stillness. She was not downstairs. He tore his way up the steps to the bedroom. "Amber," he cried. Still nothing. A sense of panic overwhelmed him. He could hear his heartbeats thundering in confusion. Where was she?

His thoughts turned back to Aura. Retracing his steps, Joel returned to the place where he left her. She smiled bravely at him, momentarily controlling the shivers of the gathering bitter night. His mood was transparent. "What is the matter?"

"She is not here." He blurted incomprehensively.

"Who?"

"The woman I have been travelling with." He took a deep breath and paused. Best not to make declarations at this point, he ruminated.

An Unknown Hour

Amber sat between two *fire ants,* wishing she had ignored her instincts. 'Go and find him. It's the only logical thing to do,' she had decided while resting at the shop. She waited patiently for four hours, wondering what had befallen her partner. Amber mumbled the words they had used. 'You are not our prisoners. You are free to walk away.' He just wanted to collect his rucksack. Back within twenty minutes. So, what on earth had happened to him? She'd paced up and down the ground floor a hundred times before deciding to strike out and look for him. There was only one place to start. The hotel.

With appalling timing, the daughter of John Byrne walked straight into a passionate planning meeting. Not that she saw or understood any of this. Amber didn't make it further than the stairway. She was quickly apprehended by guards. As she was marched into the main room, she immediately recognised Sita and Quinton, occupying prominent positions at the front of the hall. There were animated voices. Disagreement among the *fire ants.* Something was wrong, and it wasn't just her unwelcome appearance.

"I'm only looking for my friend, the African. Please. Tell me where he is?"

Sita raised her hand with a gesture of irritation. "Frankly, you and your friend are causing us a fair degree of annoyance. The pair of you keep appearing at awkward moments. Can't you see we are engrossed in something important?

She stared at the young woman before turning to Quinton. "You handle it!"

Her colleague looked around and gesticulated to one of his guards. The whispered conversation was curt. The other man swept his blond locks away from his eyes and stepped forward. "There is something you should know!"

Layton, as he was known, had received word that Joel was last seen trying to escape from a raid on the storage banks. They think he was helping another *fire ant.* Female, they said and injured. That's all we can tell you.

"What on earth was he doing there?" she exclaimed with ignominy.

"He only came to retrieve his bag."

Quinton offered a brusque response." We needed him earlier. Couldn't risk letting him go. Sounds like he has been useful." He paused as if choosing his next words carefully before telling her that her friend would have to wait.

"The next stage of the plan happens now!" Quinton barked. The earlier mumblings of discontentment had subsided as the remaining *fire ants* roared their cries of anger.

'For our fallen comrades! Our fallen comrades", they yelled.

"And you, young lady, will be joining us. We can't leave any loose ends behind."

***

Joel removed the last piece of bandage from Amber's bag. It carried the pungent smell of a familiar owner. He half-smiled in recognition of its use in the treatment of his own wounds three weeks earlier by the *gatherers.* He would undoubtedly wash it this time. But She was missing, and her bag was still there. He tried not to speculate about what might have happened.

Joel's thoughts now returned to the young woman he had rescued. Cleaning Aura's wound with as much water as he could spare, he applied the last healing paste to the arm. It had browned in colour from its original green texture, but he hoped its therapeutic qualities were still active. The bleeding had finally subsided, and with a tightly wrapped bind, any immediate health dangers seemed to have been averted.

"Thank you, stranger, and I don't even know your name."

"I'm Joel," he dutifully muttered before explaining how he and his companion had come to be there. Their experiences at the mines, the encounter with the *Separated,* and escape with the help of Marcos. It felt good to tell somebody else about all this. He quickly glossed over the tragic accident that befell Yolina, briefly sketched their arrest outside the protected tree zone, and their eventual arrival in Worcester. Aura soaked up the tale with a blend of fascination through clenched teeth. There were no painkillers in the rucksack to ease her discomfort.

"What about you?" Joel enquired. "How did you get caught up in all this?"

Aura 's story was proverbial. A tale of betrayal, abandonment and false promises. "I guess I ended up following the only man who showed me any respect. I loved his idealism and the excitement of being with him, but I wasn't ready for the danger and violence this would bring. When he realised this, I became a liability to him."

She paused, with head bowed in sombre reflection. "He was out there with us this evening. I don't know if he made it back." She began to cry. "I'm not a brave person. Not cut out for the risky stuff. Simply haven't got the courage."

All Joel could do was listen, his heart heavy, and then he gently wrapped one of Amber's blankets around her, his mind already racing about what to do next.

Arbiters of Medicine

The AI medical centre wasn't far. It was one of the reasons the *Red Ants* had gathered to set up a base within the remains of Worcester. It was located barely a kilometre to the north, just beyond the outskirts of the old city. Alongside the data storage unit, it created two worthy targets for their rage, both within easy range. However, Quinton thought this was the most important one to hit. The storage unit was a decoy, a distraction from the main objective. Quinton hadn't shared every detail of the plan. Not even with his trusted colleague, Sita, although he suspected she had guessed why his less robust *fire ants* had been chosen to take part in the earlier attack.

As they hid behind a giant rock wall, Quinton gathered his saboteurs close to him. He stood before them, resolute and focused, his eyes burning with certainty. Amber sat between a stoic-looking woman with platted red hair and a stocky, avuncular man, probably in his forties, camouflaged in a sand-tinted tunic. They turned their heads to absorb the rhetoric.

"This is the moment, comrades. They won't be expecting another attack so soon after the last one. We have the element of surprise. Let's use it to inflict a strike they will not forget." Amber looked at the nervous expressions around her. Without warning, she was overcome by a sudden rush of fear. What if?

"Quinton reinforced the instructions. "We move around the back of the building as quietly as possible. There is a small, black door in the protruded entrance block. It has been deactivated by two of our advanced parties. Once inside, keep away from the laser beams that safeguard the drug storage bays. Ignore the loading trays and packaging anchorages.

We need to bypass the monitoring machines and get to the drugs. Once there, grab anything you can and fill your bags. If you recognise them, painkillers and healing creams are a priority, but we don't have time to rummage. These AI security protectors are fully armed and programmed to eliminate any threat to their cargo."

There were no more words. Just a cluster of hopeful nods and determined glances. And the blank expression of one young woman who had no idea what she was doing there.

***

Amber shivered as the temperatures began to drop. The loose-fitting outfit, hastily acquired before they left, was no substitute for her night coat. This one was far too big and smelled of a previous owner. The scorched hole, surrounded by faded crimson stains on the jacket sleeve, suggested that the tunic had not been donated voluntarily. Amber fingered the small firearm in her pocket and hoped for the best. Quinton snapped his fingers, and they rose to follow him. The entourage snaked through the last of the ruins and moved towards the dry riverbed. Amber considered leaving a trail of clues behind in the vain hope that Joel would discover the route and follow it. Naïve, she pondered and shook her head. Her would-be rescuer had no idea what she was doing. These wishful thoughts were blown away by the sight of the AI Centre. It looked like a recent construction of steel and stone in the half-light, like some alien spacecraft nestled in the landscape. "Quickly," Quinton barked. ''Move around to the back of the building."

As they entered the perimeter, sensors in the ground triggered their arrival. A network of laser beams burst across the path, segmenting the terrain into triangular-shaped death traps. "Keep away from the beams," Quinton screeched. The assailants managed to step away from the danger and tip-toed their way to the back of the complex. The black door came into view, and each of them shuffled through the opening. The interior was a breathtaking maze of conveyor belts, carrying hundreds of tubular cartons from five storage bays to colour-coded bins. Screeching metal filled their ears without warning, precipitously stopping the intruders in their tracks. Amber saw part of the building fabric separate, releasing robotic blocks that moved on rollers towards them. Each of the loading belts shuddered to a halt. At the same time, several red hazard lights flashed their danger symbols across the room.

"Get those drugs!" Quinton cried and moved towards the first storage area. 6Amber was still flanked by the couple she had travelled with and turned to see the man sink to the floor with a cry of pain. The robot's line of laser fire had claimed its first victim of the evening. She made a frenzied dash towards the nearest storage container, narrowly avoiding becoming another casualty. Banks of white tablets were stacked strategically and analogously synchronised with the conveyor belts. She removed the large plastic bag inside her tunic and began filling it with the blister packs. Consumed in the task, she failed to track the robots' appearance. In a sweeping movement, they cornered off the storage area and stopped instantly, like metallic sentries, before the remaining intruders. Just as Amber thought about making a run for it, the machines synchronised a broadcast of deafening menace.

Intruders stand still. If you move, you will be eliminated.

Amber looked up to see three other *fire ants* similarly surrounded by androids. One of them took his chance and was brought down by a cutting laser blow. A pool of blood emerged from his heart as he lay motionless. An overwhelming sense of fear gripped her body, and she threw her handgun to the floor. Her bag of painkillers fell from her other hand to lay next to another fatality.

With unified automation, the droids announced that the intruders had violated the security of a government building, and the consequences of such trespass demanded that they would be handed over for interrogation by human enforcement officers. The droids moved closer. Two extended rods clasped Amber's wrist and locked it before leading her away from the storage room towards the entrance of the building.

Interrogation

Amber could clearly hear the clatter of powerful engines above her before they burst through the leaden gloom and landed in front of them. Her wrist was aching from the robot's clasp. She hardly noticed the needle plunging into her arm by one of her new human escorts when they were finally released from the droid's metallic grip. She instantly felt unsteady on her feet, her vision blurred, and her eyes heavy with impending sleep. The last thing she remembered before passing out was being assisted into the *helizoom.*

"No talking," shouted one of several men in white suits, but Amber was already unconscious.

***

She woke and tried to reach for her throbbing head. The arm failed to respond, fastened by the shackle that held both hands together. Both legs were also secured to the end of the stone bed she was lying on. An undignified spectacle, with most of her clothes having been removed. From the corner of the room, a familiar figure emerged. The same speckled man with his side patches of limp grey hair that had administered the truth serum in *Gnosis.*

"So, our paths cross again, *tainted female no 18271*," he exclaimed nonchalantly. "Or should I call you Amber, as others know you? You are in serious trouble this time." The corner of his mouth seemed to curl with dissatisfaction.

She peered through his glasses to try and read his facial expression. All she could gleam was a note of sobriety.

"To say we are disappointed is an understatement," he added.

Amber became aware of two others moving towards her. One was the recognisable image of Richard Hartwood. He brushed past the man in the white coat and stared at Amber.

“I thought I made it clear to you when you were here before that you needed to avoid being drawn in to those elements who wished us harm.” He shook his head angrily. “Yet here you are, apprehended by AI security guards in the act of damaging a vital medical facility. Wearing the colours of those deluded fools, the *fire ants*.”

Amber tried to explain how she became caught up in the attack, but Hartwood dismissed her protests. “Enough!” he shouted. “Give her something to wear and bring her to the pit.”

***

It felt good to be released from the constraining slab of rock. Her cramped arms and legs tingled as they burst back into life. Apart from a few needle marks on her forearm, she seemed ok. A tunic was roughly pulled over her head, and her hands were once again, secured. Two guards led her away to the outside of the building, where they descended a flight of stone stairs. At the bottom, it opened into an empty square, bathed in sunshine.

At one corner, a small fire crackled. A pile of *fire ant* uniforms lay strewn next to it. Towards the other end, three wooded posts were set into the ground. She recognised each person who was tied to them: Quinton, Sita and the impudent Daniel. Amber was forced to stand in front of them and observe the spectacle. Each of the incarcerated bore signs of interrogation. One of Quinton’s eyes was inflamed, and he bled profusely from a wound in his neck. Daniel’s face was also puffed up and swollen, while Sita’s hands looked bruised and crushed. Amber Byrne shuddered at what might have befallen them.

“Observe. This is how we treat those who seek to destroy us,” exclaimed Hartwood. On his signal, one of the guards stepped forward with a long, serrated knife and slit the throats of each of the condemned. It was all over in a matter of seconds. The lifeless bodies of each of the victims slumped forward and were cut loose by the guards. As they fell to the floor, each was dragged away, unceremoniously, to the edge of the pit. Hartwood turned to Amber. “You should be next, young lady, but there could be another solution." She'd been holding her breath in terror for several seconds. This slightest glimmer of hope forced her to expel the air with such force that the expulsion felt like an explosion in her lungs. She wrenched as her heartbeat was racing uncontrollably. "Please, Mr. Hartwood. I will do anything you say."

"Yes. I know you will, Amber Byrne. I have read your memory log. You have been busy." He turned away to confer with a colleague. The animated whispers suggested a difference of opinion about her fate.

"We will speak further in my office."

"Bring her."

Amber was led back to the central part of the building, up the stairs, beyond ground level, to another floor. She was bound to a twisted willow chair facing a dark, wooden table there. Apart from her, the room was empty. One question was burning away in her head, and she had to ask them. Had Joel perished similarly?

After what seemed like an eternity, Richard Hartwood arrived with two colleagues. The men sat behind the table and focused their attention on her.

"Tell us again. Amber. About how you ended up taking part in a violent assault on an AI medicine distribution centre."

Amber meticulously recounted the story of how Joel and she wandered into the outskirts of old Worcester, were brought to meet the leaders of the *red ant* group and how, after initially being released, were forced to take part in the attempted theft of medicines. "I was only trying to find my companion, Joel. Believe me."

"Oh. We do.," responded one of the men. "In fact, we know all of this. The truth serum is always accurate. You told us everything."

"Then why are you still questioning me? Please. There is something I must ask you. What has happened to my friend Joel?

The men looked pensive. "That is something we don't know. We hoped that you could enlighten us," declared Hartwood.

"But I can tell you three things of importance. One. We have not yet apprehended him. Two. You have only cheated death because we may have a task for you, and three, a piece of information has come our way about your father."

Amber sat, open-mouthed with the last announcement.

"When we searched your *tainted* identification number, the lineage and DNA connection recognised someone else we know about: Corporal John Byrne, British Army. He peered down to gauge her reaction. "Presumably, your father."

Amber nodded before permitting herself an awkward smirk. "I knew he'd survive. I just knew it," she blurted out.

"He happens to be something of a war hero. Now works for the Armed Forces recruitment team. "

"I didn't know any of this," she responded, "apart from him joining the army. I told you when I was here before. I was up in the north, at the black crystal mines. Now, I'm just trying to find him. In the *Wastelands."*

Richard Hartwood moved intimidatingly close before whispering to her. "For the sake of your father, we have decided to spare you the punishment meted out to the others. But there will be a price. Come, sit here."

We need better intelligence outside these walls to monitor what is going on. More specifically, I'm talking about the resistance groups that have formed around the country, and their plans to sabotage the infrastructure we are trying to develop. It was too easy for the *red ants* to breach the perimeter of the AI Medicine Centre and the Data Centre. We need people to be our eyes and ears. Reporting such planned attacks back to us. Do you understand?"

"Do I have a choice?"

"You can choose death if you prefer. "

The other man interrupted. "Your father's profile is your authenticity card. Use it to infiltrate the resistance. Find out and help us to build a better country for all of us."

She knew what she had to do.

movement with our drones. Of course, if successful, the same conditions will apply. We also have a mandate to execute him because of his confirmed involvement in the attack on the data centre.

"I will speak to him," said a tearful Amber. "He will do this for me."

Amber Byrne reached to scratch the skin under her right arm. "Why is it sore here?" she asked. "That is our little insurance policy."

"In case…'

"In case you flee. There is an explosive device embedded in your arm, which we can detonate at any time."

She quickly removed her hand and sat there, stunned. An overwhelming sense of despair trapped her ability to think clearly, casting shadows across her plans to find her father.

***

Amber cut a dejected figure as she stepped out into the morning haze.

Her new employers had sanctioned her plea to find Joel, but there was a short time frame of no more than two days. The obvious place to start would be the shop, although she suspected they already knew about this venue. Nevertheless, her companion may have left some clues there. Her captives had given her another bag with basic supplies for a week. 'Maybe my old bag is still there,' she speculated.

An eerie stillness hung in the air as she stepped across the shop's threshold. Amber hesitated for a moment, forcing her sinews to scan every corner of the interior. Nothing but a fossilized silence, the ghosts of another time. Her heart pounded in anticipation that anything would bring a flicker of hope. And next to the chair was what she was looking for. Amber stooped to pick up the blood-stained bandage and examined it.

Gnosis had told her he had been spotted on the cameras, running from the data centre and wasn't alone. Could they have escaped and found their way here? If so, which of them was wounded? Or were they both injured?

She ascended the stairway and inspected the bed. There was little evidence that the room had been occupied recently. From the fractured bedroom window, she spotted the disturbed shape and rocks below in the yard. She held her breath and gasped. Moving down the stairs as quickly as her legs would allow her to, she pulled open the back door and, 'hand in mouth,' examined the mound of sand. The configuration of stones only confused her further. 'Was it him or his companion?'

She knelt on the ground and began to scoop away the sand until the outline of an arm emerged. Instead of the black, muscular limb of a well-built African man, the arm was thin, pale skinned and delicate. She scratched further across, and the petite features of a young woman's face began to show. Amber had her confirmation. She fell back and stared at the skyline. The brightness forced her to pull her hood over her head.

'He is still alive. I know he is!'

Alone

Amber decided to pitch down for the night at the shop, in the absence of other feasible alternatives. In the morning, she would revisit the *fire ant* centre at the hotel basement, hoping to find someone to explain where Josh might be. Beyond that, she wasn't too sure where to look.

She fell asleep in the chair, her head finally letting go of the burdens the day. Amber woke in the night, startled by the nightmare that had visited her. Despite the nocturnal cold, she was sweating. Her dream was both vivid and disturbing. Joel was calling to her from the edge of a great sea. Each time he cried out, his image grew smaller and more faded. He jumped into the ocean and started swimming towards her, but the distance was too great to cross. The waves crashed against his defenceless body until the sea devoured him in one last, crushing blow of force.

She started to cry. 'I need to keep the candle burning', she murmured. 'Until I see the flame extinguished. In truth, Amber felt more uncertain at that moment than at any time since she had left the mine.

***

She rose early the following morning, although her body still ached for further sleep. Her search for her rucksack had proved fruitless. 'He must have taken it,' she mumbled to herself. All she had now were the modest provisions given to her at *Gnosis* and the clothes she stood in. 'How would she cope with the night winds without her thick coat?' she speculated.

The journey down into the centre was slow. At every shop, she gazed, hoping to see the man she loved, but there was no sign of life. Eventually, the mangled pillars of the hotel façade came into view. It looked different from her last visit. Hollow, empty, devoid of human presence. The stairs creaked as she descended to the basement. Her hopeful shouts echoed off empty stones. The place had been thoroughly cleaned of flags, symbols and memorabilia associated with the occupants. Amber sat down despondently and looked around. In the corner of the room, some images of the ants lay torn and crumpled. Just as she was about to leave, a scratching sound from behind distracted her. Amber turned to see the pale outline of something crouching behind one of the rocks.

"I am armed!" the shadowy figure shouted. "Don't move another step. "

Amber tried to reassure the voice, "I am not your enemy. You have nothing to fear from me."

The figure moved into full view. A hunched, bedraggled-looking man of around fifty, clutching an old pistol. His hands visibly trembled as he limped towards her. ''Have you any food or water?"

Amber nodded and lifted the bag from her shoulders. "I have dry bread and something to drink." She removed the items from the rucksack and placed them on the floor. The stranger straightened his frame and looked eagerly at the offering.

"' Push them along the ground towards me, and no tricks, lady. This gun is loaded." Amber could now see his face more clearly. Like a large rodent, she thought, with a swollen head, large ears and protruding whiskers. She didn't know whether she felt pity or fear for the pathetic individual that stood before her. He tore open the food cloth and pulled out the dried bread before devouring most of it in a couple of frenzied mouthfuls. The water slurped down his cheeks, in equal measure to what he managed to swallow. 'Don't waste it, you fool!' she cried, increasingly agitated by his behaviour.

Amber plucked up sufficient nerve to challenge her unpleasant host. "Where are the other survivors?" The man put the water carrier down and looked more carefully at his visitor.

"I remember you. Before the raid. One of the two strangers."

"Yes. I was there on the first raid. But I need to ask about my friend, the African guy. Have you seen him?

He bowed his head despondently. "Only a few returned, but they left again, very quickly."

"How did you survive?"

"With more luck than some. Left behind because of this leg injury. Managed to hide when the guards came to look for any *red ants* who had returned here. I can tell you something. One of the survivors said the African was last seen trying to help an injured woman from the group." He added, rather pessimistically, that neither had come back to the hotel. Unfortunately, this only confirmed what she already knew.

"Where are the other survivors of the attack," she demanded. The man just shook his head. A couple of the *fire ants* returned and collected their belongings but immediately left. They said the guards had taken Quinton and Sita, and so had their young rottweiler, Daniel. Those in power, including *Gnosis*, are not known for their mercy regarding direct attacks upon government-protected buildings. He pointed a finger across his 'Adam's apple' to emphasize their likely fate. "I was asked to stay behind and watch the base. Because of my leg." He rolled up his trousers to reveal a swollen limb, heavily strapped in cloth bandages. A stroke of luck, ah?" He broke into a strained grin, baring a ridge of misshaped teeth. "Me and you need to stick together, girl. More chance of keeping alive." He put the revolver down and reached across to embrace her. Amber read his intention and delivered a sharp kick towards his kneecap. He howled with pain before a second blow from her elbow smashed into his nose. The nostrils exploded with blood. "That's for pointing a loaded weapon at me and stealing my food."

He collapsed to the ground, whimpering like a wounded animal.

"You and I aren't going anywhere together!"

She reached for the gun and checked the bullets. He hadn't been lying-it was fully loaded.

"I should finish you off right here, you moron!"

"Now pass what's left of the food and water back to me carefully."

He reluctantly complied.

His mood changed. "Don't leave me here, lady. I beg you."

But his words fell on deaf ears. Amber was already packed and ready to go.

"Come back, you bitch!" His words echoed around the area as she mounted the stairway and headed out, not knowing where her feet would take her next.

***

Amber Byrne pulled the hood over her head and headed into the blazing heat. She knew that this wasn't the time to travel anywhere. With limited water and hardly any food, she must conserve her energy and take frequent rests. However, she was mindful of the importance of putting some distance between herself and the obnoxious individual at the hotel. She walked south, away from the city and came across a promising house. An imposing property made of stone, within sight of the river basin. The tiled roof was remarkably intact, with just a tiny back section missing. She felt for the gun in her pocket and rested her finger on the trigger. Walking up the path, she looked around to gauge if there was any sign of life. Not a sound anywhere. At the steps, Amber reached to turn the handle on the grand, ornate door and push it open. Immediately, the temperature dropped, and she could discard her outer layers of clothing. She collapsed on a faded recliner and opened her bag to seize her water bottle. The warm fluid felt soothing on the back of her throat. There was also a chunk of bread next to it, which she munched eagerly. And then, suddenly, a moment of good fortune. As she manipulated her fingers around the base of the rucksack, she felt a bulge. There was something else packed there, buried below a sweater. Amber pulled it out and smiled.

“Oh, sweet beauty!” she exclaimed, staring at the circular shape of another large bottle, which was still full of water.

***

Joel couldn’t believe how cold it was in the cave. The Nigerian shivered and pulled his coat closer, trying to think what to do next. He’d had to move fast when he heard the swirling blades of the *helizoom* and, understandably panicked. The craft transmitted an identity beam which locked onto his arm. He knew what the outcome of this would be. His *tainted* ID number is 4867139, establishing his unique status. There was little point in running, but he just that felt he had to. Joel could see the sandstone ridge to the left and did not stop sprinting until he came to the mouth of the cave. The fact that they would have monitored his movements and knew precisely where he was, didn’t enter his head. And so, Joel waited in the damp of a freezing hollow for the inevitable. The guards soon appeared at the entrance like police enforcers from the past.

“Tainted survivor No 4867139 Joel Agwuegbo. You have been apprehended to face charges relating to an attack on a data storage facility. Present yourself for confinement.’

Joel gathered his composure and stood up before walking over to them. He suspected what was coming. It was pointless trying to struggle. The subsequent injection crushed any possible resistance as he tumbled, unconscious, to the ground.

“Bring him.”

***

Amber woke, squinting and confused. The night darkness still held its icy grip on the land. Something was glowing next to her, which, on closer inspection, turned out to be coming from her arm. The light projected a hologram on the wall in front of her. It portrayed the details of Joel’s capture, with a message for her to be ready for transportation to *Gnosis* in ten minutes. As she reached for her bag and boots, Amber was conflated about the message. Now she knew where he was, but was he still alive, and if so, would he cooperate with the proposition she had received?

***

The room stank of chemicals and disinfectant. Joel breathed deeply and tried to stretch his neck to the left. Something or someone was moving about there; the sound of muffled voices filled the air. "You are back with us again, I see," barked one of them. "Give him water."

The man from Nigeria did not need to ask the question. He realised precisely where he was. An inquisitive face appeared, carrying a bottle. The restraining bed cranked as his head was raised to receive the water. He choked a little and automatically reached out to pull the bottle away, but his shackled hands would not permit him to do so. He spat out the seepage, and it dribbled down his cheeks.

Another figure approached him. Bespeckled and balding, he looked familiar.

"Do I know you? What do you want?" croaked Joel.

The man raised an eyebrow, with a touch of incredulous candour. "As far as you are concerned, I have no name. As for why you find yourself at the mercy of *Gnosis* once again, I suspect you are bright enough to figure that out. But just in case, I will give you a clue: the attack on the database a couple of nights ago."

Joel's expression of resignation hardly required further explanation.

"The good news for you is that you are still alive. Your crime is usually punishable by death. However, thanks to the benevolence of the authorities, there is a chance for you to live."

Joel lay there manacled and frustrated, as the conditions for his survival were outlined. "You are a lucky man, Joel Agwuegbo. Your choice of female companion has given you another chance to prove yourself. As one of our 'ears', listening, learning, and reporting back to us. And according to your blood analysis, there may be another reason to keep you alive." The Nigerian looked confused.

His captor beckoned his colleague to open the door. The voice Joel most needed to hear lit up the room, crying out his name. "Joel. Oh, Joel. It's true. You are alive!"

***

Amber's fingers sought out the calloused hand of her companion. She squeezed it tightly like a frightened child. She found his physical touch calming and reassuring. It had been some time. Squeezing his limb distracted Joel sufficiently to lift his eyes towards her. He smiled as only he did and whispered, ''It will be ok.''

Richard Hartwood sat across the stone table with a younger colleague, examining an archaic paper map. ''This is where we will drop you," he announced. "You know how to contact us when you have news. Don't make us come looking for you," he added sternly.

Joel stared at the mark on his arm. Although he didn't understand the technology behind the threat the explosive device presented, he believed that it was real. Hartwood cast him a studious glance. "Don't forget to keep it always covered. A wrist strap should do it. Here!" He threw Joel a couple of brown leather bands. "There's a spare one, too." It was a big surprise to learn that they would be sent to work in *District 1: London Sector*. Hartwood had concluded that a couple of the *fire ants* may have avoided capture and might comprise their mission by identifying them. Better to pitch them in an area where they were utterly unknown. Amber looked stunned. Your mission is to infiltrate resistance groups, discover what is happening, and report back.

"Our sister research centre in the south, *Gnosis 1,* will track your movements."

Amber had no idea that there was another *Gnosis* centre.

The second man, who introduced himself as Stuart, queried their knowledge of the area. "Did either of you visit London before *the Change*?'

Amber went there with her dad, sister, and brother when she was a teenager. They had been to see the Houses of Parliament and the British Museum and saw a show later in Leicester Square. She remembered it well. Joel, however, had never set foot in the capital. Stuart continued. "As you can appreciate, London has changed."

"The old capital is now a cesspit of squaller. A dangerous place. One of the reasons why the central government has moved to the outskirts. Richmond, to be precise. Shortly after the *Change* occurred, they were advised to flee Westminster for security reasons. Our leaders are now housed in a secret nuclear bunker built under the ground, protected from the factions that spread right across the old city, even to its western outskirts. We have heard whispers of a big incident being planned by terrorists. These people are determined to destroy our work. Unable to see the bigger picture, brainwashed by radicals and madmen!"

Stuart was now shouting, puffing his cheeks and glowing red in the face. He looked like a man scarcely able to contain his anger. A creature about to explode. Someone you might cross the road to avoid in the days when there were roads. The other thing that set Stuart apart was his physique. Unlike so many of them, who had withered away to a skeletal version of their former selves, this man maintained a powerful build. Broad, muscular shoulders supporting a chiselled torso, the muscular frame of an elite soldier or athlete. Somebody who could look after himself in a fracas or an emergency.

"We've caught wind of something being planned. That's why we are dropping you in Twickenham, not Central London," Hartwood continued.

He placed a reassuring arm across his colleague's shoulder. "We have said enough for now, Stuart." He turned to Joel and Amber. " Get some rest, you two. Tomorrow, you start work."

Alien Territory

Amber rolled across and searched for the comfort of Joel's body. The restlessness that enveloped her spirit was not just about what lay ahead in the morning. Her vision caught the glowing embers of the fire in the corner of the room, and she watched the flames slowly fade. It was unusually warm for that time of night. Clearly, those who lived there enjoyed a more generous wood allowance for the evening fire, she thought.

"Joel. Are you still awake?" Her companion yawned and opened his blanket to welcome her body.

" Not really. Just turning over a few things in my head." He looked gravely at her. "What are we doing here, Amber. How did we get ourselves into this situation?" She stroked his tight, knotted hair and kissed him on the cheek. "Who can say, my love? The fortunes of life. All I know is that if we keep together, we have a chance to come through this." He embraced her with all the power his arms could muster. "I love you, he whispered into her ear. We will do what we've been asked to and leave this nightmare. And then, we will find your father."

***

They woke early, with the sound of exigent voices in the hall. Within minutes, a stern-looking man in a military uniform arrived with new rucksacks for them. They were bigger and more robust than the old ones. "Put your other items in these," he instructed them. As if reading the question that was about to leave Amber's lips, he emphasised the dangers of not looking authentic in the city. "As you can see, these bags are a little tatty but will help you blend in better. Everything inside is re-cycled." His Scottish brogue reminded her that there were parts of the United Kingdom she had heard virtually nothing about since the *Change.* Amber lifted her rucksack. It felt heavy. Joel was already investigating the contents of his bag. "There's twice as much drinking water in these!" he exclaimed enthusiastically. "More food, too."

Amber grinned. She looked like a little girl who had found a hidden sweets store.

"Right, you two. Breakfast is inside your bags. Let's go." He began moving away at pace. They quickly fastened their backpacks and scuttled after him.

It wasn't long before they stood before the *helizoom,* dwarfed by the giant blades that propelled her. It was bigger than any helicopter she had seen before, protected with menacing laser guns at both the front and rear. They were beckoned forward with a pair of scruffy young men who had joined them. "More spies," I'm guessing, grunted Joel. Neither of the men spoke to them. They just exchanged vacuous looks devoid of all expression. Within minutes, they were airborne, whirling up into the same azure, cerulean sky that greeted them daily. They observed substantial cobalt-shaded streaks of haze through the window, hanging as if suspended by hidden ropes and created by the hand of some colossal artist. Only fifteen minutes elapsed before the towering stadium at Twickenham began to loom below. Behind it loomed a charred mass of grey and black, the remnants of a once prosperous and powerful London suburb.

A message rang out to all passengers:

Two minutes to landing. No movement of human life forms detected within one kilometre of the surface. Safe to activate drop.

Their surly Scottish protector appeared from the front of the craft with last-minute instructions. "Remember: we require updates. If you don't make contact for 48 hours, you are history." Like something exploding, he blew a raucous, hostile sound from his lips. "It's not pleasant," he added with a truculent stare."

The *helizoom* twice circled the remains of the former English rugby stadium before descending to a few metres from the ground. This once home of English rugby had survived the destructive winds better than many buildings. Two roofing sections had collapsed, giving one-half of the arena the appearance of an ancient Greek amphitheatre. There was no evidence of any movement below. As the craft hovered some five metres above the ground, ladder ropes sprung from the floor, and they were instructed to climb down to the floor. Seconds later, the *helizoom* disappeared into the firmament, shrouded in the red cloud of toxic dust, leaving their human cargo like discarded packages. The irrepressible heat immediately drilled into their faces with alacrity.

"We need to find cover," shouted Joel. "Let's try those buildings over there." He pointed to the properties that lay beyond what was left of the stadium carparks. They pulled the hoods over their heads and ran towards the first house within a row of damaged terraced properties. The door opened easily onto a corridor lined with green floral wallpaper. At the end was a large sitting room with broken panes of glass leading out to a small garden. They sank into the remains of a grey, stripped sofa and began peeling off layers of clothing.

"Phew," declared Joel. "And I used to think it was hot in Nigeria!" He began unpacking the rucksack's contents for a closer look at the provisions. The usual basic ingredients were present. Dried bread, vegetable paste and water. Plenty of water. They would not need to replenish this for more than a week if careful. But there was something he wasn't expecting. A yellowish, sweet-smelling bar of something with a hint of peanut. "This is good," he enthused, thrusting the cake treat under her nose. Neither of them could remember when they last tasted peanut crisp. They permitted themselves the smallest of morsels, just enough to stimulate their tastebuds. Anymore, and all semblance of self-control would completely vanish! They sat back, purring with the unexpected snack.

Joel continued to remove what was in the rucksack. A small hunting knife was found at the bottom, with the item he sought.

"Here it is, Amber." He held up the compact communication device. Keeping his grasp of the object, it eventually lit up in operational mode. "They said to hold it tight for at least twenty seconds," Amber interjected.

"Yes. I'll remember."

As promised, his companion found another device located in her bag. "A twenty-second hold and a full twist for the contact bleep. And forty-eight hours to report back. Let's just hope we have something to say to them."

She noted the two-day countdown dial on the spherical object, ominously reaching for the lumpy implant lodged just below her wrist.

"Need to keep these wrists covered," she added, "just in case."

***

Each evening, they would need to undertake the laborious task of meticulously going through the details of their new identity. That way, there was hope that they would ingrain the story into their minds. Whatever happened, there could be no hesitancy, no mistakes. They were now Peter and Ella, desperately trying to unite with Ella's family after being trapped by her own lengthy illness thirty miles south of the capital. At least some of the elements of the story rang true. *Gnosis* had fabricated a yarn around the need to find medicines for her mother before she succumbed to a deliberating fever. The family friend, who had shared this with them, had now conveniently been killed in an accident, thus removing the only one who could verify the tale. Joel is now 'Peter,' an African student who was studying politics at the University of Reading. Like many, he became trapped in the UK by the *Change,* having befriended 'Ella' at the Leatherhead Garden Centre, where they both worked part-time. Both had been given information sheets to learn about the real people their characters had been based upon. 'Each is now conveniently deceased,' they had shared. A tight-knit story to unleash upon anyone looking to probe the authenticity of their deceit.

***

As the unrelenting heat finally began to fade, they made a note of the position of the house and hid their rucksacks behind a chimney screen in the front room. The *helizoom* captain had announced that there were no humans in the immediate vicinity of the stadium site, but they suspected it was only a matter of time before they came across local people. They stepped out upon what remained of the road. Flanked by the rusted remains of old cars and vans, they headed deeper into the once, affluent streets. After twenty minutes, 'Peter' suddenly stopped. ''What is it?'' she quizzed. His eyes had been drawn towards a house set back from the road. ''Look! Over there, by that greenish coloured property with the decorative wall. There was movement beneath the canvas roof. Something rustling in the garden wreckage. And there she was. A girl of around fourteen years of age. Hair like twisted corn, clothed in ragged blue overalls. She finally noticed them and ran inside. All they could here was 'mum, dad, outsiders.'

Ella and Peter stood frozen, in their tracks. The door opened cautiously, and a man emerged carrying an old shotgun, slung across his shoulder. He wiped his brow with his shirt sleeve, grasped the gun, and pointed it in their direction. ''What do you want?'' he bellowed. ''We do not welcome strangers around here.''

Amber realised she needed to choose her words carefully. '' We mean you no harm, friend. Just a *tainted* daughter trying to find her sick mother.''

''There is no sick woman here.'' He studied his visitors with a guarded expression. ''What is her name?''

Amber poured out her carefully concocted tale, punctuated with emotional pauses, to foster sympathy. Joel just bowed his head in silent appreciation of the performance. Without lowering his weapon, he continued to quiz her. ''So how have you travelled to the outskirts of London?''

The experiences journeying towards Worcester had furnished them with vivid examples of how to avoid the fiery daytime cauldron and the angry night winds. With the assistance of Joel, they described a couple of challenging encounters, embellishing the stories with imaginary characters. The girl's father finally lowered his gun, seemingly satisfied with Amber's account. He pointed towards the building next to his house. A brick annex with its roof still intact.

''You can stay overnight there, but I expect you to be gone in the morning. There is no spare water here, but if you can avoid the river controllers, there may be some available, under the surface of the Thames riverbed.''

''Thank you for your kindness.'' Joel responded, without any mention of the copious stock of water they carried. ''I'm Peter and this is Ella.'' He extended his hand towards the girl's father, but the gesture was ignored.

''Keep away from the girl. She is not used to strangers these days. ''

''Of course. We will wander down to the old river when the heat subsides.''

They walked across to the annex building and pulled open the door. It was reminiscent of the old 'granny' flats once built for elderly parents. A metallic walking frame still lay parked in the corner, next to the back door. A blackened fireplace bore testament to fire activity there, in the past, but there was little sign of its former occupant.

''I'll check out the upstairs,'' Joel declared. From the bedroom, he could see the remains of the road that once connected Twickenham to Richmond. Although two miles away, the once imposing river town, nestling alongside the Thames, seemed like an alien world. One part of the famous bridge that straddled the river, was still in place. There was little need to repair the damaged section. It was now possible to walk across the basin without getting your feet wet.

A large metal-sprung bed lay pushed against the wall. The duvet was still resting over it, clinging to its former life, like a prop on a stage. Joel reached for the contact sphere in the bag and read the countdown dial. Fifteen hours. By the time they woke up the following morning it would be twenty- eight and counting.

''Let's see what's happening down by the old river, Amber, before the winds pick up.'' She nodded and grabbed her outer coat. They walked the short distance to what was left of Twickenham town centre. It was ghost-like, apart from the whimpering of a solitary dog, somewhere in the distance. The Thames basin came into view; a twisting canyon of gauged out rock, a little wider than the Severn. There were flickering lights on the far side and human figures.

''Stick to the story at all costs,'' he implored her. ''If our deception is discovered, we are as good as dead.'' The terror in her eyes did not require further confirmation.

They climbed down the rocky edge into the basin of the river and moved towards the lights.

''Stop right there, you two.'' The menacing command was accompanied by the familiar clicking of manual guns. ''Who approaches the river controllers?''

Amber nudged her companion. ''Let me do the talking.'' She looked up and smiled at her interrogator. ''Just an anxious daughter and her boyfriend looking for my sick mother. '' A second man appeared, draped in a bizarre chain of old fish bones.

What is the name of the woman you seek? He shouted.

Amber hesitated, before burbling out: 'Charlotte Maher.'

''Charlotte Maher, you say,'' the burly inquisitor repeated. He scratched his head revealing a deep scar under his fringe. ''Never heard of her! His eyes narrowed. ''How do I know you aren't making all this up?''

''She was a healer and lived alone in Burton Street, this side of Twickenham.'' The swiftness of his partner's response surprised Joel. The emerging words forming were put on hold. Internally he was aching to protect her. 'Stay calm, my love. He can't check this out.' The other man approached and muttered something in his colleague's ear.

''Bind them.''

''I have just instructed somebody to check out your story as we speak,'' he continued. ''Meanwhile, you two will stay here. ''Have you anything to trade, strangers?''

Amber clearly did not want them to rifle through her rucksack. ''Untie me and I will see what I have,'' she pleaded. With reluctance, the man complied with her request. Within a hidden compartment at the base of the bag, she extracted a gold necklace. ''It belonged to my grandma,'' she exclaimed. Josh looked on, incredulously. He had never seen her wear the item. The fish -bone carrier pulled a magnifying glass from his belt and carefully studied the item. '' I'll give you some food and water for it,'' he grunted. Amber stood, dwarfed by the man. Towering above her, he was nearly two metres tall. Covered in crudely carved tattoo's, his face swollen red by too much contact with the sun, he presented a frightening figure.

He placed the necklace in his pocket. Joel watched two women emerge from the ladders which led to down below the surface of the ground.

''Give them some food and water!''

The man untied Joel and handed them both a plate. ''They call me Harpoon,'' he disclosed. ''On account of my skills with this!'' He stroked the short spear loaded upon the aquatic gun. ''Now I hunt different creatures.''

''I'm Ella and this is Peter'' Amber volunteered, but he didn't seem to be listening.

***

Neither Joel nor Amber was sure what they were eating. It appeared to be some kind of meat and vegetable broth. As if reading their minds, the added with a smile, ''there are still plenty of rats under the ground, if you know where to find them.''

Amber choked on her stew. Suddenly she no longer felt hungry. He observed her discomfort. '' Around here we no longer have the luxury of preference. If it moves, we eat it!''

Twenty minutes later, a nervous looking woman in her forties appeared. ''Their story checks out, Harpoon. There was a woman of that name living in the street.'' She turned to Amber to break the bad news. 'I'm afraid she died a couple of months ago of cancer, we think. I'm sorry.'' Amber knew she needed to respond in an appropriate way. ''The crocodile tears flowed in abundance as she summoned every ounce of distress and paraded it accordingly.

Josh contributed to the charade by throwing his arms around her and trying to look distraught.''what will you do now?'' Harpoon enquired. ''I guess we will return home. But first, we need to visit the house and see her grave,'' her 'daughter' replied.

''Is it safe around the town? Do *Gnosis* operate around here? Joel asked.

At the mention of the organisation, the attitude of their hosts changed. The atmosphere darkened. With renewed suspicion, they fired one question after another at the couple.

'What do you know about *Gnosis*?' Why are you asking us about them?' Harpoon stepped forward. 'Maybe they are spies after all!' He picked up his harpoon, fully loaded, and pointed it at Joel. The realisation that his name was directly linked to the weapon for good reason, only heightened the tension.

'' Do not be alarmed. It is just that we have had bad experiences with them. Arrested. Interrogated.'' exclaimed the African.

''So why are you still alive?'' Harpoon asked. They sketched a story about the *Green Zone,* stumbling across the *fire ants* and wrongfully being accused of assisting them during an attack.

A second *river controller* appeared and joined in the interrogation. It was only the story of her dad and brother serving in the military, which seemed to pacify them. ''I also lost members of my family in that fucking war,'' he said. ''We should never have gone there, '' he continued, bitterly. Amber almost mentioned her dad's name but realised the error just in time. At least their anger had now been deflected towards a different target.

Joel sought to seize the initiative and blurted out, ''We hate *Gnosis* and all it stands for! The elitism, the injustice of it all. Ordinary people, like us, the *tainted,* need to fight back and force them to share our country's meagre resources more widely.'' Amber raised an eyebrow and felt like applauding her partner's rallying cry but thought better of it.

Harpoon listened carefully to Joel's rhetoric. ''What lengths would you go to to prove that these are not just empty words, African?''

''Whatever it takes,'' came the curt reply.

''Does that include rebellion and murder?'' he persevered.

''Desperate people must do desperate things.''

Amber interrupted before her companion got ahead of himself. ''We both know how to use manual firearms, and clubs.'' Harpoon gave out a raucous laugh as he assessed the physical strength of the woman stood before him. ''I'm sure you can, young lady,'' he added with sardonic mockery.

Our fight in London will not be won with sticks and handguns. It will be achieved with our brains.'' In that moment, his suspicions rose as Joel sensed there was something of a veiled threat in his words. But more importantly, they had their first glimpse of dissent against the government. Josh risked a final question. ''Do *Gnosis* and the other government bodies leave you alone out here, Harpoon?''

''By and large, they do. If there is no trouble.'' He peered into Joel's eyes. ''And you, Peter, ask too many questions.''

''I will now ask you one. Where are you sleeping tonight?'' Josh described their encounter with the elderly man and young girl. ''We know him, and we also like to know where any strangers base themselves.''

With that, 'Peter' and 'Ella' left the riverbed and returned to the town. As they approached the house, they saw the girl. Still on the porch, sat on her makeshift swing, staring aimlessly out towards the sky. They greeted her but she did not answer. As they came to the annex, the man emerged from the house. ''She is mute,'' he shared. ''Hasn't spoken since she watched her parents killed in a local riot, last year. I'm her grandfather. I do what I can to keep her safe.''

His pained expression was barely contained. He looked at Amber. '' Did you find out anything about your mother?''

''We met the river controllers, and they had some information about mum,'' Amber disclosed. ''Not good news, I'm afraid. She has passed on.''

''Probably for the best, girl,'' he muttered.

''I will bid you farewell now.'' With that he retreated to the house, without casting another glance at them. Amber and Joel sleeked across to the extension building and prepared to settle down for the night. They ate the dry bread and green paste with renewed enthusiasm. After sampling the rat broth earlier, it tasted better than it had ever done.

''We should contact *Gnosis* in the morning'' sighed Amber. At least we can report that we are following up a lead.''

''Barely,'' mouthed Joel.'' But it should keep our arms from exploding.''

Recruitment

With the winds less brutal that night, they both sank into a rarefied deep sleep. Joel eventually woke, startled by a vivid dream that had plagued him at night. In his vision, a formidable figure emerges from a desert storm, hands bloodied, clutching his heart, and calling out to him. The words are lost in howling winds, but he seems to be offering some sort of invitation. The man is old and has no facial features, only the impervious outline of a powered shadow. As he draws closer, pliable trees which flank his passage, quickly wither and die. And with the proximity of his presence, he too crumbles away, leaving just bones scattered upon the ground.

Joel sat up and wiped the sweat from his brow. Staring out at the night sky, he ponders the dream's meaning. There is no clarity in the confusion of the story, but he senses it has significance. Is it a warning or a prediction of what will come? He looks at his antiquated wrist panel. It's 5.30 AM, and the sun is beginning to penetrate the darkness. Joel reaches across to hug his sleeping partner and tries to extricate a little of her tranquil peace. He gently kisses her forehead and whispers, 'I love you,' before turning on his side and drifting back into light slumber.

***

Amber was woken by the sound of footsteps next to her. Joel looked down and smiled at her while playing with the communication sphere from his bag. "Are you all right, Joel? You look tired."

He ignores her question and buries the images of his dream in a part of his memory where they won't easily be reached. "We must speak to them this morning," he mutters to her. Amber had been dreading the reality of the task. 'Should they wait a little longer?'

"Two hours before time's up." Her reminder was hardly needed.

"Shall we ring them from here?" she continued. They agreed it might be wiser. "You stand watch at the window in case we attract any attention," Amber suggested. She reached across to her rucksack and lifted the sphere out before switching the device on.

"What will you tell them?"

"The truth. We have contacted local people and are close to finding out something important."

"But we haven't."

"I know, but we need to give them a story to keep them interested."

With that, she pressed the activation button and passed on her message. The response was short, automated and functional. *Keep us posted.*

As they walked away from the annexe, the sun-bathed roofs of central Richmond lit up the morning haze before them. In a neighbouring house, a young girl sat on a twisted swing and followed them with her eyes. She did not speak. Her silence a testament to the trauma of another uncertain day. In the background, the ethereal figure of her grandfather, his protective eyes still guarded, watched them leave.

To their right, rising like an ancient earthen mound from the river basin, was the crest of Richmond Hill. The adjoining park, now a desolate zone, was once a vibrant oasis where lush flora thrived alongside deer and people seeking fresh air and recreation. Some of the more opulent mansions surrounding the park had survived relatively intact, but their once prized views were now a carpet of brown and red dust. The isolated skeletons of once great trees stood withered, rooted to the ground like curious pieces of abstract art. All life sapped from the stems, leaving only brittle, crusty stumps as a haunting reminder of a different time.

A familiar voice called out to them just before Richmond Bridge came into view.

"You are heading the wrong way. Come with us. We have work for you to do." Joel and Amber turned around to see the imposing figure of Harpoon walking towards them. He was not alone. Their protestations and questions fell on deaf ears. Those with Harpoon carried a selection of weapons. One held a large axe, another a longbow and quiver, while a third had a rifle strapped across his shoulder. Not surprisingly, Harpoon's marine spear gun hung menacingly from his waist. Eventually, the latter sprung a question of his own to Amber and Joel.

"What would you be willing to sacrifice to save your country?" He peered at the couple, waiting for an acceptable answer. Joel immediately jumped in with some patriotic rhetoric. "Whatever it takes." He thumped his chest with his fist, eyes bulging in anger.

Harpoon permitted himself a smile and looked at him curiously. "Where are you from, then?" The man from Nigeria understood the barely disguised racist tone.

"This is my country now." He turned to Amber. "A place where our children will have a chance to flourish."

Harpoon, a weathered man with a glint of determination in his eyes, seemed satisfied with the answer and beckoned them across." Here. You are going to need these." He thrust a spear into each of their hands.

Amber noticed they were moving west, away from Richmond.

They soon left behind the last of the outer streets and strode through former fields peppered with scattered rocks and debris. Soon, they were back in Twickenham, but they carried on until they reached the dilapidated remains of the antiquated university campus of St. Mary's, close to the Thames River, in Strawberry Hill. From their position, hidden among the rubble of several old houses, they gazed at the curious remains of an 18th-century Georgian Gothic building. Some sections seemed relatively intact. But what grabbed Amber and Joel's attention was the imposing black metal fence of some five metres in height that surrounded the grounds' perimeter. Beyond the fence lay several clusters of barbed wire, separated by a central pathway in which guards, clad in military clothing patrolled the outer area with what looked like laser guns. Perched upon four posing support towers rested larger weapon assemblies flanked by giant searchlights.

"Wow. What is this place?" exclaimed Joel in bewilderment. "It looks like some sort of prison."

"This, African, is where the new government currently resides since the Parliament buildings collapsed. It was built by the son of a former prime minister. A guy called Walpole. If you ask me, it looks like a fantasy palace with pointed towers and ancient walls." He paused as if bored with his own rhetoric. "More importantly, this is where we strike a blow for voiceless ones like us!"

Amber's glance at Joel was enough to remind him that they had been in such territory before. They both knew how it ended. Her mind was a whirlwind of panic-laden, disjointed thoughts that slowly merged into one clear issue. How would they escape from this predicament? How could they warn *Gnosis* about what was happening? And finally, how would they escape from there.

***

Joel knew at least one of them needed to make the call. "I'll do it!" he shared with her.

"No. They will be less suspicious of me, I think." She looked across at the large boulders to her right. "Over there. I'll say I need the toilet. Be ready to make a run for it if the *helizoom* appears to pick us up."

***

"Need the toilet? Just take a piss here, like the rest of us, woman!" One of Harpoon's male assistants stood listening to her request with indifference. "But it's going to be messy," Amber pleaded and smiled expectantly. "Ok. Ok. Just make it quick. We don't want to be stepping in your shit, Lady." Joel watched her meander through their ranks to relieve herself behind the rock. A hand suddenly appeared upon his left shoulder. "I don't expect you to be joining her," the voice bellowed. "Think she can manage her ablutions on her own. Don't you?" Joel re-focussed and sprang a question to his questioner. "When do you think we will attack?" The grizzled man in his fifties delivered a curt response without even looking at him. "When we are ready, son."

Meanwhile, Joel became distracted by the steadily increasing number of individuals arriving. They trudged past him wearily, suggesting some had travelled all day. These strangers unfurled and carried bizarre banners embellished with emotive slogans denouncing the government and crying out for change. Others were camouflaged to fit in with the rock-strewn landscape's browns, reds, and oranges. Some exchanged obscure greetings, but the ones with exposed arms were all identified by the same calling card, the numerical mark of an untouchable forever branded in their arm. Joel whispered to his accomplice, "There are nearly a hundred faces here. What on earth have we stumbled across, Amber?"

***

Amber squatted down behind the rock and pulled open her rucksack. The device was carefully lifted from its hiding place and activated. In a hushed voice, she beckoned her controllers.

Speak, tainted number 48273. Do you have something important to report?

She cleared her throat and shared what was happening around her.

Yes. We've detected a significant surge in the movement of bodies in the vicinity. An attack is imminent, the urgency in her voice mirroring the gravity of the situation.

'We also believe so.' Almost forgetting the subject of their exit strategy, she quickly probed the voice about when they would be extracted.

The helizoom will be there. We have your coordinates.

The voice vanished, and Amber was left with a sense of uncertainty. She pulled her trousers up and returned to the camp.

“You took your time, “the assistant bellowed. Amber sheepishly shrugged her shoulders and re-joined Joel. He looked anxious. "They say we will get the call to attack soon. Was everything ok with them?"

"I think so. A different voice answered this time. More nonchalant, vague. At least he confirmed they would extract us when the time was right."

"When the time is right!" This only added to Joel's mounting anxiety. Feeling the weight of the situation, Amber took his hand and placed a reassuring kiss on the back of his palm. "We need to stay calm, my love,' she whispered, her voice a soothing balm in the face of impending danger.

***

Despite the uncomfortable ground, with its sharp edges and un-yielding rockface, the pair slowly drifted off into semi-sleep. Their heavy eyes were lifted by a sudden kick. “No time to sleep, outsiders. We attack now!”

The sound of hover- blades grew louder as a transport plane broke through the clouds. “Here he comes,” shouted Harpoon, defiantly. “Sneaking back to his lair, like the coward he is.”

“Who?” enquired Amber.

“Why the premiere, of course. With possibly his three acolytes. The protectors of the three new districts in England. They won’t forget this night.”

Harpoon seemed to command a position of importance among the would-be attackers as he barked instructions to those around him. “You two come along with me. We will strike at the left gate.” As the *helizoom* drew closer, it swooped down over their heads and hovered on the inner side of the college wall. They could see the obscure outlines of four figures disembarking from the craft. They were soon joined by a dozen heavily armed guards, who formed a shield between the outer gate and the arrivals.

"The place does not look that well defended," one of the others cried. ''Do not be fooled by appearances," shouted Harpoon. The old university buildings you see are only the entrance to a far more expansive defence. That lies underground, in a network of tunnels and chambers. We are going to destroy as many of these as we can." He paused as if hesitating to add something.

"Destroy them with our limited weapons?" the man queried. Harpoon turned to him in disdain. "Of course not." At this point, he picked up the large rucksack next to him and pulled out an electronic device. "But with these, we might."

Harpoon had been waiting for this moment. "We have ten of these incendiary units. Above all, we must protect these devices in our lives. It has taken months to assemble these bombs. People have already lost their lives constructing them. If their efforts are not to be in vain, some of these devices must reach the tunnels. To detonate them won't be easy. Some of you may die, but your achievements will long live in the minds of those who come after us."

Extolling the noble virtues of self-sacrifice did nothing to allay the fear that Joel and Amber could see in the faces around them. These were not highly trained soldiers, protected with sophisticated weaponry. Just *tainted* wretches like themselves, desperate to grasp a better life from the hands of those who already did. Joel gazed up at the mushrooming clouds gathering above them. The night sky was starting to flex its power. He realised that the moment had come.

Amber grabbed his hand. "This time, we stay together at all costs."

The Assault

Harpoon rallied his supporters, a diverse group with a wide range of skills and characteristics. Amber and Joel, the second cohort of attackers, were joined by six individuals, each with their own unique traits. Among them were two senior men, their advanced age etched across their faces, a quiet and nimble youth, and a rugged looking middle-aged woman named Laura. Their armaments were as varied as their personalities, with two spears, two antiquated handguns, and a homemade shotgun. One of the older men, carrying a large bag, introduced himself as Will, a man of mystery who inferred he had an important role to play in the assault.

"If the first group fails to deliver their parcel to the western elevator, we go in with ours" He pointed to his bag. "If we are to succeed, friends, you need to protect me with your last breath."

***

With some caution, the first wave of attacks began. The response from the government forces was brutal. A blistering eruption of laser fire lit up the space where the first cohort now stood. Bodies soon littered the ground. Few made it to the wall. Military guards began to comb the area for survivors, displaying little mercy for the injured. Harpoon gazed upon the scene, seemingly unaffected by the outcome. Already, his mind was racing to identify something to give to the second group as a signal of hope. He looked at the sky. The fading dusk was slowly providing further camouflage as they meandered slowly through the rocks towards the open space, stretching across towards the gate. Amber and Joel watched the towers direct their search beams towards the invaders, locating their position before striking with laser beams. Several attackers fell to the ground, cut down by their deadly rays. Others reached the wall, where a small metal door to the left was now ajar. Amidst the shouting and confusion, a loud explosion was heard as one of the rucksack bombs detonated. This seemed to prompt further activity from the security services, who pursued those who had begun to squeeze through the door. Meanwhile, soldiers scampered around the wall's far side, where another door had opened.

"Be ready," Harpoon instructed them as they waited to join the attack.

"Now!" he shouted and pushed them forward." Follow me!"

Amid the dust, smoke and confusion, the left door was still visible. "Head towards it, quickly!" he shouted and dispatched his fish gun at the first guard that blocked his way. The man fell back, a short spear penetrating his protective suit through the heart. He stopped briefly to pull the spear from the man's body before carrying on to the entrance. Joel saw the man with the bag fall as a laser blast blew away a section of his upper torso. He immediately snatched the bag from the ground and carried on. Amber, meanwhile, made sure she matched her partner, stride for stride, as they followed Harpoon through the aperture. Somehow, they managed to side-step the laser assault and push through the door. It was un-unnervingly quiet, away from the chaos unfolding outside. Before they stood a few hardy souls who had fortunately made it inside. They were busy trying to open an electronic lift door with metal bars. Harpoon pulled a rucksack from one of the victims and shouted to stand back. They crouched down behind the imposing steel girders that supported the interior of the wall as Harpoon placed an explosive device next to the lift.

The blast almost lifted them off their feet. Thrown against the girders, Amber winced as the metal bit into her back. She looked down at the floor. No sign of blood, only bruises. As the smoke dust and smoke dissipated, the sound of voices at the doorway prompted the dishevelled figure of Harpoon to rise from the safety of his zone.

"Quickly! Into the elevator."

Peering into the lift, it became immediately apparent that there was a new challenge. Although the elevator door had been blown open, the explosion had also taken off one side of the lift. They looked down where the door had been to see a line of knotted cables.

No matter how many times Harpoon pressed the descent button, nothing happened. He looked at the elderly members of the group and demanded their rucksacks.

"You two stay here and cover our backs. We need to climb down."

The despair on their faces required little amplification. Their fate was sealed. Amber grabbed their leader's arm. "Do I assume 'we' includes us two?"

"If you can climb down, it does."

He realised it was a good moment for a little encouragement. "It's not too bad. Reckon about thirty metres, I think." His words, meant to inspire his colleagues, but no more than a flickering candle of hope in a desperate situation. They quickly faded in the silence of the elevator shaft.

Joel pushed himself forward. "We'll do it!"

***

The cables were warm and rough around the edges. Amber tensed her wiry muscles and wrapped her belt around the hanging lines of metal flex, easing her way to the floor below. As her feet hit the floor, she breathed an enormous sigh of relief. Joel was already standing there with Harpoon and the young man who had formed part of their group of six. In front of them lay a passageway, chiselled from the rock that quickly split in four directions. The gabbled sounds of irate voices suggested that their presence was already detected.

"Our intelligence about the underground chambers suggests that the right-hand tunnel eventually leads to the power hub where the politicians meet," Harpoon shared. He conducted an impromptu check on the state of their firepower. Joel received a nod of approval when he presented the rucksack. "Good work, big man. That's two incendiary devices we still have." Young Zane had acquired a laser gun from a fallen guard, while a Harpoon's supply of bolts and a couple of spears gave them some hope of apprehending the senior legislators further inside.

However, their objective was no more than a glimmer of hope. In reality, it seemed a futile gesture. No government organisation, even a dystopian one like this, would leave itself so vulnerable again. Their experience at Westminster had exposed weaknesses in security that had required urgent attention. Despite several costly refurbishments over the years, this warren of ancient bricks remained vulnerable to intruders. An attack on the main entrance of Parliament just before the *Change* had done severe damage and forced a re-think about how to lockdown segregated parts of the building to avoid another severe breach. The experts had concluded that the position of Westminster could no longer fend off an attack by organised and well-armed dissidents. Most of the population didn't know that five years before the devastation caused by the *Change*, major renovation work at St. Mary's University had begun, masquerading as essential repairs to the fabric. In fact, it was an extensive programme of underground development, fortified with a nuclear-resistant chamber and facilities to survive there for several months. All this meant that the insurgents were never going to achieve their aim.

As they entered the right-hand tunnel, a heavy metal shutter dropped from the ceiling without warning, barring their retreat. Nevertheless, Harpoon strode forward, determined to deliver his bombs. The tunnel began to broaden before two parallel laser grids descended behind and in front of them. They were utterly trapped. The grids started moving closer together until there was barely enough room for the visitors to stand between them. A loud voice boomed out to leave them in no doubt about their predicament.

You are guilty of a severe breach of national security and will be apprehended immediately.

A line of heavily armed soldiers with reinforced bomb protection gear appeared from a side channel. They shone a scanning device on each of the intruders. At the same time, a narrow passageway opened through the laser field.

Tainted No 3451, lay down your incendiary devices and walk through the protected corridor.

Harpoon's need for heroism was unbridled. He reached for one of the bombs in his backpack to be met with an immediate burst of fire to both legs and arms. He tumbled to the ground in a pool of blood.

Seize him, the voice demanded. Four soldiers entered the protected corridor and lifted the bloodied body of Harpoon onto a stretcher while another examined the contents of the bag. After a couple of minutes, he signalled that the bombs had been de-activated:

All clear, Commander.

The youngest of the insurgents was then directly addressed:

Tainted No 40131. Place your laser gun on the floor and step forward.

Dripping with fear, the young lad obliged, mumbling something inaudible about being sorry. He was literally stopped in mid-sentence by a barrage of laser fire.

Tainted No 40131 executed for treason.

Amber choked with the smell of burning flesh.

Tainted No 48272. Place your spear on the floor and step forward.

After obeying the order, her eyes turned towards Joel. In one instance, every moment she had spent with him over the last few months merged into a single declaration. She placed her right hand over her heart and approached him with the other. He wiped a tear from his cheek and replicated the gesture. Then he turned away, unable to watch the inevitable.

Tainted 48272. Walk towards the soldiers.

Confused, he looked up to see her escorted away.

Tainted 5029. Place your weapons on the floor. Walk towards the soldiers.

***

The room was dark and musty, with small, monastic-like windows. It reminded Amber of the ancient abbey she had once visited with her parents in Yorkshire, sieved with dark corridors and tiny rooms where religious monks once slept. There were few changes to the image she had drenched from her memory. Except for one noticeable difference. The steel door that prevented any escape. At least her heart had stopped beating like a frantic hospital monitor. When she began walking towards the soldiers, she feared the worst. Two bodies lay lifeless on the floor around her. Instant chastisement for their participation in the attack. Were they to suffer a similar end? And what fate had befallen Joel? Was he, too, now expendable? At least he didn't perish in the chamber. They had both been taken to an interrogation room, where truth serum and brain monitoring equipment had seemed to verify her account of events. As she sat in the depths of silence, Amber pondered her situation. Had *Gnosis* forgotten about them in the heat of the attack? Were they no longer of further use to this mysterious arm of government? Was Joel sitting in another cell asking the same questions?

The sound of approaching footsteps quickened her thinking. The door crashed open, and a tall, drawn-looking man in military garb beckoned her forward.

"Seems there is more to you and your friend than we initially thought. *Gnosis* has corroborated your story. They're sending a *helizoom* to pick you up and return you to Midland. It will be here within the hour."

With something of an afterthought, he added," Oh, and well done today."

It didn't feel like a job well done to Amber. One by one, she pictured the people they had met and furtively deceived. Harpoon, young Zane, Laura, and the two senior men. Ordinary people, much like Joel and herself. Not for the first time, Amber had been moved by the courage of such *tainted* souls. Foolhardy, maybe, but they were trying to make their country a fairer and more equitable place. The secretive work that Joel and she now did, by comparison, left an unpleasant taste in the mouth.

Amber had to ask." And Joel?" she blurted out.

"Of course," he smiled. "He will be arriving shortly. His timing was perfect. "The smiling face of her friend suddenly appeared. There was no need for words on this occasion. The African threw his muscular arms around the woman he loved and kissed her.

"It is over," she whispered in his ear. "We are going back to the Midlands."

They were brought to another room and given food and water.

"I never even realised that this place existed," she shared with those sitting at the table. One of the men, in military uniform, cleared his throat and spoke to her. "That is the way we want it to be. The government must be safe in conducting its business without fear of threat. Without the stability to plan provisions for food, water and medicine, we will all perish. Do you think we want to kill these people who attack us? They must learn to be patient, and life will improve for them. In time."

Joel raised an eyebrow. He couldn't wait to free himself of the yoke *Gnosis* had placed upon them.

Their heads spun in unison like the four sets of blades that powered the *helizoom* into the skies. The same dazzling light that blinded the naked eye each day. They shaded their faces from the power of the sun's glaze and tried to get some sleep. Neither of them had anything to say. They just wanted to be alone with their thoughts.

Amber woke, startled by the sound of a side door opening. *Two minutes to landing,* the speaker informed them. The craft dropped out of the heavens and landed within the *Gnosis* fortified complex in Sector Two, The Midlands. The commander of the craft approached them as they un-buckled their safety belts.

'Richard Harwood is waiting to meet with you. Accompany me to the security centre.

***

Joel watched Hartland enter the room they had been placed in. He thought *Gnosis's* leader was looking rather pleased with himself.

"Ah. My intrepid spies have returned. Am I right in thinking you are unarmed?" They nodded simultaneously. "Excellent! I told my sceptical colleagues that I had a good feeling about you two at the start. We are pleased with your work. "

He dropped the jovial grin and stared sternly at them. "We knew there would be an attack upon St. Mary's, but we were not sure exactly when. Your information confirmed the date and unusual time of day. It allowed us to strengthen our security. A pity we were betrayed by one of our officers with the gates, but he has been dealt with. It just goes to show it is difficult to trust anyone, these days. We have also apprehended the ringleader. Disappointingly, he was once one of our informers. Somebody we gave privileges to, as a river warden, on the Thames. I think you knew him as Harpoon. Fortunately, he did not succumb to his wounds before we managed to extract everything that was in his head. Suffice it to say there will not be another attack on the new parliament building for some time.

But what to do with you two, I ask myself?"

Amber had been biting her lip for long enough. "You promised you'd release us from our role if we provided you with information. Surely, we have now fulfilled our pledge."

The *Gnosis* official did not respond well to her outburst. "In matters of national security, it is us who decide when your work is done, lady." Irritated by his own anger, Harwood squeezed the sheet of paper he held so hard it fell from his grasp. Regaining his composure, he took some deep breaths before picking up the sheet and continuing. "You two know a great deal about how we operate with issues of national threat, so any release from your duties must be conditional. That said, I have decided to let you continue your journey home, Amber Byrne, together with your companion. However, we may call upon you again in the future. Your father is proud of your work and looks forward to seeing you again." At least the second part of his statement would be true, she mused. Joel was itching to say several things, but a glance and shake of her head convinced him to hold his tongue. Harwood informed them that the meeting was over. "Of course, we will furnish you with new backpacks with enough provisions to keep you nourished on the final part of your journey. Stay safe. I am sure we will meet again one day." With that, he left the room.

The two of them were once again alone. "What do you make of that?" thundered Joel. "*We may call upon you in the future.* I don't know about you, but I'm done with *Gnosis*!

Amber sat there in a pensive mood." I agree, Joel, but we must not let them know this. Not yet. At least they are allowing us to leave."

PART FIVE

Homeward Bound

The journey back to Amber's village of Lurnham was mercifully uneventful. Utilising strategies employed on their earlier travels, they slept in isolated buildings, avoiding built-up areas with all the additional dangers that urban places carried, and, most of all, avoided other people. When they opened the rucksacks on the first day, they were surprised by the generous food and water rations. Joel had initially complained about how heavy his pack was when they left the *Gnosis* compound.

"Maybe you are losing your strength, big man," she laughed while disguising her struggle to lift her bag.

Amber couldn't help but dwell on Richard Harwood's words. He had seemed genuinely impressed with their covert operations. But were these ample supplies in their bags a sign of his genuine support? They would undoubtedly help them stay solid and hydrated. Yet, the question remained, would her father and sister be waiting for them at the end of this journey?

The three days and nights of isolation that followed gave Amber ample time to ponder what they would do if her father and sister couldn't be found. Perhaps they would stay at the cottage, if it had weathered the storms. Try to find work. There would be no returning to the north. She managed to push some of these thoughts aside, hoping for the best. As for Joel, she couldn't imagine a future without him by her side. He had been her pillar of strength for the past couple of years. She owed him more than her life.

***

On the third evening, they crossed through what was left of the woods she used to play in and headed down the dusty path into Lurnham. It was unnervingly quiet. The only voices to be heard were their own. The sense of gloom was palpable as they finally approached the old cottage. It looked like a derelict witches' lodge from a children's storybook, ready to ensnare the unexpected visitor in the half-light before dark. It was difficult to see where they were treading. The front door was blocked with a large metal rod across the middle. Something indefinable slogan had been painted on the door. Joel decided to wander around the side of the building. “We don’t need to worry about the entrance,” he shouted back. “Look! We can get in here.” One side of the outer wall had crumbled, leaving a sizable hole to climb through. They eased their way in and switched their time devices to ‘torch mode.’ “Wow, “she sighed. “Just look at the damage”. Brick and stone were strewed across the dining room floor. They shivered as the night air began to bite them. They mooched through each room, slowly avoiding the obstacles on the ground. Joel made his way upstairs, hoping to prevent his partner from stumbling over the bodies of her loved ones. After checking each bedroom, he shouted down, “Have you noticed yet?”

“Noticed what?”

“There is no furniture here. Neither chair nor table, bed or wardrobe.”

“Yes. It does look a bit spartan.”

“They are clearly not living here.”

“Joel. I know it might not be ideal, but I’d like to spend the night here. Just one, for old time’s sake.”

“I’d better find something to make a fire with, then.”

She ambled up the stairway and cradled his face with her hands before kissing him on the lips. “Thank You.”

They found a corner of one of the bedrooms and laid their blankets together. Joel broke a few chips from the old branch and spread the three pieces of wood above them on the metal plate he found at the back of the kitchen. He placed it on the concrete floor. After several attempts with his flint, the embers finally smoked, and a small flame appeared. Within minutes, the modest fire was valiantly attempting to keep the dropping temperatures at bay. "It won't last long, so enjoy," exclaimed glumly.

They opened food from the bags and washed it down with bottled water. Joel listened to Amber's stories about their childhood at her family home until sleep took hold of both as they held each other beneath the blankets to share their warmth.

***

Amber woke to the crisp aroma of wood smoke. It reminded her of those childhood days when her father would be up early to chop wood for the fire. Everybody had morning fires then, despite the damage known to the environment. The release of carbon from the flames was the least of their worries. Even before the *Change*, staying warm was more of an immediate priority. She forced open the bedroom window and poked her neck through to identify the source of the fumes. She identified the location of three buildings down on the same side of the street. 'Wasn't that the Warton's property'? she whispered to herself. Amber remembered the two blond-haired twins who had become friends when they were about ten.

Stream and Suzzie. They had travelled together each day on the bus to the senior school further up the valley. There was a sudden urge to burst down the street and bang on the door. Do you remember me? She would bellow. But a sense of reality held her back. That was thirteen years ago. Better to tread cautiously and find out a little more first. She looked across at the contented face of the man she loved. He looked so peaceful, lying there in her parent's old bedroom. He was beginning to stir. "I'll boil up some nettle tea if I can find a pot," she whispered.

As she passed the living room, she stopped in her tracks. The iconic family photograph on the wall is now just a blank space. But in that space, faded words rose from the stonework, drawing a tearful reaction. "Joel. Come here. I think I know where they are."

The couple stood rereading the message.

Amber

Your sister and I are alive, holding on to a glimmer of hope at government unit 214. We live in the belief that you, too, are safe and hope you can join us one day.

Love,

Dad

“What are these government units, Joel?” He shrugged his shoulders. Possibly some sort of protected housing? He speculated. “Maybe my dad knows the right people,” she mused. "We need to find out where this unit 214 is, and quickly. Let’s ask around in the village.”

***

After eating, they packed up their bags and headed into the village. The first stop was number twenty, three buildings down. They could still smell the residue of the fire, although the plume of smoke had lessened. “Go on then,” said Amber. Joel thumped the outside door with his hand several times. A front room curtain was pulled back to reveal a young, yet haggard-looking face, seemingly aged beyond her years.

“What do you want,” responded a voice from the house. Amber stretched her neck to try to identify the person. “Stream. Is that you?” The woman stared back at her through the window, confused and agitated.

“Who are you. How do you know my name?”

“It’s Amber. Amber Byrne. Remember, we were friends when we were children.”

The woman scratched her head and peered at her visitor again. “Amber, you say.” And then, as if a light had suddenly been switched on, she laughed boisterously.

“Yes. I remember you now. The skinny girl from number seventeen. We were at school together.”

Her expression changed. “And who is this?”

“This is Joel. My friend.”

“Can we talk to you?”

The woman came to the door, grasping a large kitchen knife. “I’m on my own these days and can’t be too careful,” she added apologetically.

Stream Walton beckoned them inside. After sharing a pot of nettle tea with her visitors, she pulled an old picture album from the cabinet. “Remember this?”

Blowing away the murky dust, a familiar image emerged from the page. Her eleven-year-old self. She was standing outside *Green Places Early Education Centre* with her sister, Emerald. Next to them were the unmistakable blond figures of Suzzie and Stream.

“I think your mother took this picture. I recall how happy we all were, then,” exclaimed Amber. The Byrne daughter had to ask. “What happened here, Stream. Are your mum and dad still alive?”

Stream strained her face to answer. The pained lines on her forehead made the words difficult to recite.’ “Dead. Dad was shot for stealing food from our local distribution base twelve months ago. Mum perished from illness shortly afterwards.”

“What about Suzzie?”

The stream became tearful. “They took her away. Said I couldn’t look after her. Heard nothing since.”

“Who did this?”

She wiped away a tear. “*Gnosis.*” Stream composed herself and described how their once thriving community of two hundred or so people, had been whittled down to no more than twenty. The village is dead. Every survivor does what they must do to survive. Joel saw the sadness in Amber's eyes and tried to change the subject.

"Do you know what unit 214 is?" he asked the woman.

She reflected for a moment. "I think you are referring to the special domestic units for influential *tainted* people. They have been setting these up for the last eighteen months. I gather they get government support with food, water, etc. They are scattered around the outskirts of towns and villages, I think. I know one thing. To become part of Gnosis and live within the community, you need to have a strong connection and be invited. Our local doctor was contacted to live in one when his house was destroyed by the storms."

"So how do we find out where no 214 is?" persisted Joel.

"I think your best bet is to enquire at the distribution centre. It's about a mile outside Lurnham." She went to the window and pointed out the direction.

As her visitors rose to leave, Amber withdrew a large section of flatbread from her rucksack, together with one of the full bottles. "Take these. We have plenty."

"You always were kind, Amber. Thank you. Please come back another time. It gets so lonely here"

With that, they said their goodbyes, and the couple set off for the distribution centre.

Unit 214, The Wastelands

A Summons from On High

John Byrne squirmed as the military vehicle pulled up outside his compound. These days, such visits were rarely the harbinger of good news. He watched the soldier climb down from the driver's seat and approach him. He was clutching a document in his hand. John stepped forward in anticipation.

"I assume you are Byrne. Lt. John Byrne? Sir, this paper is a notification that the army requires your presence at a military workshop tomorrow. It will be held at the *Gnosis* research base in the area. A truck will pick you up at 0900 hours sharp.

"Can I ask what they want me for?"

"Read the briefing sheet, sir. It will tell you what you need to know."

With that, he returned to the vehicle, started the engine, and quickly vanished from the farm.

Hawk and Emerald had been watching in the wings.

"What's all that about dad?" He began to scroll down the paper.

"It seems that they want me to do some recruitment work with a couple of new army veterans."

Emerald's face sank. "Don't worry, love. It's not a mission. Says I'll be back at 6.00 p.m. tomorrow. Hawk ambled up to him with a wide grin. "Maybe they will give you a couple of assistants to persuade even more people to sign up. They should have asked me first. I'd have done a good job!"

"I need you here, Hawk," he exclaimed wryly. "Someone's got to keep this unit safe."

***

The next day, the same military vehicle returned to their compound. It sounded its horn to beckon John, like a muezzin heralding the arrival of the morning sun, as it stretched out its arms to dazzle the landscape. Standing at the top of the perimeter ladder, John was already waiting, rubbing his robotic arm. It had become a noticeable habit. His army uniform had been brushed carefully the night before, with his medals of honour, flanked by three ***'s, pinned carefully to his lapel. While dressing, he saw his face in the broken mirror. It resembled an old picture he held of his dad. John Byrne saw a pale shadow of the man he had once been. Gaunt, scrawny, with swollen bags of skin around tired eyes. His jacket hung across his shoulders like an oversized stage prop. Emerald and Hawk had asked to go with him, but he had declined. "Best I go alone. You know, hush-hush. Army business."

In the truck, he opened the letter and reread it.

We want you to help us train a couple of injured soldiers. Show them how to draw from their experiences, just like you did, to promote a sense of 'never say die' heroism on the battlefield. We understand your health issues are getting worse. Once these veterans are ready, we will not require your services so often, John. Getting these men up to speed as soon as possible is in your best interest.

He certainly wanted to let go of this recruitment work for the army. He was tired of pretending that all was well. Instead, he craved to spend his last years with those he loved, preparing for the inevitable end. But why were they meeting at the *Gnosis* Research Centre? It didn't make sense.

Twenty minutes later, they pulled up outside the shining towers of *Gnosis.* John cast a forlorn glance back at the food and firewood distribution centres nearby. With the use of transport, it was nearer to unit 214 than he realised. The driver escorted his passenger to the security gate and radioed a message about their arrival. Three heavily armed guards appeared and escorted them inside. John was aghast at the size of the interior. A labyrinth of corridors and tunnels with adjoining networks of rooms joined to form an enormous matrix of human activity.

Men and women in white coats, some in overalls, fully masked and hooded, busying themselves with numerous experiments and activities. Overgrown plants, edible fruits and vegetables saturated the air with their distinguishing smells. They sent his nostrils into a frenzy, with memories of a different time when such succulent flavours were commonplace at the dinner table. They carried on beyond giant computer systems and machines to a closed section. Their guard brushed past the huge *NO ENTRY* signs before reaching a black metallic lift. All five men entered the elevator. John watched the lift descend through several levels before stopping at area five.

Warning: Higher grade clearance required to proceed further

John was bewildered. "What is this place?" he asked his driver.

"All will be clarified shortly," he whispered.

A metallic arm shot out of the lift wall. "Place your biological arm in the recess. This may sting a little." Two of the guards manoeuvred his upper limb into the device and waited. A sharp pain made him flinch as something entered his arm. "What was that?" he winched.

"Just an insurance policy, Lieutenant."

The outer door suddenly parted and opened into what John could only liken to a giant electronics factory. Except what was being processed was not machines but humanoid figures of every shape and size in various construction degrees. "What is this place?"

A new voice from behind him provided the answer. "This, Lt. Byrne, is the future!" John turned to see a tall, grey-haired man wearing the military stars and rank of a general. "Welcome to the world of EHS. Enhanced Human Status."

He pointed to a blue door on the left. "They are waiting for us."

***

Two soldiers sat in medical chairs attached to various tubes and cables. John guessed the first was around thirty and the other a little older. One appeared to display a mop of black, curly hair, but when he turned his head, John could see it was only on the right side. The other side was bald, swollen and badly burned across the skull. It was also noticeable that his left arm hung limply, like a broken tree branch. He tried to stand up to greet his visitors, but a pronounced limp made it difficult. After all, half his right leg was missing. "This is your replacement, John. Wallace Cusack. He has recently returned from Ceuta; a place I believe you remember well. Like you, he survived a massacre out there. He also sustained quite appalling injuries, the like of which few survive. However, we can help him, as we can Ben over there. In short, rebuild these men, make them stronger, more able to demonstrate why we will win this war against the militant migrant's movement." He put aside his rhetoric for a few seconds and turned to look at John. "We want you to mentor them."

The older man looked less badly injured but carried a blank disposition that suggested he was not completely tuned in to what was happening. "This is another of our heroes from the Spanish border. Ben Wheatley. We thought we'd lost him at one point, but the cognitive enhancement treatment we have administered has restored him beyond his former mental capabilities. In short, he has received an upgrade. Part artificial intelligence and part human cognition. Come, let me show you."

John wasn't convinced about the 'cognitive enhancement' improvement. He looked more like a zombie. A distinguished character with sprigs of white hair, wearing large circular spectacles and a medical gown, was attending to them. He turned to greet John. "I'm Prof. Stephen Goldstone. Welcome to my workplace. I hope the injection didn't hurt too much. It's a precaution we needed to take."

John caressed the point of impact on his arm before responding. It had hurt and still throbbed. "I'm intrigued," he exclaimed. "What is it for? To stop bringing infections into *Gnosis?*"

Goldstone raised an eyebrow. "In one sense, yes, but more an infection of the mind than the body. What you are about to see is highly classified and controversial. We need to guarantee your loyalty. Any breach of this could create mayhem outside. That is why the explosive device has been inserted. Look! We all have them. (pointing to his arm) National security demands that we have the power and the means to eliminate anyone who shares this knowledge with those who might be considered a threat. Don't worry about the liquid bomb. It will only be detonated if we construe you have failed to observe the bond of silence."

John's mood had plummeted. He detected a movement of Goldstone's mouth that betrayed a hint of a smile. He suddenly felt trapped in a contract with people he neither knew nor trusted. This wasn't the military he recognised. This was something far more sinister.

"Time to get to work, John."

Goldstone pulled down a large three-dimensional image on the screen before them. It showed the bodies of the two injured soldiers. Next to each was a live cam status picture of various interventions taking place with a status update on each. The first was labelled 'blood transfusion, the next was 'digestive upgrade, the third referred to 'muscle and bone density' reinforcement, and the last was 'cognitive stimulation.'

'They're completely rebuilding these poor buggers,' he mumbled.

Goldstone continued. "The arm we gave you twelve months ago was merely a prototype, John. We'd say it was groundbreaking at the time, but as you know, it's not without its drawbacks. Now we have moved a stage further. Taken a magnanimous decision to provide these men with the latest innovative treatment. Something we have been working on for a while with AI. We call it EHS: Enhanced Human Status. A parallel programme for women is also under construction. He pointed to the male images. "Similar to your experiences, lieutenant. Not just because of their battlefield valour or use to us in army recruitment. The future of our nation depends upon this. If we become like gods, our species will withstand the onslaught of extreme weather and human chaos. We stand at a monumental point in history. Each of us will eventually realise our superhuman potential." He hesitated for a moment before deciding to expand. "The major obstacle to this pioneering development is us. However, at present, there are simply too many people to treat everyone."

The meaning of all this was beginning to sink in for Lt. Byrne. That is why the work of *Gnosis* so secretive, hidden behind armed towers and gates, he mused. The reason why an explosive device has been inserted into his body. Those on the outside would never accept such a monstrous philosophy.

"It is not for everyone, and if the massed voices of the *tainted* found out, there would be even greater chaos," Goldstone surmised. John slumped into his chair, barely containing his sense of despair. He looked across at the general. He was nodding all through Goldstone's explanation. He is doing his best to present a positive slant on all this. "Just imagine it, Lt; how raw recruits will react to military service if they know we can completely rebuild them, even from serious injury."

John's replacements stirred into life. It made him feel nauseous. "I want you to share as many tips with these men as you can," the general exclaimed. "Explain what strategies have worked and what didn't go down quite so well. You'll find they now have an excellent memory and attention to detail."

Byrne gazed into the eyes of the two soldiers in front of him. Although they seemed animated and keen to engage, there was something missing. He was no theologian, but the word that came to mind was 'soul.' How much of their inner selves had survived?

Reunion

Ambers heal was throbbing. It was trying to tell her that she needed new boots. However, her spirit was leaping ahead with expectation. "They said it was about two miles down this track," Joel shared. He clutched the badly drawn map given to them by a peevish storeman at the food depot. "There aren't any alternatives," his companion responded curtly. The dusty road twisted away towards a range of pinkish-red hills. There were no identifiable ruined settlements of any kind on the horizon. "They said the farm is in a crater. We might not be able to spot it until we get closer." His response seemed to pacify her anxiety. Despite the pain in her foot, they increased the pace at Amber's insistence. "Come on! We need to get out of this heat."

They navigated through a Martian-like landscape of rock-strewn boulders and endless banks of sand until they finally saw the crater submerged beneath the ground. Joel stopped in his tracks. "Talk about isolated!" He saw the raw emotion in his partner's eyes and embraced the woman he loved. "Come, Amber.

I'm looking forward to meeting this family of yours."

***

The only sign of life in the crater was the outline of a figure hammering something against the outer wall. Closer inspection revealed the image of a man with long, golden hair. He soon spotted them and rang a warning bell to alert the others. As they arrived at the perimeter, two men and two women lined up in front of them. The bearded man with yellow hair challenged them with a warning:

There is no food or shelter here for strangers. Be on your way!

He emphasised their resolve by angrily pointing his spear at the visitors. The other man held small rocks in his hands, ready to throw them. The younger of the two women, brandishing a large knife, squinted and shielded her eyes from the burning sun. Amber took a step forward, pulled back the hood of her coat and made direct eye contact with Emerald. “Don’t you recognise your big sister?” The younger woman’s mind recalibrated several times within seconds, as recognition finally gripped her.

“Oh my God. It’s you, Amber. It’s you!” She dropped the knife and ran to embrace her kin. We had almost lost all hope, thought you were dead. In the name of all logic, how on earth did you get here.”

“We would have liked to travel in a luxury vehicle, she joked, but the reality is we have walked all the way from the black crystal mines in the north. It’s been some journey.” She turned to the man at her side. “This is Joel. We’ve travelled every minute and mile of the last few months together. I couldn’t have done it without him.” The man from Nigeria lowered his gaze and blushed with pride. He plunged his hand into Emerald’s. “She is the most extraordinary woman I have ever met,” he declared.

The others stood by cautiously, trying to make sense of their arrival. Hawk had put his spear down, smiled, and nodded with approval. Meanwhile, with tears running down her cheeks, Hope could no longer restrain herself. “Oh, Amber, your mother would be so proud of you.” She embraced them both and kissed Joel on the forehead. “Thank you, thank you for looking after her,” the grey-haired woman declared. Raul grabbed the African’s hand and shook it vigorously. “Gracias, Senor. You are most welcome.”

Amber’s eyes were probing the outside buildings like a radar gun. “Where is he? The old fella, dad. Is he still alive?” Emerald could sense the nervous energy on her sister’s face. “Don’t worry”, she nodded. He’s been hanging on to a thin shard of light that you would return one day. No matter how faint, it has kept him going. I can’t wait to see his face.”

Emerald interrupted. “Dad’s not here today. He is working with the army. Recruitment stuff, I believe.” Hawk was keen to amplify. “Says he’ll be back before the *Change* arrives, later.”

“Come inside, you two. It’s not a luxury, but we have the basics for survival. We have so much to talk about. We want to hear everything about your journey,” enthused the younger daughter.

***

An hour passed in much merriment and laughter. Hawk had opened the dusty bottle of Spanish red wine he found in a dilapidated cellar near the town. Raul remonstrated that it tasted more like vinegar but took his glass. There were tales of how John had acquired the property and how each incumbent had joined unit 214.

Eventually, the sound of a vehicle engine rose above the voices. Hawk cautioned them. “Joel needs to come with me so we can hide him. Remember the numbers quota.”

And so it was that the bedraggled image of John *** Hons. Byrne appeared at the rim at the top of the ladder which he had climbed many times. He took his time descending, for another fall might always be his last. The residents suppressed their exuberance until the noise of the army van faded into the wind.

An ebullient Emerald greeted him with a kiss. “You need to sit down.’” That is very true, my girl. It’s been a long day.”

“No, I’m not talking about that.”

“What are the rest of you grinning about?”

“We have visitors, Dad.”

“What? Out here. Who are they? All I can say is that miracles do happen,” and with that, Amber stepped out of the dimness. “Hello, Dad, I’ve finally found you!” John stumbled across to hug his elder daughter, hardly daring to believe it was true. He kissed her cheeks and clasped his older daughter like he would never let her go of her again. “Is it really you, Amber?” Tears carved channels down his wrinkled cheeks. “You can let me go, now,” she remonstrated. “You are crushing the life out of me!” He looked at the young woman who stood before him, sand-swept, older than he remembered, heavy-eyed with the trauma of a journey nobody in their right mind should have made. His last wish had come true.

Consumed with pride, he sought some explanation. "How on earth have you got here?" he finally blurted. All his eldest daughter could do was celebrate with every sinew of her being. "I couldn't have made it without Joel." She pulled him across and presented him to her father. "My protector, my companion, the man I love," she confessed.

John cradled her face again. "You know, I never gave up hope."

***

It was getting late. The skyline was already mixing and twisting her night colours together. They all knew what was coming. "Hawk, bring the spare blankets to the bedding area," John instructed. Hawk nodded but whispered in Emerald's ear. "We need to check they were not followed. The unit regulation is clear: no more than six people." She grabbed Hawk's hand. "Have you time to check for vehicle tracks in the sand?" He had his hat and outside coats on before she'd barely finished the sentence. She planted a kiss on his cheek. "No more than fifteen minutes, love."

As darkness descended and the winds rose, Emerald gazed anxiously out the window. Her partner arrived back, shivering and moresque. "There's no sign of any vehicles," he announced. "We are good for tonight!" The others had sat down on whatever they could to enjoy a communal meal. The occupants of unit 214 were surprised at the rations their newcomers had. "You can thank *Gnosis* for that," exclaimed Joel. "We had to do some work for them. They were grateful." Mention of the scientific centre brought sombre groans.

"They only care about the government and themselves," John responded. "Yet today, I, too, entered the hallowed gates on army work. It's just mind-numbing what they are doing there, but more of that later. "Eat!"

***

John drew Amber to his side as the others began to clear away. "Come with me, Amber, I need to talk to you. They moved towards what was once the farm's dining room and sat silhouetted against the candlelight." For a few seconds longer, he closed his eyes and bathed his troubled soul in the soothing sight of his daughter, seemingly returning from the dead.

"Do you know how these units work?" he enquired.

"I know there is a maximum of six people."

"And now we are seven."

"Don't worry, Dad. We will find another unit with vacancies. Hopefully, not far away. After all, you are not the only one who has worked for *Gnosis*." There was an awkward silence. This revelation both stunned and intrigued John in equal measure. Josh and Amber had yet to disclose their spying activities in previous discussions. "And did they promise you places or permission to form a new unit?" he enquired.

"Well, not exactly." Can we hang out here for just a few days?"

John was anxious. "It's not that simple, Amber. They have regular checks on people, ignoring the rules. He looked sternly at her." We are all at risk if the quota is exceeded; they'll kick us out to live at the mercy of the elements."

"Guess we need to think this through more seriously," she reflected.

His father nodded. "I'm already on to it."

"Tell me more about Joel?"

Amber described her time at the crystal mines, how he had protected her, their escape and incarceration at the hands of Urgon, their struggles to stay alive among the 'red ants' and the unusual circumstances by which they came to work for Gnosis. "I love him, dad. And I owe him my life. We are now inseparable. I go where he goes."

Tears were forming in her father's eyes. Wiping them away, he realised he had to find places for both. "You may be wondering why I can't ask other residents to leave. You know that Hope kept this family together when your mother was ill and brought you up as her own. Raul, a bystander, a stranger, dragged my wounded body away from certain death at the hands of enemy insurgents, placing himself in the line of fire. I wouldn't have survived without his heroism.

"Hawk has been more than just Emerald's love - he has been my right hand in keeping everything running smoothly." In my heart, I could not ask any of them to leave."

"We will check out all our options, Dad. Don't worry."

"Where are you going in the morning?"

"Back to the old village house until we figure out a way forward." John knew it was pointless trying to remonstrate; he had little alternative to offer. "He kissed her on the forehead. "Stay safe. I'm due at the store's depot tomorrow. Emerald and I will see if there is any talk about you."

"And we'll check where we stand with *Gnosis."*

***

The problem of squeezing seven people into six places was an issue concerning all the residents of unit 214. Hope had been the first to approach John. She cited her advancing years and increasing fragility as a reason to leave the farm. “I know I’ve not got long,” she said. “Let me do this last thing for Bethany and the girls. I’ve been watching Amber and Joel together since they arrived. You can see how much they love each other.”

Raul had also volunteered to leave the farm. “Some things are even more important than friendship, John. She is your flesh and blood. I will go to solve the problem.” John had shaken his head.” No, my friend. There is no distinction between what you and Hope are to me and my blood kin. You both stay." None of these conversations were reported to the others.

For John was hatching his own plan. He'd decided to take a risk by not informing the food and fuel centre about any personnel changes. It seemed that no one had seen their visitors arriving, and they hadn't been in contact with outsiders. The next food collection day was the following morning, with the wood delivery arriving the day after. He reckoned it gave him almost two days to resolve the dilemma. Lies would have to be told, and deceptions maintained, but his utilitarian thinking was clear: he would do whatever it took to benefit the group.

***

It should have been the best night's sleep he'd dared to enjoy for many years, but Amber and her partner's unexpected arrival had unearthed a terrible dilemma. About why there was no room for her. Dam! he should have anticipated that she wouldn't be alone. Nor would she have expected to find an extended family living with her dad. Amber felt confused. Why had others emerged with claims to live there? Her father had tried to explain the circumstances in which Hope, Hawk and Raul had come to form part of this new family, but she didn't seem convinced. Also, his internal radar had picked up suspicions from both Raul and Hawk about Amber's partner. She too has wondering if this might be about Joel's race and background. An unknown outsider from a distant continent. They agreed to meet back at the unit the following day and assess the options open to them.

***

"No, Dad, I'm not watching you virtually crawl all the way to the food centre. We're using this. Hawk will join us today." Despite his mumbling, John knew they were right. He stared at the crudely fashioned cart in front of him and frowned about the quality of the joints.

"We haven't got your background in wood," Hawk joked, ''but it's the best Raul and I could do."

Like Inuit figures from an old artic sleigh scene, Emerald and Hawk pushed their shoulders into the leather straps and pulled the old man along. It wasn't comfortable, and moving the cart through the sand was far from easy. However, he had to admit that their progress was faster. He could concentrate on the landscape before them and ignore his pain for at least thirty minutes.

Outside the store, the guards laughed at the arrival of this desert chariot.

"I think Fr. Christmas is paying us a visit today, guys," one shouted in mockery. John fumbled for the tokens in his pocket and passed them to Emerald. She squeezed his excellent shoulder to remind him to behave himself while locking her fingers in Hawk's hand to reinforce the need for all of them to avoid trouble.

"We had a couple of wanderers asking about you the other day," one of the guards shouted to John. Hope you haven't taken in any strays, army man."

Hawk was quick to respond. "No. They were just visiting. They left to stay at my old cottage in the village. They know the quota."

"Better tell the truth, or there's a price to pay. He looked at the statuesque figure of Emerald, strong and defiant in the sands. I've told you before, lady, there's always a place for a pretty face in my house. He wiggled his tongue over a row of broken, yellow teeth and belched loudly. "Some catch, eh," Hawk whispered in her ear.

"Emerald thrust the tokens on the stone counter and repeated the numbers they needed to hear:

Five adult residents at unit 214

The familiar rustle of food bags was heard behind them as their request was processed.

"One crate of wood for delivery tomorrow: 214," echoed behind them, and with that, the strange entourage set off home.

***

Joel and Amber were frantically attempting to contact *Gnosis* at a clearing outside the family cottage. No matter how many times they rang the link code, their communication boxes failed to respond. Josh shook both devices in frustration. The look on their faces suggested further explanation was futile. Amber stared at the tumbled remains of the east wall of her family house. "Guess we'd better start trying to repair this place, "she croaked.

Joel threw his muscular arms around her. "We will find a way.'

Honour

Amber couldn't feel her toes. It had been a bitterly cold night. They had been wildly optimistic about the protection still afforded by the tethering, insecure walls of the old cottage. There had been little they could do to shield themselves from the onslaught of wind that swirled through the gaps in the east wall. Even the single log her father donated to help ease them into sleep had given only momentarily release from their shivering. They had abandoned the lower level during the night and sought refuge in the small bedroom upstairs that she once shared with her sister. There, they lay until exhaustion finally took its toll, and they drifted into a light sleep.

Amber reached across for her partner, but Joel was already up and busy trying to warm a small bottle of water by igniting an un-burnt end of the log. "We can't live like this." He shook his head pessimistically. "Maybe we can find somewhere else."

Amber thought of her old school friend at the end of the street. Would Stream take them in if they could provide for her?

The sound of a vehicle rumbled into their road, and two armed men jumped out. They looked across for evidence of a particular property they were interested in. Joel stood outside the front door, arms folded, in stoic defiance.

"Ah, so. You are here, are you," one of the men shouted across. "We had a report of a possible 'numbers' violation at one of the units. Your ID, please. Amber had joined them, looking anxious. They presented their forearms for checking. "And you are staying here?" the other man enquired. "Rather you than me," he mocked and returned to the van. "*Tainted* migrants located," he shouted through his communication device. 'Status satisfactory. No further action needed.' With that, they pulled away without another word.

"Phew!" Amber exclaimed. "Just as well we've given them some evidence we were here."

"Nevertheless, I think we need to explore other options. Starting with Stream."

***

It took some time to bring Stream Warton to the door. She brandished two large kitchen knives this time and looked even more petrified than on their last encounter.

"I wasn't expecting to see you so soon, Amber." She looked to both the right and left of them before cautiously welcoming them into the house. A large wooden plank was placed across the inside of the door. "Now I can relax. So, what brings you two back to me so soon?"

***

John was woken by the sound of coughing. His eyes followed the culprit as they moved towards the waist pit in the neighbouring room. The door remained ajar as the familiar outline of his daughter, bent upon her knees, disgorged the contents of her stomach. He quickly rose and followed her into the toilet area. "Are you ok, Emerald." She lifted her blushed face and nodded. "Come on, Dad, it's still early. Let's return to our beds." Later that morning, she returned to the communal cesspit to repeat the ritual. John caught Hawk's arm and led him to the kitchen area. "Tell me, son. Is Emerald, ok?" Ashen faced, the young man could only respond with his own question. "Has she told you yet?" Told me, what? "I think it's for Emerald to tell you." His worst suspicions were confirmed when he managed to get her on her own for a moment. "Yes, Dad, I'm pregnant."

John's head was in a tautological spin. The joy of becoming a grandfather; the practical horrors of what would lie ahead. For a moment, he stood transfixed, trying to process the announcement. Then his large protective arms embraced her with the bearhug that was so familiar to her. "So, the family lives on," he smiled. Hawk appeared at the door. He was uncertain about John's reaction to the news. He didn't need to worry. "Congratulations, young fella. So, you are going to be a dad!" Hawk shared that it had not been by intention. "Nevertheless, we could soon be eight in number," lamented the sickly Emerald. John was only too aware of the new scenario. Childbirth was an increasingly precarious experience, especially for the *tainted.* There would be few certainties about the outcome. But the child could survive.

John said he wanted to be alone for a while. He retreated to his private area, a curtained-off chair and small desk, upstairs, at the rear of the farmhouse, where he kept his personal items. Reaching under a pile of papers and books, he lifted the shoe-sized wooden box and placed it on the desk. The lid loosened, and he removed the medal he had been awarded for surviving the massacre in Morocco. He flicked it like a coin as if he was tempting fate for an outcome. Next, he removed the military revolver that had been his constant companion while in the army. The box of ammunition, which sat alongside, was checked carefully. Six bullets. Each fingered, massaged, manipulated. In his head, there was the name of someone he loved on each of them. He put the items back in the container and re-placed it under the papers. There were urgent decisions to be made.

***

The news about Emerald's condition didn't stay hidden for long. Most of the inhabitants of unit 214 had suspected that the recent coughing and wrenching were indicators of morning sickness. They said nothing, but no one could avoid pondering the implications of another mouth to feed. John, meanwhile, remained unusually quiet during the day. Raul had withdrawn from the group, suggesting he had an upset stomach. He returned briefly for a bit of food but, again, disappeared to rest. John was suspicious.

Meanwhile, Amber went to find Emerald. The sisters were locked in conversation for some time, and their voices were raised, suggesting tension. Eventually, Amber appeared looking flustered. "Don't ask!" was all the others could muster from her.

Once again, Hope approached John. "Let us speak," She pleaded. The leader of unit 214 could tell from her expression that it wasn't good news. "The situation with Emerald has only cemented further what I said to you before. I will leave the unit to make space for a new generation of Byrne's. " "And where would you go, Hope? What's left of the old town? The village? How would you survive on your own? And besides, Emerald will need you more than any of us when the baby is born. I can't do that sort of stuff, you know that, and Hawk will find it challenging, too." She smiled benignly and held his hand. "He hadn't finished. "And another thing. Bethany would never forgive you if you abandoned the girls now. It's out of the question. You must stay" "OK. At least until the first few months are out of the way." She sleeked away in the knowledge that at least she had tried.

Given Joel and Amber's encounter with the *Gnosis* guards earlier, he was prepared to risk one more night of keeping them at the unit.

***

The light had barely taken hold of a new day when John woke suddenly. He thought he'd heard the door shut. Curious, he wrapped himself in a large, shaggy blanket and moved toward the farm exit, but was distracted by the white paper note standing proudly above the fireplace. It was simply addressed to 'John.'

My friend

The time has come to thank you, amigo, for all your kindness in the last few years. I understand the impossible choices that now need to be made, and I'm making mine today. Yours is the new family I clung to when my own perished in the fighting. I will always be grateful for the support and love they have given me.

Until we meet again,

Raul

John moved to the window, but there was no sign of the Spaniard. Now, there was one last task to complete. He moved past the communal bedding area and blew a silent kiss to each of the sleepers. Then, dressing himself in his army uniform and night coat, he removed the revolver from the box and loaded one bullet. The front door opened without a sound as he left the farm building and painfully climbed the steps for the last time. The sound of gunfire shattered the early morning silence. Hawk was first to the door, hardly noticing the absent shapes in the bedding area. He stood transfixed, staring at the lifeless body of John Byrne*** Hon, lying spread-eagled on the ground. His daughters, distraught and traumatised, soon joined Hawk. They needed no explanation. He said he would protect them, kept his promise, and made the ultimate sacrifice. Joel and Hawk carried his body back into the compound and covered it in rock. 'Like a flower from the dust,' Emerald whispered between the shedding of tears. Amber had found the note from Raul. "Do you think they planned this?" she speculated.

"Eight into six, eight into six," her sister repeated. Once tearful eyes had been temporarily dried and the reality of what had happened began to sink in, Emerald gathered them around the old, rickety kitchen table and announced. "This is something Dad put together a while ago. She opened a lengthy letter and removed it from her coat. "I know we have all had private conversations with him about worst-case scenarios, but this document outlines what needed to happen when Dad eventually passed on. It delegates the responsibility of the unit leader to me. Of course, this predated the unexpected return of my older sister. I will take up the mantle but want my sister Amber to share this challenge with me."

Amber nodded in acceptance. "Life here will carry on as it must,' she exclaimed. "We must try to develop, not just survive. Dad would not have foreseen it any other way."

Emerald smiled and returned to her statement.

"The food and wood rations will continue to be collected. I will update the personnel list for the stores and for Gnosis. And the child in my womb will herald a new period of hope. We must find a better way to work with our privileged community behind the white gates. It is the only way forward. Each member of Unit 214 slapped the table in agreement.

Unit 214, Sector Three, The Midlands

(Twelve Months Later)

The loss of their father, in such unexpected circumstances, was a heavy blow for the Byrne sisters to endure. It took several weeks to sink in. Hope stopped speaking to the others, so consumed was she in grief. Hawk and Joel busied themselves with tasks around the compound to distract themselves from the trauma. As Emerald approached the full term of her pregnancy, the atmosphere brightened, and everybody, including Hope, pooled their energies towards ensuring every possibility of a successful birth. The outcome was a healthy boy who they named Axel. Emerald seemed to recover quite quickly from the experience and soon completed the fortnightly visits to the food stores, accompanied by Hawk. Unknown to her, he always carried John's revolver in his pocket, just in case. The guards displayed some cynicism when they heard the news about John, but her father had anticipated such a reaction. The position of *Guardian of the Hearth* at unit 214 had been transferred over to Emerald and witnessed, on paper, a month before his demise. And there was good news to raise everybody's spirits. The growth centres managed by *Gnosis* had produced increased yields that year, leading to larger rations for the units. In a new development, *Gnosis* was becoming increasingly interested in the plight of new births. Young Axel Byrne now had access to three monthly monitoring checks at a new medical facility next to *Gnosis*.

But something even more extraordinary happened halfway through the year: the scientists constructed an atmospheric intervention that caused the night clouds to discharge rainwater on the land below. It only lasted for twenty minutes but led to unrestrained rejoicing and frantic attempts to collect as much of it as possible in containers. Everyone held their breath when *Gnosis* shared the news that some neighbouring countries had conducted similar experiments, and it might be possible to re-activate the process again.

***

Amber and Emerald had taken several weeks to arrange the memorial gathering. Although the news grapevine was starting to improve, the logistics of 'word of mouth' communication remained slow. Twelve months previous, the occupants of unit 214 were surprised when their news pods ran a short report on the death of John Byrne. There was nothing about the circumstances of his demise, just a glowing tribute to his work in the army and his status as a war hero. It did, however, alert a couple of John's old army buddies, who managed to come to the event, as did his former boss, General Fletcher. Even a representative from *Gnosis* appeared to show their respects, with one of John's recruitment successors. They all said pleasant things about his exploits in Morocco and subsequent training role. Perhaps John would have been more thrilled by the unexpected sight of Raul trudging back into the farm that morning. The warm welcome he received brought tears to his eyes. Although a little thinner and now greying around his beard, he explained that he'd managed to find work looking after a widowed friend of one of his old customers. As they stood around the grave's site, another sound would have warmed the cockles of his heart: the cries of a young toddler in her mother's arms - His grandson.

Hawk and Joel had humped four large pieces of granite to a site at the back of the farm. They now formed a rectangle-shaped monument. The largest of these pieces of rock had been inscribed with images of a hammer and chisel. Tools John had respected. A few wise words about the importance of family, sacrifice, and love that Amber and Emerald had composed had been carved into the rock. The sisters linked arms, shielded their eyes and looked up to the firmament. Amber whispered to her gently. 'This is not the end, Emerald, but a new beginning. It was what he would have wanted."

THE END

Printed in Great Britain
by Amazon

50050657R00149